PROMETHEUS IGNORED

JOHN D DESAIN

ISBN-10: 0615686087
EAN-13: 9780615686080
Library of Congress Control Number: 2012915317
CreateSpace, North Charleston, SC

For Zhuo Zhang,
thanks for all the inspiration

Chapter 1:

It Takes Time to Build.

I can't, said the ant.
— Polly Cameron, author

There was a time when a civilization was judged by the great works the society erected. The ruins of the ancient world stand as reminders to the present that here was once a great civilization. There once were people so prosperous and powerful as a societal unit that they poured their very souls into their public buildings. They had humbled the very gods in the sky and now had them dwell in the houses they erected for them. Some of the buildings had practical societal benefits: astronomical charts to tell them when to plant, when to store, and when to go to war. Across the land mighty rivers were diverted from their natural beds and brought to the expanding capitals so that fountains, baths, and drinking water would be plentiful. There were also giant entertainment arenas constructed so people could spend their precious leisure time enjoying poetry, battles, and plays. In their time these great societal works stood to make neighboring civilizations frightened and envious. These

1

monuments proclaimed: *here is how a society can do great things because it has an organization that allows it to wield great power.*

The construction of these great works was not done without great cost. The society poured the kingdom's coffers into the works, for in the greatest ancient civilizations, even the most practical public buildings were built with a sense of aesthetic delight and megalomania. These were supposed to last forever as the very fabric of society, just as the gods stood forever in the sky as the fabric of the universe. Not only was money thrown into the efforts, but workers would slave away for years to construct the monuments. Bodies would break and crack under the exertion to produce the biggest, most technologically advanced buildings of their generation. The workers needed food to fuel their efforts, and only the richest societies had the resources to support not only the basics of life—food, water, heat, and shelter—but also the basics of society: art, architecture, and institutions. It was understood that there would be great costs when societies constructed the very culture that would persist not just for the here and now, but for generations beyond the reach of imagination.

Today modern visitors to these ancient lands can still see the great temples, arenas, state homes, and burial grounds—monuments erected by a past society that was willing to sacrifice everything for the state. They still stand even though it has been eons since not only the makers perished, but in many cases since the civilization itself perished. It has even been eons since their conquerors also collapsed in a cycle of exchanges of the crown. Nevertheless these ruined societal structures sit to be observed by modern visitors, reminding them that here once stood one of the greatest civilizations on Earth. When you pass by the ruins of the once-great civilization, you are temporarily transported back to that long-dead society. Visitors may still bow their heads to pay their respects because they too may be among the decedents of the people who produced what was once the very best of human culture. They are reminded that within them is perhaps also a chance to experience the very best.

Modern elected officials wield less power than the ancient kings, of course. The overthrow of the kings created a need for new, great public buildings. These buildings were not meant to house the ever-changing invisible gods of the sky and the tombs of their earthly representatives. Public buildings of the modern era were meant to house the public government and its great societal works. Modern society created a new, modern government of the people, by the people, and even occasionally for the people. The modern new societies once again erected their public works with both practical and aesthetic purposes. The goal of course was to reproduce those ancient societies, but this time with a new purpose. No more wasting societal coffers and lives on temples to invisible beings of the sky. The modern public works were built, as always, to remind those who came after them that their societies mattered. Temples were replaced by monuments to great societal moments and achievements: statues of great leaders, monuments to great military victories, great laboratories, and libraries containing the society's knowledge. In the past a great king, priest, or emperor was needed to focus the society into cultural achievement. But in the modern world, individuals—as part of the collective whole—would have to band together to make a government that could do great things.

The modern world, it would seem, also spared no cost for the construction of items beneficial to the society. At first great marble structures were built to remind people of their great past and to impress upon them that their government today would be as important as those of the past. Booming populations, however, produced an ever-growing need for practical buildings. A government of the people and by the people required a lot of people. These people who did the work for the society did not directly produce food, shelter, heat, and water. These government workers placed strain on the modern society just as they did in ancient times. A practical societal builder didn't have to simply worry about whether society had enough resources to build what needed building; he or she also needed to worry about whether the people would allow those resources to be used. In ancient times an official in charge of food production only had to convince the king of the need for a new grain silo. The modern government worker needed to convince a collective majority of the people—or at least their ever-distracted, duly elected public representative. There was the new problem that many officials didn't represent districts that were involved in grain production at all. Also there was the temptation of money to be made from controlling how the grain was made and who made it. The government was supposed to be for the people, but in a society where rich corporations were people, there was money and power to be gained if certain people went without. A few scared people without grain might change who did or didn't have power in the government of the people, by the people, and for the people. In a place where not building a silo might gain you advantages—even if a few suffered for it—silos were often difficult to build even if the society needed them.

In ancient times civil servants could be placed into positions at the discretion of the rulers. A king could appoint whomever he pleased as his priests and civil servants. The new modern government of the people, for the people, and by the people at first worked somewhat like a kingdom. Those in power through wealth or election could still place their favorites in charge of civil service jobs. Unfortunately those who saw people as equal, regardless of race, color, or creed, tended to also want equality among government workers. Soon civil service examinations, affirmative action, and promotion based on merit (rather than political connections or sex), became the law of the land. Civil service reform removed the mystic aura from the civil servant. Civil servants were now common, everyday workers, not equal (or near equal) to those who had power, as in ancient times. If the state jobs could not be had by natural born merit or political connections but by some earned merit and hard work, then it was determine by those in power that these workers were now to be considered just another form of the common people. Common people could make do with more common surroundings—not some expensive and expansive public spectacle reserved for the few. By being able to obtain public jobs previously reserved for the privileged, the common people inadvertently caused the end of the grandness of public works that had been their natural domain since antiquity. The few were not going to pour out money for the commons when the commons were reserved for use by everyone, and *everyone* included mostly common people.

A great monolith of a building, made of the finest Vermont marble from a bygone era of grandiose public boldness, was Tammy Usher's unwanted destination today in the future postmodern world. It was built at a time before civil service examinations robbed government workers of their natural, unearned merit. It was once a shining beacon of a bygone era of civil construction, but now it was a beacon for what became of the commons now that they were seen as merely common. The old building was very imprac- tical for the everyday postmodern workings of the employed. It had been built with large, open public spaces and small, uncom- fortable side offices. It was built in an era of personal communi- cation and public display—not the era of remote communication and public distrust. Worse still, as building codes were updated, inelegant compromises had to be made for fire safety and acces- sibility for the disabled. The greatest indignities to the original architecture no doubt the compromises made to accommodate the sheer volume of workers. Soon the great, open marble spaces were filled with mazes of felt-covered particleboard cubicles. False drop-ceiling tiles covered the ornate, mural-covered ceiling, and cheap polymer-based tiles covered the floor. The best workers could get promoted from the cubical maze into side offices, which promised rugs and a little privacy. The William Henry Harrison Federal Building for the Department of Transportation had seen better days. It certainly was not the kind of state building Khufu envisioned when he built the pyramids of Giza, but then again that was because pharaohs were always in it for themselves. If Harrison himself lay dead in the maze of cubicles and temporary partitions that now occupied the William Henry Harrison Federal Building, surely no one would notice for a few weeks.

Tammy was forced to physically come to work this month. Through the great vision of cost efficiency, it was determined that far too much money was spent maintaining facilities for government workers. A tax was thus levied on government workers who spent too much time at work in government buildings. Thus showing up to work was costly for government workers—well, at least the unlucky ones who worked in government-owned buildings. The lucky ones worked in leased buildings where the government paid another company to own the work space for them for a small lease fee. While the lease fee was generally more than the cost of maintaining a government-owned building, oddly government workers, when faced with needing new accommodations, often preferred to lease a building rather than purchase one outright. People like Tammy who worked in historic buildings, such as the William Henry Harrison Federal Building, had to find other ways to work around the tax laws. While the tax was in theory used to pay for the maintenance of the people's facility, in reality it was a small fee applied to government workers that gave them little incentive to actually arrive at their work place. Particularly with the great networks of computers that allowed people to work from home, coffee shops, and—the most preferred of all—bars. It was thought that in postmodern times more people passed their driving exams by visits to the local bar than by going to the Department of Motor Vehicle Safety. With all the ways to work around the law, one would think the tax would've been removed; instead it was federally mandated that every other month government workers had to spend time at their actual federally designated place of work origin so that at least some money could be collected. This was Tammy's mandated month to be at the official office. She was not happy.

Tammy preferred working in her home office. She had spent the better part of ten years constructing her office. She had a specially made ergonomic chair designed by NASA. NASA may have found space-exploration funding lacking, but it discovered a cornucopia of funding by having the world's top engineers design office chairs that made your back feel less bad after a day of sitting in front of a computer. Every bar in DC had them so people could get there work done and still have a back that felt great. It was said that if a person rode to Mars sitting in one of those chairs, he or she would be able to simply jump out of the spacecraft with only a mild strain in the neck at the end of the three-year voyage—if he or she was still alive. If not, that was one less chair that needed to be sent up for the next mission. The chair was not perfect, but with a few more years of vigorous testing, who knows what the future of space-travel research might offer in terms of office-furniture technology.

She had found the perfect antique desk at a trendy reclamation shop to go with her space-age chair. The shop specialized in visiting thrift shops and finding unwanted furniture that looked trendy enough that with cheap refinishing (or better yet no refinishing) it could be resold to people looking to spend premium dollars to look trendy by buying used reclaimed furniture someone else had given away for nothing. On the desk she had two lovely potted plants of violets and thistles. She had decided she would not allow vulgar artwork to adorn her office walls. Though no one would visit her at the home office, if one should catch a glimpse of her home office in a video conference, she wanted to project the sturdy solidarity of selflessness that goes along with a perfectly planned, personalized home office. Planning was her career, and so a planned home office was a must. If there was one thing Tammy knew how to do, it was how to plan.

She had found a perfect computerized reproduction of a French impressionist painting of flowers in bright pastels. It was obvious that a digital photograph of the nineteenth-century original had been hastily scanned and used to guide another machine designed to place blobs of acrylic paint on a canvas in a jerky motion that attempted to simulate the original impressionist pastel painting. Tammy thought the computer reproduction nicely captured the warm feeling of the French impressionism without the vulgarity that comes from original artwork created by actual human French painters. The final touch to the home office was a nice, framed picture of her favorite dog, Chester A. Arthur, who was never allowed in the home office but whose picture was always allowed.

Her first mission of the day at the official work office was always the same. Tammy stopped by her department's Efficient Mobile Temporary Office Information Unit of Personalized Central Information Gathering and Distribution. In the old days, this was just a cubical with a secretary in it. Actually in the postmodern age it still was. Consultants discovered, however, that it was cheaper to create more prestigious-sounding titles for jobs and work spaces than it was to create more prestigious jobs and work spaces. The secretary was a shrinking art form. The consultant had discovered that the "support" staff was a cost overhead for the more expensive primary "economic-driver" workers. This tended to make your primary "economic-driver" workers "look" more "expensive." Quotes around random words were also known to have this effect. The consultants had thus recommended that personal-secretary work be shifted to one giant secretary pool. The pool quickly moved to what is called an *offsite location*. Then the offsite locations were privatized as secretary centers so that one secretary unit could do the office work of several departments and/or companies at once. Finally it was theorized that the secretary would simply be replaced by a computer. Before this occurred, though, another consulting firm discovered that the advice of the first consulting firm had led to the primary economic-driver workers spending much of their time not doing primary, economic-driven work, but instead repairing copy machines, fixing computers, moving office furniture, screwing in light bulbs, cleaning bathrooms, making travel reports, and brewing coffee. This consultant firm recommended adding cheaper support staff to do the less primary work so that the people hired to do important, economic-driven work were actually doing that type of work. This nearly caused a war between the two consulting firms. Luckily a third consulting firm was hired to find a compromise so that no physical violence occurred. In the end the companies lost their secretaries and added Efficient Mobile Temporary Office Information Units of Personalized Central Information Gathering and Distribution in their place. But really to you and me, they were just secretaries.

Tammy found her secretary, Luke, sitting in his cubical listening to a new age book on his personal portable mobile electronic device (some called them PPEDs, but others didn't because they thought it was a stupid name, although everyone agreed iPPED was a cool product name—because one letter makes a difference). As far as Tammy understood, new age stood for two things: (1) the oldest ancient herbal remedies, medical practices, and associated fitness exercises such as yoga and (2) the newest slickly marketed self-help philosophical fad technology.

Tammy had no interest in self-help e-books; she was always suspicious of advice that promised help but was only effective until the next edition was released. She preferred the old-fashioned method of reading words printed on a page or at least electronically generated on a page-like screen. Also she loved reading English stories written by sweet, old English ladies about people who travel to exotic, romantic locations around the British Empire so they can be murdered most brutally. A good mystery novel had a sufficiently foreign detective of quaint professional mannerisms who managed to sort through the twisting plot to its satisfying end of united lovers and just desserts for the murderer(s). Tammy herself had an idea for a Finnish detective who was a talking cat with a mustache who solved murder mysteries on various forms of exotic public transportation. She never started the book, though, because she didn't know anything about Finland, and writing would be a long bother with no point since no one was likely to read her novel. Also she hated the thought of someone listening to her novel instead of reading it, particularly because she was certain they'd never do the Finnish meow correctly. Some novels, alas, are best left as dreams.

"What is on tap for the day, Luke?" asked Tammy.

"I'm working on elevating myself beyond the third excited quantum state of mental cognitive positive elevation. I can feel I've moved to the second state last week after I understood why my mother forced me to play junior soccer," replied Luke.

Luke was at heart a good people person. Unlike most of the people in the building, he came to work every day even when not congressionally mandated to do so. Luke loved his job, and more importantly he loved to interact in person with people. This was because he not only looked for ways to improve himself, but also to get others around him involved in the process. Tammy had work to do and was pretty sure Luke would abandon his quantum state of happiness within the next month. Her goal with Luke was to accept his new mental approach process for understanding human existence and gently push him toward her goal, which in this case meant pushing today's agenda up a quantum state.

She said, "Yes, I'm pretty sure I can see that. You are practically glowing in quantum luminescence, probably because you know what the projects are for the day and were about to tell me. Oh, and why did your mom make you play soccer?"

Luke replied, "Because soccer was fun! My new book says that moms think children require simple, structured fun, often with round objects scientists call balls. Once you accept that your childhood—with its scout groups, baseball, soccer, piano practice, backyard fort building, and unconditional love—was actually fun, and not parentally implanted memories of mental enjoyment like that book last month told me, you can move beyond your parent issues. Quantum mental therapy is the road to mental happiness and well-being. Oh, Tammy, you just need to try it. I really feel in a month or two I could become the next Peter McKinnon! Now if I can understand why paperclips and thermonuclear war scare me, the book says I could hop at least one more quantum mental state."

Tammy's mind started to wander from Luke's latest happiness theories toward the question of who was Peter McKinnon. She knew she had heard the name before. Unable to conjure a face, she moved on mentally. She said, "I'm pretty sure instant global vaporization by the detonation of nuclear weapons is not an irrational fear. Now how about we get to today's schedule?" She still had high hopes for moving the conversation ever so slightly toward the end goal.

"Oh, Tammy, thinking like that is why you'll always be stuck in your ground state. Now you have a Mr. Johnstone in the early morning via video conference, a Ms. Katy after that with another video conference, and hmm...." Luke paused. "You have an actual flesh-and-blood meeting with a real someone in your office. Let me look him up for you. Oh yes, I remember now—it is that inventor fellow. He was trying to see you all last month. Apparently he doesn't understand that you can be at your virtual office without being in this building. He insisted on a meeting where you two actually meet. Now before we start the day, remember to take your wood extract for the Googatta tree. Scientists can fly a man to the moon, but they can't cure the common cold. The ancient Googatta tribe discovered that wood extract prevents cold symptoms. I've been taking it for three years, and I haven't been sick once. I can see it in your eyes—you haven't been taking it at home like I recommended. Oh, Tammy, where would you be without me taking care of you?" Luke handed out her daily dose of wood extract.

Tammy pretended to be thrilled by the thought of the taste of the wood-extract pills. She thanked Luke and took her pills and her mental note of the day's schedule with her toward her office. Her work office was a hastily constructed space that had been carved out of a much larger office space. It was built with drywall and the usual false drop-down ceiling; its incandescent bulbs hummed slowly, casting yellow-brown shadows throughout the room. The lights were set flush into the false ceiling and rigged to a motion sensor in an effort to save taxpayer money by not illuminating the room when it was empty. Unfortunately the motion sensor was not smart enough to know the occupancy status of the room with a hundred percent accuracy. A person occupying the room but sitting relatively still sometimes failed to trigger the sensor. For instance being at the desk was not enough to signal to the sensor that the room was indeed occupied so from time to time Tammy had to wave her arms wildly in the air to let the sensor know she was still in the room. A cold metal desk sat at one end of the small room. On the desk sat a several-generations-old computer device and a small metal container that held coffee. A small sticky note on the coffee read, *"Here's your morning coffee. Don't forget to take the wood extract! Love, Luke."*

Tammy wandered over to her desk to start the first day of the month away from her comfortable home office. She smiled at the note and reluctantly placed the wood-extract pill on her tongue. Closing her eyes and wincing, she washed the pill down with some coffee. The coffee was one of the few joys of the work office. The administration didn't provide coffee, so the employees communally purchased it as part of a coffee club. Tammy was in charge of the club and made sure it always stocked her favorite coffee. She loved her coffee—well, not the coffee itself. She wasn't interested in pure coffee itself; she loved the idea of coffee in general. Her ideal coffee was mocha filled with two containers of simulated cream, two cubes of artificial sugar, and just a hint of real raspberry extract that was added just for taste.

She sat down and wiggled the computer mouse. Her screen lit up with the day's e-mail. Luke had sent a copy of the schedule, and he had already filled it out with helpful notes next to the names. There were happy faces for people he thought Tammy might want to conference with and unhappy faces for those he thought might bring a daily dose of trouble. Today's menu had two unhappy faces and a question mark. Tammy frowned and decided to surf through her other e-mails. E-mail was a source of secret joy for Tammy; she never knew what someone might send. In her e-mail she would find invitations for exotic mining opportunities in Africa, time shares in the Caribbean, lost banking fortunes of eastern Europeans, and South American penny stocks sure to explode in value. E-mail made the world outside the office seem like an exciting place indeed. Of course there was tragedy as well: little girls with a cancer that could apparently only be cured with greeting cards; men with various erectile dysfunctions; cats, dogs, and children recorded doing precariously dangerous, yet surprisingly amusing things; and of course Slovakian billionaires imprisoned by Ethiopian pirates who needed her help in rescuing their lost fortunes. There were also the daily humor e-mails certain to have some endlessly forwarded comic list or joke. These were OK for a quick distraction. But for her the best e-mails were the chain letters—the lucky leprechauns who granted you a daily dose of good luck, but only if you passed him on to your friends, and of course he would curse you forever if you didn't.

Sure the "junk" e-mail seemed pointless, but it beat the actual work e-mails most of the time—e-mails from busybody coworkers who justified their existence rehashing uninteresting business conversations for the twentieth time in proper business-letter form, often with full-color pie charts. People mistakenly thought uninteresting or trivial information would become interesting to Tammy if presented in pie form. If faced twenty or thirty pie charts a day, you might look forward to a visit from the lucky leprechaun too. He might not actually grant you any luck or really be able to curse you to damnation, but he never expected you to look at pie charts.

Tammy glanced up at the wall of her office. She had placed two pictures on the wall. It took three months for them to be approved as inoffensive material appropriate for normal business days as well as for casual Friday. Casual Friday had been designated as the first Friday after the first full moon of the month, unless the month had an odd number of days; then casual Friday fell on the following Thursday, unless the new moon occurred too late in the month so that no Friday or Thursday was available. In that case there was—to the relief of the office—no casual Friday that month. No one knew why casual Friday existed—they just knew that it did. Casual Friday was the law of the office, and everyone feared casual Friday. You dared not dress too casual lest you project that you did not take business seriously; but you also feared not dressing casual enough lest you appear ungrateful to receive casual Friday with all the good spirit management had bestowed upon it. There was an entire series of books written on how to look casual while not being too casual to maintain proper business professionalism. Luke had recited it word for word at least twice to Tammy. Tammy thought the writer was surely a billionaire by now. Tammy herself never read the material because she didn't like the dress the model wore on the book cover.

The pictures on her wall were the sole source of character and charm in the room. Tammy selected them because she knew the office censors could not deny they were work related. There was the charismatic portrait of James J. Hill staring down from the wall on what remained of his railroad empire. Centuries earlier Hill had single-handedly built the Great Northern Railroad—well, single-handedly if you don't count the hands of all the Irish, Chinese, Swedish, French, and Italian laborers and craftsmen who performed the actual labor. Hill had various rich investment partners as well to be sure. But certain history books ignored these details because they were less glamorous, and it was more romantic to attribute great deeds to a single man with a single mission. It was Hill after all who had the vision of building this transcontinental railroad. The everyday laborer…well, they might have had visions of their own, but they were not lucky enough to have the resources to pursue them.

The remains of Hill's Great Northern Railroad were still there in the postmodern world—literally there in Tammy's office, represented by black train lines on a computer screen on her desk: the official train schedule "big board." Tammy was in the federal Department of Transportation's subdepartment of light-rail and rail. Specifically she was in the planning and scheduling department. Her job was to manage the trains and make the trains arrive on time. The computer big board of rail traffic displayed little green, yellow, and red circles to show Tammy where train traffic was moving on time, behind, and in trouble. On a good day, the board sat at green and yellow, and Tammy simply had to deal with office routine. On a crisis day, a colored circle on the board would turn red due to weather, natural disaster, poor maintenance, or poor planning. The first two were often beyond Tammy's control, but the other two brought countless headaches to fix. Today the morning board was green and yellow. Many an angry rider believed Tammy could control the weather and the water level of rivers. Tammy would assure them on the phone that if she had those powers, she would not be in a mid-level government job. Irony was generally not effective on angry callers who expected the impossible and were not going to get it.

The average everyday citizen could not get through to Tammy on the phone of course. The government had created an effective computer-controlled train complaint "help" line. The line was run by a giant computer whose voice was selected specifically to give the caller no reassurance at all that his or her call mattered, no matter how often the computer reassured the caller it did matter.

The computer had a complex menu system, subsystems, and sub-subsystems with categories specifically designed to not represent the ten most common problems an average caller might have. The hope was that the caller would go away having failed to find his or her complaint on the list. A truly persistent caller could navigate the maze of menu options to finally arrive at the "speak to a real human" option. The real humans specifically selected for this task had as little knowledge of rails and trains as possible. Unfortunately nearly every other country had a more sophisticated rail system than this country, so support staff could not be outsourced offshore. Luckily, thanks to "pay-for-schooling" programs, most real humans in the country had acquired little-to-no information on the function of either trains or light-rail. Pay-for-schooling programs were good at teaching children how to pass standardized tests by making sure to properly fill in ovals with number-two pencils. Had the rail lines worked by filling ovals with number-two pencils, the help line would not have functioned since the real human might have been able to actually help the caller. But to date no railroad had successfully integrated oval-filling technology into its operations. Thus the phone help line worked brilliantly so long as you needed no help.

The callers who got to speak to Tammy weren't your average Joe the plumber, Pip the piper, or even Miss Havisham the totally should have just gotten over it. No, the callers were generally other members of the Department of Transportation or, worse, politicians at the local, state, and most-dreaded federal level—people who thought getting a seat in the House of Representatives was like being anointed king of France by the pope. To listen to them on the phone was not productive. Most were privileged and extremely deluded on the subject of train scheduling. But they were, of course, absolutely necessary for Tammy since the big ideas of train management could only be acted upon with their approval. They would call Tammy, and Tammy would explain to them that they just had to accept that cows sometimes got on tracks. The cow, she assured them, did not cross the tracks because it knew the senator was having an important vote on limiting federal spending on food stamps. Tammy would suggest that the senator look on the bright side: with less federal money available for food stamps, at least poor people might get some track-kill cow meat every now and then.

The other picture on Tammy's wall was an old reprint of a flier from the Orient Express. Tammy would stare at it during particularly difficult teleconferences where she felt like murdering the people on the other end and then getting away with it.

How a lowly federal worker came to have the power to get the trains to run on time is not directly related to the pictures on the wall, but it's an interesting story. The great trains lost so many riders over the years that the government finally stepped in and took it over in postmodern times. The least profitable units—the passenger trains—at first were federalized, but as the energy sources of coal and chemicals needed for the car society dried up, the freight train companies let the postmodern government take over the cost of the tracks as well. Finally climate change pushed the gas automobile and the coal plant to the edge of extinction, and socialism claimed the whole rail system. The Department of Transportation, in charge of the people's commons, and more specifically Tammy were now in charge of the greatest of all transportation systems—the train.

A small window on Tammy's computer screen opened up to reveal Luke. "Hello, hello, we are on time and on the rail, ready for that nine thirty a.m. He looks like a hydrino-state thinker to me. No quantum elevation there for sure. His briefing packet included many very colorful pie charts, and it's in your in-box," said Luke's head on the screen.

"Luke, don't speak badly about the West Coast regional manager. He is bound to speak badly enough all by himself," Tammy replied.

With that Luke's screen box disappeared and was replaced with a countdown clock—just two minutes until Mr. Johnstone appeared. Tammy quickly began to look up his charts in her in-box. She chastised herself. Seriously—for a person skilled in time management, she had wasted far too much time this morning daydreaming about trains. Now she had to scramble for the charts. If she didn't find them, he would offer them over My Time. My Time was the name of an incredible information delivery system that allowed someone to take over your computer screen and share his or her screen with you. You could see the person's presentation without the need to follow along yourself. It just had one disadvantage. The other person had control of your screen and you were forced to follow along with him or her. Tammy thought her time was precious, not to be just given away to My Time, especially by the likes of Mr. Johnstone. She was panicking now with only thirty seconds left to find his e-mail with the charts. The dread of getting on My Time and being forced to work on his time and not her time was sinking in. Finally there was relief. There was the e-mail sandwiched between an offer to sign up for a free Bible verse of the day and another e-mail containing an exciting bid to lower her boat insurance. She clicked on the icon to open the charts just as Mr. Johnstone arrived on her screen.

Mr. Johnstone was speaking: "Seriously, Tammy, I'm surprised I still need to talk to you on this subject. Now as you can observe, the metric depicted in the pie chart on page five of three hundred eight..."

Tammy smiled with relief. Mr. Johnstone was one of those self-focused people who believed the rest of the world was as focused on his ideas as he was. He started his presentation when he started it and ended it when he ended it, just assuming the other people were there with him, computer technology be damned. Apparently he hadn't bothered to wait until the video conference had started to begin his presentation. He probably assumed everyone was on My Time, which meant his time. This self-absorbed naïveté was his only redeeming quality, Tammy thought. By finding that e-mail, she was lucky enough to have missed his first four slides!

"Now we can't run the city train system without addressing these key, core central issues," Mr. Johnstone droned on.

Tammy was a big-picture manager. She preferred to read the introduction slide and the conclusion slide, then move to her in-box and hope the lucky leprechaun had arrived.

Tammy spoke, "Mr. Johnstone, please, can we focus this discussion on the big-picture items. Help me help you by giving me the point and telling me how I can help you."

"I am discussing big-picture ideas," Mr. Johnstone replied. "Indeed all three hundred eight of these slides focus on the big picture. To understand the big picture, you need to know all the little pictures. The devil, Ms. Usher, is in the details. Indeed if we turn to slide one forty-eight, I have a bar graph where I cleverly changed the bars into small devils to demonstrate this point."

"I am sure you did," Tammy said. "I was hoping we could boil this down to one word to start with. For instance, I have no clue what you are talking about. I mean, at all." Tammy was desperately trying to move toward any picture—big or small—that clued her in to the conversation she was having so she could plan how to end it.

"Ms. Usher, I am getting to the point. I am definitely at the point. The point is here on every single one of these three hundred eight highly crafted charts. They all have the same single central point—a point I am sure we can both agree upon. A point that will no doubt be a point which, when this meeting ends, we will remember and take home. On page two hundred seventy-six I clearly depict this point in cartoon form from a cartoon I found on the Internet that produces a moment of much-needed levity but also clearly hammers home this point to everyone involved."

Tammy scrolled to page 276. There was a cartoon with an obese orange cat, a dog, and a caption about Italian food products. "I don't see much about trains on slide two hundred seventy-six. Perhaps levity is not the best way to get to your point, Mr. Johnstone. Perhaps verbally might be the best way to clarify the point to everyone. And by everyone I mean me as there are only two of us in this conversation, and I am counting on one us knowing the point. That one of us is you, I hope. Please get to the big picture, Mr. Johnstone."

"Parking," said Mr. Johnstone, coming to the point. "My point is parking, Ms. Usher. Parking. One cannot run my city train system and not have enough of it. My trains need more parking: bus parking, bike parking, motorcycle parking, taxi parking, and private automobile parking. In simplest form, I need more parking. Remember: our train's slogan is 'leave the driving to us,' but they can't leave the driving to me if they can't drive to me and park. A cost-estimate analysis by my cost-analysis department shows increased train parking would increase ridership by eight percent over ten years!"

So it was parking again, Tammy thought. She'd suspected as much. Tammy was in charge of trains, not parking. It was a simple fact that was simply not understood by her regional manager. "Mr. Johnstone, my department is, as you know, in charge of trains. My cost analysis shows your trains in your system have ample parking. I simply cannot build more train parking given the current rider levels. Empty train yards do not help keep the trains running on time," Tammy said.

"But they wouldn't be empty if we built more parking of other kinds. Clearly the big picture isn't just train parking but includes all the smaller pictures of other types of parking. On chart one eighteen, I show the big picture that includes both the train station and its parking. Parking has to be part of the discussion. How can we have a big-picture view and not see parking in the picture? People don't and won't ride if they can't park," said Mr. Johnstone, making sense.

"I agree that your big picture, Mr. Johnstone, includes parking, but not my big picture. My picture begins and ends with the trains and keeping them on schedule. As I believe I told you before and will tell you now, there simply is nothing in the department's mandate about parking non-train-related material," Tammy explained.

"But surely they are integrated. Look, chart two thirteen has a clear flowchart showing how parking is related to the overall operation and its mission. How can people ride if they can't park! It would be like eating pudding without eating your meat first."

"Perhaps they could walk to your stations," answered Tammy.

"Walk? Slide two seventy-six clearly demonstrates that a cat who is that fat isn't going to be able walk to any train station. Cats don't get that fat by walking to train stations. I thought that message was clear!" Mr. Johnstone exclaimed.

"I truly sympathize with your needs and your request, but I simply don't do parking. I suggest once again that you consult your local authorities and politicians on increasing your parking needs. We just don't do regional non-train-related parking here. Let me briefly explain what it is I do. I see from the big board your trains are all running on time. That's the big picture to me. Your parking situation does nothing to keep them on time, and in reality more riders may severely hamper my ability to keep them on time. If you need to work on integration and expansion of regional transportation systems, you need to call Betsy Miles, the federal Department of Transportation's managing director of system integration. I can feed you to our help line so you may try to contact her," Tammy said.

"If you look on chart seventy-six you will see Betsy does not take my calls anymore. She claims I haven't filled out the proper forms. I did fill out the proper forms, but then she said she needed them in triplicate. Then I did that, and then she said she would need them in an electronic triplicate file. I refused. Where does the form filling out end and the work begin? I have my principles, and this is a good one!"

"Complaints about interoffice communication problems are also not my department," Tammy explained. "You might want to try the federal interoffice communications department and see if they can help you contact her."

"Well I am going to finish this presentation now," said Mr. Johnstone. "Now on chart five of three hundred eight, you can see..." Tammy shrank Mr. Johnstone's screen pop-up and muted the volume. She really did feel for his problem, but it was not her problem.

Poor Mr. Johnstone had good ideas, but he lacked the communication skills and wit to see them fulfilled, thought Tammy. The Mr. Johnstones of the world never saw their good ideas come to pass because they refused to understand how the system works. People like Tammy and Betsy were just mid-level civil servants who kept public systems running as best as they could. The big ideas needed influence from the top of government and then down to people like them. To get big-picture ideas accomplished, Mr. Johnstone needed influence, and he'd never shown the ability to influence anyone. In the world of office politics, many good ideas died due to a lack of understanding of proper communication. Mr. Johnstone was destined to give the wrong presentation to the wrong people at the wrong time over and over until retirement. Tammy thought she would never make that mistake. If a truly good idea came her way, she would make a plan to make it work. If there was one thing Tammy was good at, it was planning.

Tammy's mind moved to her next obstacle—the meeting with Ms. Katy. Katy ran line management for the lines associated with Missouri, Kansas, and Texas. She was cold, calculating, and efficient—traits Tammy admired. Katy also unfortunately had an office next to Casey Jones, a young, hard charging executive type. He was wasted on the train-management side. Unfortunately Jones was the type who refused to work at home. This led to his manipulation of the system to obtain an extra square foot of office space. Since he actually used his office and was willing to pay for it, Tammy hadn't foreseen a problem with this. But the square foot had to come from someone, and that someone was Katy. During the past year, an interoffice war had erupted over this one square foot. Sides were taken and no victory was in sight. Tammy glanced at the big train-scheduling system—still only green and yellows. As problematic as a train delay slipping to red was to Tammy, interoffice wars between "adults" were infinitely worse.

Luke's head appeared on her screen. "Looks like that next appointment is ready to go. I see Katy has elevated her state since the last office-space discussion."

Tammy understood that Luke had a certain affection for Katy over Casey in the interoffice war. Luke apparently caught Casey using his ballpoint pen without express written consent. Casey pointed out he needed the pen to actually fill out the consent form. This argument had not worked on Luke, and Luke informed Tammy that he and Casey were no longer on speaking terms. These were grown adults, Tammy had to remind herself.

"I can see a certain mental positive ionic glow about her for sure. No doubt that Casey got stuck with the extra mental electrons because he gets more and more negative every day," said Luke.

Tammy sighed, "Well, thank you, Luke. Since the big board shows we are without crisis today, I guess we can start our weekly office-space war. Patch her into my office PPED, Luke."

The computer electronic box containing the head of Luke shrank into oblivion on Tammy's screen, and a new head box appeared. Seriously, thought Tammy, why do we ever have to come to the office? Few people even bother to come around to see you in person, even when we're in the office. Tammy had read in a magazine that people tended to be meaner to each other when they didn't have to physically face each other. She was sure the use of interoffice electronic communication instead of face-to-face contact only exacerbated the pettiness of normal office routine. Since interoffice wars were a nasty business to begin with, she was sure the communication system turned them into a full nuclear crisis and made dealing with them impossible.

Katy had the eager look of a cat ready to play with a mouse. "I'm sure you're aware of the interoffice-space committee's decision six months ago to reduce my office space by one cubic foot, which is approximately point zero two eight cubic meters to you and me. This decision was based on a faulty understanding that a certain Casey Jones—whose employee level is no higher than mine, I should add—was determined to utilize his office fifty percent more than me. I believe this shrinking of my office was both in error and in spite of my superior office-space efficiency. Why should I be punished for being more efficient, more compact, and a better custodian of office space? I know you are aware of this fact as I sent a one-page briefing chart that summarizes my position on the subject."

Tammy remembered the chart well. She was aware that Casey forewent any fear of higher taxes and actually came to work every single day. Due to his more frequent office use, he had put in a request with the interoffice-space committee to expand his office. They agreed that because he was in the office more than workers who telecommuted, he could use more space. Katy found the logic in the findings flawed. She pointed out that Casey was married with three children. It was only natural he would come into the office to avoid his wife and children. She argued the committee was punishing the unwed woman for the simple fact she did not reproduce and had no spouse to avoid. While Tammy felt there was some merit to her argument, the simple fact was that office space was in short supply, and a person who used his or her office could probably use the space more than someone who avoided the office at all costs.

Tammy replied, "I believe we wrote up and submitted that complaint to the interoffice-space committee, and I certainly approved a discussion on this issue for you. It's not my fault the committee gives more weight to usage in their considerations, Katy. I do not see what more I can do on this matter."

"Yes," Katy replied, "but I found in the office-approved decoration and decor manual that one living terrestrial member of the

Plantae kingdom is allowed in the office provided said member can adapt to artificial lighting and requires no additional lighting other than that available during working hours. The terrestrial member must acclimate itself to the allergies and allergens of the office complex's general assembly. I have located the terrestrial member I wish to use in my office, but it simply will not fit in my office unless I have my additional one cubic foot back. I have written up an interoffice-space request form to obtain one cubic foot of space to accommodate my terrestrial member. I seek from you your signature to move this issue to the committee for further consideration."

Well that was it then. Katy had figured out a new angle of attack. She purchased a plant.

"Let me get this straight—you want the interoffice-space committee to grant you one cubic foot of space to accommodate a plant. You want this space to come from Casey's one cubic foot of space—space the committee determined he needs to accommodate a conference table for human visitors to his office. Basically you want the committee to value your plant over one of Casey's human business associates. It's not that I'm unwilling to put this item into the interoffice-space committee's agenda; it is, however, unlikely to be approved."

Katy started to get angry. Her head moved closer to the camera and started to fill more of the box on Tammy's screen. Despite a rather nice makeup job, including what Tammy was sure was a new eye shadow, Tammy could see that Katy was turning redder.

"I know this already," Katy said. "Casey has the committee stacked in his favor. Both Ted and Alice share a commuter electric-van pool with him. And worse, Casey is one of the designated drivers of the van pool. You know van pools generate an artificial bond of security between people. They should have excused themselves from ruling. But did they? No. I have written a formal complaint on this subject as well. On top of that, I am no longer sharing verbal communication with these people. I told them as much using a notepad since I refuse to speak to them. Oh, and that Stanley on the committee is a common thief. I caught him taking two snacks from the coffee club snack drawer. Everyone knows only one snack per working day is allowed, and I'm sure it wasn't the first time with him either. How can I hope to win a fair hearing when the interoffice-space committee is full of so many cheats and liars?"

Tammy had long suspected that Katy's difficulties with the committee stemmed not from the committee's corruption, but from the completely unlikable aspects of Katy's manner. Tammy wondered if Katy realized that not talking, not sharing pens, and constantly complaining about people was a poor way to gain the sympathy of fellow coworkers. Tammy appreciated in some aspects Katy's new tactic. The office-decor manual was a clever new angle and would no doubt generate a vast counterattack from the other side. Tammy had to decide whether the extra drama was worth it. While it was probably best for all involved to simply let it go, pettiness, it seemed, helped these people get their work done. Tammy worried that work performance might slip without the interoffice spats. A certain amount of productive unproductive activity seemed to generate productive results. Some people joined clubs, some spent lunch at the bar, some chatted online, some had not-so-secret affairs, and some had never-ending spats. Such activity could be viewed as unproductive, but Tammy believed it helped her employees avoid becoming apathetic. Isn't that why things like the interoffice-space committee existed? The committee's job was to regulate and accommodate unproductive productive work in the workplace. A workplace full of humans behaving like perfect, efficient robots without the negative aspects of human interaction might make Tammy's job easier, but since people need people, this was surely the most productive method any office had found. Tammy would pass the new plant angle to the committee and sit back and see how the interoffice war proceeded.

"Katy," Tammy said, "I have considered this new logical approach to this difficult and vital office issue, and I will forward it to the interoffice-space committee. I appreciate your high level of productivity during what is certainly a difficult and high-stress situation, and I am sure the interoffice-space committee will find a solution that accommodates all individuals involved."

A large smile spread across Katy's face. It was a small victory in the long war. Her face shrank on the computer screen. "I thank you for your support in this matter. I will fill out the appropriate forms and have Luke place them in your in-box. I assure you this situation will not affect my work." With that Katy's head shrank to nothing on the screen.

Tammy was pretty sure Katy's work would not be affected. Indeed she was certain Katy would work extra hard to continue to try to win favor with Tammy—as if Tammy could really be made to care about this issue. Tammy was sure, however, that such activity did increase productivity. Once Casey got wind of the situation, he would surely elevate his work level as well. Indeed the two had constantly been trying to out produce each other. Their productivity was good in general, and their managed lines were among Tammy's most on-time services. Tammy would rather have hypersensitive employees who fought over trivial things than unproductive, uncaring employees who didn't care about anything. The passionately despondent business-first employee, she found, was always the least productive in the end. The one who tried to clean up inefficiencies in the system almost always made the office less efficient, always at an enormous price. The worker who talked about how much he or she worked and complained about lazy workers was almost always an unproductive worker. People who spent more time in the office got the same amount of work done as people who spent less. They just expanded the same amount of work to fill the extra time. Katy and Casey might have wasted a lot of time, but they also got things done. In the end it seemed that organizations needed a little inefficiency to get things done. In Tammy's mind there were people who got things done and people who didn't. The extra goings-on were just noise in her perfectly running machine.

It was now Tammy's lunchtime. After lunch she would have to meet with some inventor person. What a bore, she thought—a person with some idea so important it required a one-on-one interview. The morning had brought her someone with a good idea who had no idea how accomplish it and someone with a meaningless idea who knew how to get maximum inaction. The first person never got anything accomplished; the second got her work done despite the busybody arguing. Overall the morning was a wash, Tammy thought. Who knows—maybe Katy would get that extra square foot back. Then Casey would counter it in some way. At least it would be slightly amusing for a while. Oh well—office silliness and a green-and-yellow train board. It felt like a good time to go to lunch. She texted Luke, "At lunch—do not disturb," then headed out the door.

The building had at one time a rather nice cafeteria. It had these great sticky buns that contained about one million joules, which sounded less fattening than saying it in calories. They also made fresh bagels every day. At that time the cafeteria had a sandwich-and-salad bar because they believed college-educated workers were smart enough to construct their own sandwich or salad without aid of others. But the cafeteria had fallen on hard times.

Now the fresh pastries and bagels were replaced with pre-formed, life-shortening sugar snacks. The make-your-own bars had been replaced by worker-constructed sandwich lines in which little old ladies constructed your sandwich for you at glacial speeds. First they would ask if you wanted bread. Yes, you wanted bread since it's not technically a sandwich without bread. Without bread a sandwich is not a sandwich but a pile of unrelated food objects on a plate. Next they asked if you wanted everything on your sandwich. You would reply yes, I want everything. Next they asked if you wanted lettuce. Yes, you wanted lettuce since lettuce was considered a subcategory of *everything*. Then they asked if you wanted mayo. Yes, once again mayo is another subcategory of everything. You thought it was implied once again that the word everything included everything even things of the class of mayo. Do you want chicken? Yes. You would then get angry and explain that you wanted everything they might ask about, so they should just go ahead and put it on. If they did not understand what everything meant, why did they ask if you wanted it? Then they would ask if you wanted mustard. The cafeteria was definitely not what it used to be, Tammy thought.

Tammy figured that was the nature of cafeteria food in general. It's not that cafeterias had to be bad but that the food quality tended to trend in only one direction. Every cafeteria has someone who doesn't like it enough to complain to management. Complainers will always voice their concerns, but satisfied people do not feel the same drive to have their voice of happiness heard. Happy people tend to think their happiness will go on forever and that no action is required on their part to maintain it. Thus when the cafeteria contract is up, the company management faced with only complaints will go in a new-worse direction.

Tammy preferred to eat alone. Her day was filled with enough virtual people. She had been taught in management class to never eat alone and that a lunch was a time for social gathering and contact. She found this was true and that the best business decisions were often made not in meeting rooms but at lunch. But PPEDs allowed social contact at all times. She was never truly alone. At any moment a thousand friends, virtual friends, coworkers, relatives, and strangers could video conference, chat, e-mail, tweet, blog, text, or—in a moment of old-fashioned sensibility—just call her. She even had Chester A. Arthur wired in so he could bark-activate instant communication if he felt lonely without her. In the postmodern world, one did not have to fear ever being truly alone, so Tammy ate alone hoping to get a few moments of peace before the rest of the workday was upon her. She decided to have the daily special, which was Texas-style eggs in a brown sauce. A sign next to the daily special read that due to the international observance of Egg Freedom Day, watermelon would be substituted for eggs. The meal was about the quality Tammy had expected. If you went in with low expectations, you were rarely disappointed at this cafeteria.

Tammy arrived back at the office in time to see the train board light up with a few reds. The question wasn't whether the board would turn red on any given day, but whether unexpected reds appeared. A quick look at the afternoon trouble areas showed that today's failed on-time arrivals were your typical failures. She looked for action items, but the situations were all running nominal crisis with no action items. Fishbone diagrams of the crisis had been started, and the failure investigations were tracking to closure. She took down a note to call the Chicago office. Really, they should work on reducing the number of nominal train delays. She would offer her wisdom on getting their nominal late arrivals in less late.

Luke's head popped up on her screen. "Hello, fellow coworker. I expect you had a superior lunch and you are cationic to start our afternoon? The book says that one cannot achieve proper quantum energy states without a well-fed quantum motor. I trust you did not forget your afternoon face-to-face meeting. Indeed, your fellow meeting attendant has already arrived."

Tammy wasn't interested in meeting anyone new at the moment. She had fishbones and flowcharts to go over; she didn't need a distraction. Luckily the government had a cure for such a situation—paperwork.

"Luke, has the fellow meeting attendant filled out the proper TITTP forms? I see no point in seeing him face to face, or at all, if he is not properly formed. I've already had to waste my morning on one such person. Granted it was an internal matter, and I had to meet the person, but an external matter is totally different."

Luke was pretty sure Tammy was instructing him to give the visitor what the layman called *busywork*. Luke responded, "Unfortunately said visitor came last month while you were at home. Frustrated by the lack of face-to-face personnel at office, he sat around and filled out the Technical Information Transfer to Technical People forms. Indeed he completed the whole of Heilmeier's Catechism form in triplicate! He even did it on actual paper with an actual writing instrument and included a digital copy on an electronic media." Luke held up what appeared to be some type of electronic storage device. "I don't even know how to read these into the system anymore. I'm afraid you might have to just meet this one since he is as properly formed as any visitor ever."

Tammy was frustrated. Really, what was the point of government bureaucracy if only the totally the wrong kind of person could use it? "Very well. Show this person in."

"His name is Bob," Luke replied, "and according to his full technical biography form, he was some type of scientist. Good luck with this one; he seems very eager."

Tammy's office door opened, and a man in his mid-forties with graying hair and a slowly falling midsection came in. He was dressed in the finest mass-produced department-store business suit that she thought he could probably afford. His remaining hair was freshly cut, and his beard was trimmed. Under his arm was an impressive stack of paperwork.

"Please have a seat, Dr. Bob. What exactly is your last name?"

"Just call me Bob. Everyone does," said Bob.

"OK, Bob. Who are you, and why exactly was it so important to meet me?"

"I work for the patent office in Cleveland. The office is, well, sort of slow at times, and I started to look at trains in my free time. Trains are my hobby, you know. I have a beautiful N scale set up at home. Anyways I noticed much inefficiency in your system. Do you realize the International Northwestern Pacific Rail is using 848 Red Barons when they could save the government over a million per year upgrading to 852 Slick Willies?"

Tammy was a little disgusted—some model-train amateur coming in to her to tell her her job. Of course she knew this! Did this amateur know what it would take to make such an upgrade? No, of course he didn't. "Thank you for coming and telling me my job. If that will be all, I have a very busy afternoon to get through."

Bob didn't get up. "I'm not finished yet. I mean, I just used an example of things I noticed. It got me excited, you see. I started modeling your train system on my computer. I came up with several train-scheduling sequences that could upgrade your programming and timing system. I patented them, in fact. I was hoping people would quickly pick up on these great ideas and enact them. Then I realized no one else had noticed that I had done this. I had built a better mousetrap, and no one was beating a path to my door. So I thought I needed to come and pitch these upgrades. We are talking about a point-five-to-two percent efficiency increase by using these train-scheduling software upgrades. An even greater efficiency is possible if track-and-train upgrades were implemented. More efficiency could be achieved with changes in fuel usage formulation, and the addition of a small number of track lines in peak travel areas. For a small upfront implementation cost, my train-scheduling proposal could save the government billions. Most important, millions of travelers will get to enjoy a more pleasant and efficient transportation system. Now I am entrusting this proposal to you. I hope my documentation is long enough."

Bob got up and put the paperwork on Tammy's desk. Tammy looked at the mountain of electronic media and pointless paperwork. Was it long enough for what? To annoy her while sorting this pile out? Yes, it was certainly long enough for that. But was it long enough to not be a pile of jargon and gibberish? She didn't know.

"Well, a good proposal is sized appropriately," she said. "A bad one is either overinflated or not important enough to justify more than a page. As the great emancipator said in reply to how long a man's legs had to be, 'Long enough to reach the floor.' From the size of this pile, I would say you could reach the floor and then some. Seems to me you might be a little overinflated."

Bob sat back down. Tammy craned her head around the mountain of paperwork. She did not want this busybody out of her sight while he was in her office.

Bob replied, "Well, I think what Abe meant was a good idea is always a good idea, and a bad idea is always a bad idea. I mean, a man might have legs two inches shorter than they are now, but they always reach the floor no matter the length. Just like a good idea is always a good idea."

Tammy was getting more annoyed. How dare he explain her analogy to her! "Yes, you are very clever person, Bob. I daresay I never heard of a clever person ever working for a patent office. Well, you have delivered this to me, but all this needs to go through our technical-review process first. I don't sit as judge and jury for any proposal. You really should've submitted to them first by mail."

"Of course I understand that," Bob replied. "The Postit Corporation does not deliver mail to government offices, as you know. By law, the US Post Office is only allowed to exist here in DC, so I thought if I had to go all this way to mail something, I might as well deliver it in person. I thought I would go to the top first. I figured if I convinced you of its worth, I could gain your advocacy. I often work in the technical-review process. People involved in that process often can't sort out a good idea from a bad one. They create a mountain of bureaucracy to cover the fact they have no idea what they are doing. But an idea submitted from the top of management will get a more solid hearing because, while they still may not understand the proposal, they always understand how to kiss up to upper management. So I am here on a mission to gain your advocacy."

Bob was making Tammy even more annoyed. She disliked having to come to the office today; she disliked having to meet with coworkers; she disliked working through the predictable schedule delays. But those were her normal job functions, and no matter how much she disliked them, secretly deep inside she must have loved it or she'd have left years ago. No, she really disliked the person who assumed something. How dare he assume the technical-review committe at the Department of Transportation was full of idiots! As far as she could tell, it actually *was* full of idiots, but how dare he just assume as much. How dare he assume his ideas were any good! It would take her weeks to sort through this mess. But what if the idea was actually good? Tammy always told herself. If a really good idea came her way, she'd do whatever it took to push it through.

"Look, Bob," she said, "here's how it works in my department. I love good ideas. I'd love to give you my advocacy. I will person-ally send this to technical review. I will make sure you personally speak with them to ensure they understand your proposal. If they come back and tell me the idea is good, I give you my word I will do what it takes to implement it." There, she thought, what more could he expect of her?

"But if I could just spend a little time with you and talk you through it—"

"I have given my word. If there is value here, I will act on it. I simply have no more front-loaded time to give to your proposal. I am a very busy person. These trains don't manage themselves, you know. I have a whole grid of troubles to work through. I will be in touch if there is merit here, I assure you."

Bob got up and headed out the door. He briefly looked back at Tammy as he left. Was he disappointed? She thought so. Really, what did he expect? Advocacy? She would do everything she could if the technical people approved it. But it was doubtful they would. They loathed new ideas; the process loathed new ideas. Old, bad ideas that had been tried and had failed a thousand times had that tried-and-true comfort about them. It's like an old friend you don't like: but you're glad they never leave because at least you know what to hate about them. The unknown was scary. The world took a long time of good ideas to build; a bunch of comfortable bad ideas kept the momentum going, but a truly horrible idea could destroy the world. Was this new, unknown idea good, bad, or truly horrible and disastrous? Who really knew? That's why people hated new ideas: the world had taken a long time to build, but it would take only a second to wreck it.

Tammy looked at her screen of meaningless blinking green, yellow, and red. What good did it really do anyone? It was just a bunch of blinking gibberish busywork. She frowned. She looked at the pile Bob left on her desk and started digging through it. She pulled out the cover sheet and started to read it.

Chapter 2:

The Demon-Haunted Office

God doesn't play dice (with the universe).
— Albert Einstein, former patent clerk

The early days there seemed to be more people doing science for science's sake. Sure there was the possible danger of excommunication or being burning at the stake, but most scientists managed to remain unroasted. Science back then was more open to just inquiring about the natural world. It's doubtful that Nicolaus Copernicus could have passed a committee technical review based on Heilmeier's Catechism. *How long would your research take?* It took Copernicus a lifetime of scientific inquiry to produce a piece of scientific thought on our solar system that he published on his deathbed. *How is it done today?* They used the Earth-centered model in Copernicus's day because they thought the sun went around the Earth. *What's new in your approach, and why do you think it will succeed?* Well, the old approach had all these weird cycles within cycles to get empirical models to remotely match the motion of real objects in the sky, and even then it sometimes failed. Unfortunately Copernicus's model also used circular orbits in his sun-centered model of the solar system, and thus he didn't eliminate the circle-within-circle epicycles. Thus it wasn't any simpler than what came before; to the layman it did not work substantially better than previous models. *Who cares?* Judging by how little his book was read, not many people cared right away. *What are the payoffs?* Even if Copernicus was right, there was almost no payoff in terms of money. Regardless of whether we correctly understood the movement of the sun and the earth, the sun would continue to move in the sky from day to night as it always had. And getting burned at the stake, like Giordano Bruno did, didn't sound like a great payoff either. Poor Copernicus couldn't have passed the postmodern research-proposal process. One might say he was slightly more right than what came before, and his bold thought, approach to science and rather impressive use of Arabic mathematics helped inspire people to start using the scientific method to solve problems.

Bob took the commuter train into the heart of DC to take part in the postmodern science-proposal process. This time his destination was the Warren G. Harding Building. He was promised this was the best place to get an honest appraisal of the technical content of his proposal. He was going to have a meeting with the chief technical officer for Tammy's division. The Warren G. Harding Building loomed cold and slightly decrepit before him. The building's top inappropriately looked a little like a teapot. As he stood outside ready to enter, there was a buzz in the leather-bound carrying pad under his arm. Bob took out the case and opened it. There was a *pop* sound, and Luke's head appeared on the screen of his PPED.

Luke's voice beamed out: "Hello, our intrepid tribal scout Bob. Our tribal chief Tammy has asked me to remind you of today's special meeting. I'm reading the most fascinating book on office tribalism and how, through mastering tribal politics, you too can become your own tribal chief. I thought as our tribe's new scout, I would be your guide into the current scary unknowns before you. You must remember that our technical-assessment office is much like all our other offices except it contains a high degree of tribal trolls. The key to impressing trolls is to not use force. Don't try to beat them over the head with facts and information. They won't know what to do with such things anyways. Just go with the flow until they are good and passivated by the sound of their own bloated egos, then stab them with the steely tip of your proposal spear and run."

Bob was slightly amused by the pessimism. He worked in a patent office, after all, and technical assessment was part of his job. The technical-assessment officer here certainly wouldn't be much different from the one where he worked.

"Thanks for the advice. I'll try to sum up his quantum mental level and go from there," Bob said with a self-wink of delight.

Luke replied, "Oh, I'm so done with mental quantum physics. I see now the road to true mental happiness runs through tribal assessments. And let me repeat: don't feed the trolls too much. Now just enter the north side of the building. The elevators will be on your left. Get in the northernmost elevator, and take it to the basement. When the elevator doors open, follow the yellow painted line on the floor to your destination. Good luck, scout." With that, Luke's head blipped off.

Bob liked the idea of being a scout. He was sorry to hear Luke had given up on the quantum stuff—not because it was likely to go anywhere, but because it seemed more energetically sold pointless advice. Office tribalism seemed so primitive. If you were going to sell people pointless platitudes, Bob thought, they should at least be space-age modern in feeling. Bob followed the instructions and arrived at a dented elevator door. The door struggled to open. Bob stepped inside the elevator. The numbers one through ten ran up the side of the floor panel. Under that was a red button (B) that Bob assumed must be the basement. He pressed the button. The elevator closed and started down with a jerk. It then stopped and paused a second between floors. Then with a sudden jerk in the opposite direction, the elevator came to life again. Bob slowly descended into the bowels of the Warren G. Harding Building.

Bob exited the elevator in the rusting, cement-floored basement. The walls were cracking and watermarked. Various piping and electrical conduits ran on top of the walls and on the ceiling. A small, yellow painted strip on the floor directed Bob to walk down the gloomy, under-lit hallway toward the technical-assessment office. The hallway had an unpleasant odor of mildew and disinfectant cleaner clearly meant to mask the mildew. The combination actually created a new smell less tolerable than mildew. The yellow line ended abruptly at a dirty, light-blue metallic door. Painted on the door in big black block letters was *Technical Assessment Office*. Under that was a piece of paper held by masking tape. The sign read, *Sigmund Marbles, chief technical assessment officer and notary public*. Below that was a small magnet with the word *IN* on it. Bob entered the office.

The office was no more attractive than the hallway leading up to it. A patchwork of throw rugs covered the concrete floor. An assortment of posters for Norwegian death metal bands covered up the peeling wallpaper. The wall peeked out in gaps between the posters to display watermarked wallpaper with cherry blossoms on it. The wallpaper could be at least a century old, thought Bob. The office was decorated with what looked like curbside furniture that neither matched nor even appeared to have been manufactured in the same decade—or century, perhaps. There were two mismatched filing cabinets, a minifridge with a microwave placed haphazardly on top, a half dozen rolling armchairs in various states of disrepair, a round meeting table with a cobwebbed, disconnected speaker phone, and dozens of empty pizza-delivery boxes. There was also an abundance of unclassifiable random debris scattered about the room. The back wall had a pyramid of empty plastic bottles and cans—mostly soda and energy drinks—with a sticky note above them that read, *It pays to recycle.* The center of the room was dominated by a huge plastic desk on roller wheels that had sat in the same place so long they had partially sunk into the floor. On the desk were various plastic collectable figurines of comic-book characters, anime figures, and random untraceable figures from long-forgotten video games. A large monitor sat on the center of the desk on a cardboard box. Several side monitors sat next to the main monitor. Cords from the monitors ran under the desk to an ancient desktop computer that had the same general appearance as the rest of the room. The computer was a collection of found parts that fit together in a mosaic of computing technology from the past six decades. It made wheezing noises as it apparently struggled to live another day, probably five or six decades past its expected lifetime. On top of the computer sat a giant instant coffeemaker that appeared to endlessly drip coffee into a burned, stained-glass coffee pot. On the bright side, the smell of burnt coffee was probably the least offensive odor in the room. On a chair behind the desk sat Sigmund Marbles.

Sigmund Marbles was a rotund man, perhaps in his early twenties, wearing a superhero T-shirt that was supposed to be covered up by a too-transparent white button-down dress shirt. He might have been older, but the décor of the room suggested a young boy rather than a middle-aged man. Perspiration stains covered the armpit areas and the back of the dress shirt. The room's air vent hummed at full force, working overtime as a brave soldier to try to keep up with the heat output of this large man. Despite the AC system's hard work, the large man still had permanent beads of sweat on his hairline. His ruddy, pockmarked face peered out from behind the computer screen to examine Bob. A meaty arm pointed to a random chair, and a voice boomed out, "Have a seat."

Bob moved to the chair with the least litter on it. He removed a few pizza boxes from the chair and looked around for a waste receptacle. When he couldn't locate one, it occurred to him that such a receptacle might exist in this room, but it was probably buried under garbage like everything else. He placed the boxes on an adjoining chair already full of garbage and sat down on the now clear but rather stained chair.

"It's ah…rather an interesting place you have here," said Bob.

Sigmund seemed oblivious to Bob's clutter plight and continued typing on his computer. "Sorry for some of the disorder," Sigmund said, "but it's hard to get the cleaning crews down here. Bunch of snobs those janitors are. Plus I don't trust them not to touch my valuables here. You know how it is everywhere. They force us free-spirit genius types into out-the-way places because we refuse to conform to their stupid rules." Sigmund's head was still concealed behind his computer screen as he typed away. "Help yourself to a seat and stuff. I'll be with you in a sec. I just got to finish this incredibly witty and sarcastic rejoinder on this chat site. My God, people are so incredibly ignorant. Know what I mean? Can you freaking believe this idiot and the crap he writes? This person says that Ultra Alien Man flies due to a small antigravity device in his boots. Can you freakin' believe that? Holy crap, User001 is such a total clueless fucking moron. Everyone fucking knows fucking Ultra Alien Man comes from a fucking planet with a larger-than-Earth fucking gravitational field. I mean everyone knows this shit—even my mom. This dude is stupider than my fucking mom. A planet with that kind of gravity stuff happening—of course he had to develop natural antigravity organs to be able to function on such a planet. I mean everyone freakin' knows that, right? I mean hello, Einstein, page the patent office and tell User001 to file a patent for being an original moron. Ultra Alien Man ain't no weak-ass human superhero forced to use technology to overcome his natural weaknesses. . Ultra Alien Man is a natural superior human being, only he's an alien. I mean he's smart enough to make an antigravity boot, but this fuckwad don't get that Ultra Alien Man doesn't have to."

Bob actually could freakin' believe it, and he wondered why people needed to swear so much while putting down other totally anonymous people. Bob had always figured a superhero flew because the plot depended on it, and if the plot didn't need him to fly, the writers would not have had him fly. Bob wondered how there could be a correct, factual answer regarding a purely fictional character who was doing something physically impossible. Bob also had trouble figuring out what this had to do with him. Puzzled, Bob asked, "Is there really a way to describe impossible fictional situations in an absolutely correct fashion?"

Marbles replied, "Of fucking course. There is a logically absolute correct and proper answer for every question, dude. If you are a rational being and use reason as the governance of your thinking, then any intelligent person will reach the same fucking conclusion on any subject. There is simply one correct answer to any question. To answer the fucking question, I being a superior being simply let reason be my natural guide to where to focus my senses. I take into my brain the information I have acquired from my senses and then use my reason again to identify correctly the absolute truth in information. I identify this knowledge as either absolutely true by definition or false and thus forever unimportant and fucking stupid. Think of me as the Indiana Jones of intelligence, because, like Indiana Jones, I will not end my endless search through the dark corners of the universe to find knowledge, armed only with my whip of reason. Once I've discovered a piece of knowledge, I lock it up in a crate and store it preserved forever in an immutable state in the endless warehouse of information I call my brain. From this process I have been able to increase continuously my intellectual capacity to the point I am simply a superior thinker compared to most men and women. I am, as you can see for yourself, an extremely intelligent person, which is why

I occupy this dignified office and sit in judgment of inferiors such as yourself. Here, let me show you my intellectual capacity."

Marbles stopped typing. He started to rummage through scattered papers that the action figures on his desk were holding down to prevent the air conditioner from blowing them across the room. Once a piece of paper hit the floor, it would surely be hard to distinguish from the other one thousand random papers scattered about. Sigmund Marbles shrieked with delight as he found what he was searching for. He lurched forward over his desk to hand the piece of paper to Bob.

Perplexed, Bob glanced down at the sheet of paper. Sigmund went back to ignoring Bob and typing on his computer. The paper had the heading, "Marble's intellectual growth chart." Below that was the following graph:

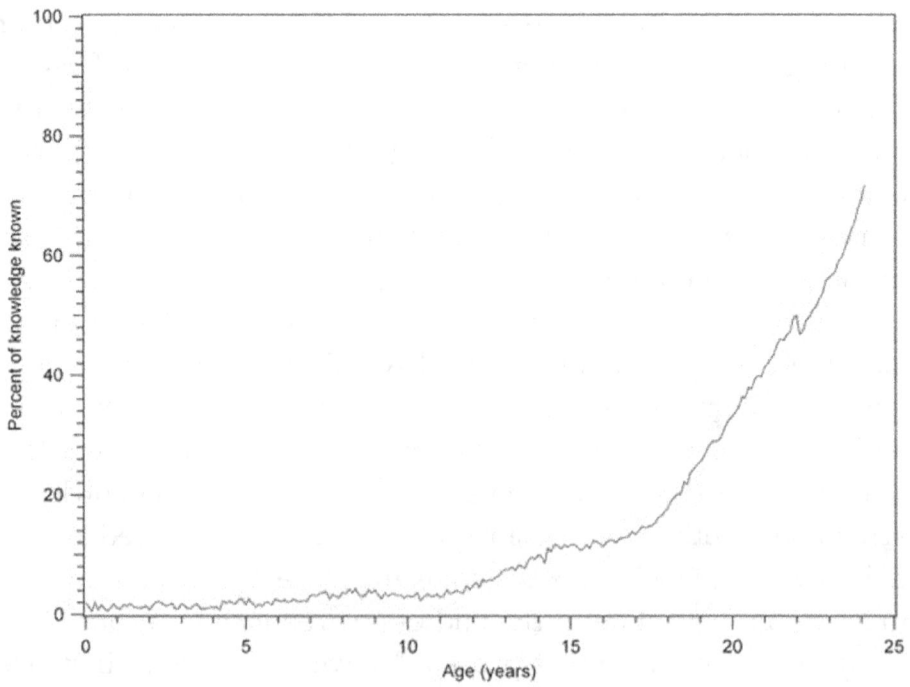

The graph was completely nonsensical to Bob. He turned the paper upside down in hopes it would clarify the meaning. No luck. He turned it back right side up. Bob wondered if it was worth asking about it.

"I'm a little confused about this chart," Bob finally said. "How can you possibly know what one hundred percent of all knowledge is unless you already possess it?

Marbles didn't look at Bob but continued banging away on his keyboard. "I know what is and isn't knowledge and how much I've obtained because I use the computer program AF-FIRMATIONSHU."

"What is that? I never heard of it."

Marbles laughed. "What is it, you ask? It's only the most fucking brilliant fucking computer search program that was ever fucking created. The program knows from your inputs that which you already believe you know. Based on those inputs, it filters all the information on the Internet and only brings you correct information. You see, I know the information it brings me is true based on what I already fucking know is true. It filters out all the bullshit false truths I know could not be fucking true, because if that shit was true, it would invalidate something I fucking already know as the absolute fucking truth. No more fucking bullshit in my searches that mucks up my fucking thinking, man. When I'm on AFFIRMA-TIONSHU, I only see clearly delineated truth as I know it. I can then go on other Internet sites and spread those truths to teach the ignorant and stupid—like probably you. No offense, but I assume with you asking questions and shit that you're a fucking stupid ass."

Feeling actually insulted, Bob decided to ask an innocent question that might cause a little trouble for Marbles. "But what if you believe in something as truth from the beginning that is not true? You know, something stupid like that Hitler and FDR were on the same side politically because they shared the common interest of going to the bathroom. Using this program aren't you bound to only get more information that supports this totally stupid and blatantly false idea? How does this program help increase your knowledge if you can't correct a really bad mistake?"

Marbles stopped typing. Apparently Bob said the right thing to at least get his attention. Sigmund was indeed waiting for him to speak. Perhaps he had only wanted Bob to just praise him, but Bob was sure that Marbles—like most Internet factoid bullies—wanted to show off to the small bit of the real world here in the office how smart he really was.

Marbles's face appeared from behind the screen again. "I can see how a person of such an apparently lower intellectual ladder rung on the evolutionary tree of smarts than me could think such a low-information thing. Just one second and I will astound you."

Marbles started rummaging through his desk drawers. Out came more debris: old food, sugar snacks, comic books, and new action figures in their original packaging. Another shriek of victory finally came from Marbles. With the gallantry of Sir George slaying a dragon, he handed Bob a small credit-card-sized membership card. "Unless you are a member of this, you just wouldn't understand," Marbles said.

Bob took the card in his hand. It read, *Member of the IQCIM-SIPA (Intelligent Quotient Club Member of Incredibly Measured Superior Intellect for a Person and/or Animal)*. Under that in bold black letters it said, *Sigmund Marbles Level 1 member*. Bob was familiar with IQCIMSIPA. As far as he could tell, it was just a collection of underachieving people with a massive inferiority complex that aggregated together based on a shared belief in their own inflated societal worth based on their ability to achieve scores on pointless formulaic tests. Bob had met actual intelligent people in his life. In general actual intelligent people had one shared quality: none appeared to know or care to know their IQ. Intelligent people who engaged in intellectual discourse and life pursuits seemed to assume they were intelligent enough that no card or membership was needed to justify themselves or their accomplishments. It's not that Bob thought such fields of research had no value—just that any tool could be reified beyond its range of importance.

Bob knew he was in for a hard time with Sigmund Marbles. Now that he had allowed Marbles to beat on him with authority, Bob assumed it was time to follow a path of false praise—step two of the troll slaying, as Luke called it.

"Yes, this is very impressive," Bob said. "I hear it's a very exclusive club. I have never been able to gain membership myself. I hope you can share your intellect with me and, more importantly, on my proposal that we are here to evaluate."

Marbles leaned back on his chair. The chair let out a groan as Marbles's weight shifted. Marbles grabbed an action figure from his desktop with his right hand. With his left hand, he started moving the figures arms back and forth. "Do you understand who this is?"

Bob had no clue. "A toy?"

Marbles now shifted forward in his chair causing the desk to shake as his large front struck it. He dangled the figure in Bob's face. "This is no toy! This is a collectable figurine of Judge Drak McNasty. He is merely the most important of the galactic judges sent by the council of Oberon V to judge the deeds of mankind! I suggest you show your respect. I am not your friend. I will not be sharing any thoughts with you. It is not my job to impress you; it is you who is here to impress me. Much like Judge Drak McNasty, I, Sigmund Marbles, have the job of judging humans. My job is to judge your probably valueless, stupid application proposal to the Department of Transportation. Will I do this with intergalactic laser rays of pain like Judge Drak McNasty?" Marbles now clenched the figure in his fist and shook it in anger in Bob's face.

It was certainly having an effect on Bob. If Marbles wanted Bob to think he was possibly nuts and ill-suited for his job, he had completely succeeded. Bob did what anyone who wants to get a proposal approved does—he sat there and tried not to laugh.

Marbles wasn't done yet. With great labor he rose again from his chair. He raised Judge Drak McNasty over his head, still moving the figure's arms furiously. "Lucky for you the days of us being able to just blast our way to intergalactic judgment are still ahead of us. The judge and I have our own way of going about the process until such better times arrive." With his left arm he reached down and pulled up Bob's case file. "The department gives me these forms to guide me, but what the fuck good are a shitload of forms? I refuse to use these standard forms as the basis of my judgment on any proposal before me."

Marbles tossed the file into a corner where the waste container would have caught it if it had not been buried under a pile of debris. Marbles continued, "So how will we judge you, you may ask? Judge Drak McNasty and myself will do this by judging not some mere proposal, but by judging you and finding out if you are a person whose application is worth fucking looking at. Are you ready to begin the test?" With a dramatic flourish, Marbles ended his rant by falling back into his chair with a crashing sound. He then carefully placed Judge Drak McNasty back on the end of the desk with his fiery red eyes of judgment staring into Bob's soul.

Bob was sure he stood a better chance with Judge Drak McNasty than with Sigmund Marbles. "I really don't understand why this is necessary. But I guess since I came all this way, I'm willing to do what needs to be done to get this process moving."

Marbles casually leaned back in his chair. He searched his drawers for a life-shortening sugar snack as all the physical movement had left him drained. "OK, now here is your scenario. This past week a famous scientist—whose name I will leave out since he needs no further publicity and book sales from me—went in front of Congress and told them they need to act on climate change. He claimed these politicians were ignoring the scientific facts and needed to start working toward solutions. He then explained the published facts about climate change. What would you say about this well-known scientist arguing in front of Congress for political action?"

Bob shrugged. He didn't understand why this was even a question. If it was a trap, it was a good one so cloaked in stupidity that it didn't reveal itself.

"I don't see the big deal," Bob replied. "I would at least encourage Congress to take the time to listen to an expert opinion and the scientific facts that are germane to the subject. Why wouldn't I?" Bob suddenly regretted that last statement. The fiery eyes of Judge Drak McNasty appeared to burn into him. The gothic look of the Norwegian death metal posters made the walls look like a fiery, fiendish jury. Then again maybe it was just his imagination.

Marbles grunted with disapproval He took a deep breath of displeasure and wiggled a little in his chair.

"*Encourage*, you say?" Marbles said. "Fucking figures—I should have guessed you were one of them fucks. I should've pegged you as one of those pseudo-intellectual types who pass off authoritarianism in place of respect for knowledge. Look, dude, don't just fucking trust fuckin' authority fucking because the fuck claims to be a fucking authority. Who the fuck does that fuck think he fucking is? Some fucking scientist, that one is, all lecturing our elected officials like schoolchildren. Well, I didn't fucking vote for him and his fucking scientific consensus. You fucking got it?"

It occurred to Bob that Marbles was a rare linguist, a true artisan vulgarian. It was said that Ernest Hemingway spent hours at a time contemplating which one word to place in certain key places in his manuscript. Marbles would never have such a problem. He had discovered the magic properties of vulgar words. Such words had the ability to replace any word without changing the meaning of the sentence. They also could be used to modify any word in the language without actually adding meaning. Most people found them convenient for occasional emphasis, whereas Marbles—a true artist—painted entire canvases of conversation with nothing but pointless, empty potty-mouth words. You would admire it as long as you weren't the one being sworn at. In any case Bob didn't get what Marbles was talking about, probably because the foul language hampered comprehension.

"I don't understand," Bob said.

Bob looked at Judge McNasty hoping between the judge and Marbles one of them could explain what Marbles was talking about. The judge only stared back at Bob with those accusing, fiery eyes. The death metal posters seemed to be moving in. Then again maybe the combination of the high room temperature and Marbles's body odor was making Bob claustrophobic. He started to think Judge Drak McNasty was too perpetually judgmental to help him out of this. Unfortunately he would have to rely on this human called Marbles, and not the plastic figurine, to get his proposal heard. He wondered if Marbles would ever stop this rant of an interview and do his job. But maybe Marbles couldn't do his job—hence the weird process. Bob wasn't hopeful at this point.

Marbles grabbed another action figure from his desk. "OK, let me explain this to you in real simple terms. This here is internationally known Professor Maxmillien Death, better known as Professor Death. Would you trust a man like this after all the times he had threatened humanity with death? Fuck no! I don't trust authority just because an authority says so."

Marbles was now shaking Professor Death in his meaty right hand while pointing in an accusing fashion at Bob with the meaty left hand. Bob wondered whether such rapid physical activity would be good for Marbles as he had notice the sweat stains on his shirt had grown by leaps and bounds since he arrived. Worse, a bodily odor was now starting to overwhelm the room's already pungent smell. Bob imagined Judge Drak McNasty being overcome by fumes and never being able to render judgment.

Marbles spoke again, this time hiding his face behind Professor Death. "Look, I'm an authority. Trust me, my weather death-ray machine is real. Now give me a million dollars in research money or I'll evolve you all back to monkeys." He moved the figure away from his face. "See, you would never a trust a guy like that. So why the fuck would you ever fucking trust this scientist fuck who is in front of fucking Congress? I mean he's just another fuck with a fucking agenda. Agendas always muck up honest exchanges of information. Here he is giving out all these 'facts' and shit, but now he's turned those facts into an agenda by politicizing the facts. Back when he was just an honest scientist working in a lab searching for facts and publishing in obscure journals that no one but geeks who never get laid read, he was doing real science. He was collecting real knowledge like I collect real knowledge. But then suddenly he gets all up in front of Congress and stuff and tells them these facts, and he's fucked it up. Now the facts are all politicized agenda, and agendas turn information into shit information. Now the fact isn't a fact anymore—it's a political agenda. And the scientist is a scientist anymore—he's an activist. You can't respect knowledge when it comes from an activist with an agenda. Look, knowledge is like shopping at the giant discount box store. We are information traders shopping in the free warehouse of discount knowledge. Trust free information where the person isn't talking about agendas, crises, and victims, but simply talking about the facts for their own sake. Never allow any authority to dictate truth to you, especially the authority of government, religion, and scientists. You got this shit down yet?" Marbles gently placed Professor Death back on the desk.

Bob understood. Not that he thought it would help his situation, but he thought he'd try to clear up the difference between what he thinks Marbles thinks and what Marbles should actually think. Bob decided to plead his case in Judge McNasty's direction just in case it mattered. "Look, I get the idea of trusting and not trusting authority. But I think you misunderstand exactly what people mean by distrusting authority. You *should* distrust scientists. Scientists and other authorities lie, cheat, and steal all the time. Scientists may have agendas, as you said. Everyone has agendas that may bias their thinking. You should have some doubt about scientists, but you shouldn't doubt science itself. In your scenario you have a scientist who gets in front of Congress. Well, what if he told the congressmen that gravity exists? According to your logic, you should now feel this man has politicized the force of gravity. Gravity now isn't a force of nature but a political agenda you can't trust to be real. Now you can't be sure you won't float up and away from your chair. I didn't see any problem with your scenario, not because the information came out of a scientist's authoritarian mouth, but because you said he was stating scientific facts and information. I trust our centuries-old science data and theories on climate change. You got it totally backward. Authorities don't validate or invalidate truth; facts are facts independent of who knows or tells them. Scientists don't go to the polls and vote for consensus or not. They read the published literature, examine the facts individually, and agree to agree or not agree with the merit of results. When over ninety-six percent of trained experts look at the same information and think it has merit, you probably should start to listen to them carefully. If I can't believe a scientist backed by centuries of scientific data on a subject, who am I to trust to inform Congress—a popular author, a European aristocrat, a paid lobbyist for the energy companies armed with myth, irrelevant factoids, and just-so stories? Me, I trust science and those people who state things that are scientifically verifiable."

Bob was done talking. He glanced at Judge Drak McNasty to see if it had any effect, but McNasty just stared back with those judgmental eyes glowing red.

If Bob had been talking to a brick wall, it might have had more effect than it did on Sigmund Marbles or Judge Drak McNasty. Marbles reached over and picked up the judge. "Oh dear, my friend McNasty. It looks like we got ourselves one of those types. You are another fucking person faking a proposal to me when it's really just a poorly concealed political agenda. Well, we here at the technical-assessment office don't do agendas. We are neither allowed to nor interested in politicizing things. I don't get political."

Political? thought Bob. He's the guy who brought the subject up! There was probably nothing Bob loathed more than pointlessly getting political. It wasn't that Bob was not interested in the organizational ways humans collectively interacted with

each other—or more importantly the mechanisms humans needed to solve the fundamental problems facing life on Earth. He
thought about the unprecedented severity of our problems, such
as the need to feed, house, and clothe each other. He had thought
about the mechanisms of government needed to deal with these
problems: a sound economy, the ability to distribute resources,
fundamental rights of individuals, the ability to maintain an
orderly society, and the means to pass on this mechanism to
future generations. Political policy was a science experiment in
which the people replaced the lab rats. In his youth he assumed
politicians carefully planned policy as a scientist plans an experiment. They formed a question as to what need to be done or
learned. They would look first to see what was known, carefully
planning the execution of the experiment and adjusting future
experiments based on past results. In his youth he assumed this
was how politics worked. As he got older, he realized that wasn't
how it worked at all. Politics would throw away perfectly working systems for no good reason and often try the same broken
failed experiments over and over again, expecting impossible-
to-obtain new results.   Bob loathed getting political not because
politics didn't interest him and not because he didn't think it
was important—no, he loathed it because politics never seemed
interested in anything actually important. Politicians spent most
of their time arguing over crap that couldn't possibly matter to
anyone. Worse, people were trained to pretend the crap they
talked about somehow mattered to them.

"Trust me," Bob said, "the last thing I want is to get political.
I just have this idea I put in the proposal you threw over there. I
think it's a good idea. I think it can get two, maybe five percent
more efficiency out of our nation's transit system. It is based on
sound principles and a good understanding of current technology
and how to manage it. Please base any judgment of this proposal
on the facts contained in it and not on some political ideas. I assure you I have no desire to get political."

Marbles grunted. He slowly rolled the chair over to the garbage pile the folder sat on. The wheels of his chair sank heavily into the carpet making the trip slow. "What the fuck? I used to have a garbage can here. Where the fuck is it? I need to e-mail those fuck-ass janitors. I don't really like doing that, you know. Last time they came here, they stole Judge Drak McNasty's sweet cherry motorcycle. That shit is a limited-edition collector's item." He picked up the folder and started the long, slow journey back to his desk. He mumbled, "Don't want to be all political and shit, huh? Too bad for you, because you're going to have to if I find this folder's contents to have merit."

Bob was surprised by Marbles's sudden change in tone. Had he gotten through to Sigmund, or was the man just sugar crashing? Who cares. It felt like some progress had been made. He had touched the folder!

"What do you mean I'll have to get political?" Bob asked.

Marbles stared at Bob as the judge might have. "Shit, you can't be serious, can you? Holy crap, man, you can't just walk in here and change the fucking train-transit system! People got their fucking livelihoods on the line here. Don't you understand how the system really works? They sold the government the trains, but then the government sells the system right back to them to manage. It's a fucking shell game paid by our tax dollars."

Bob was confused. Was Marbles talking sense or nonsense again, or was sense actually nonsense? "But Tammy Usher manages trains for the Department of Transportation. I mean, if her office approves these changes, then everything is set, right?"

Marbles laughed. "Crap, man, that's how it isn't. I mean, that sounds reasonable, but that ain't how the shit works." Marbles grabbed another action figure off his desk. It was an attractive, scantily clad female figure with dimensions unlike any real woman. "Look, man, this is Miss Amazing, and she will stand for Tammy. OK, her department does manage the train accounts, but she doesn't actually manage the trains." He then reached over to another figure. It was a fat, evil-looking figurine wearing a military uniform. "This is Commander Barron von Euro. He owns a private company that actually manages the trains and the tracks and makes the money. Sure, Miss Amazing keeps an eye on the schedule and oversees cleanup of delays, and the private companies are supposed to follow her office's regulation. But she can't actually make such a bold move like your plan without approval from Congress. I mean, the train companies write that into their contracts just to make sure some do-gooder like you doesn't mess up their finances. On page sixty-eight you call for a switch from the SR4500 to the LM1230 because it is cheaper to maintain, is more fuel efficient, and has higher performance standards. You can't make bold moves like that, man, without a lot of yes-men saying yes!"

Bob was starting to get Marbles's line of discussion. More to the point, he realized Marbles had after all at least looked at his proposal. So this whole game before was apparently a show to amuse Marbles. The whole situation was actually nonsense, and yet in this case the nonsense was reality. People generally assume reality has to be reasonable, and thus reason can be used to understand it. Sadly so many human logical constructs appear to be anything but reasonable—well, reasonable at least by the standards of what Bob considered reasonable.

"So in order to get any part of this proposal enacted, I have to get congressional approval? How does anything ever get done here?"

Marbles laughed again. "In the old days, the government used to just pour money directly into its departments, but government workers, so I'm told, are generally thought to be lazy good- for-nothings—fat fucks sitting on their asses doing nothing all day, like a stupid, thieving janitor. All fucking stereotype bullshit, if you ask me. I work harder than any fuck in this country and have to deal all day with fucking lazy-ass idiots. Like I said, when the shit hit the fan and private industry needed the government to pull them out of debt and back into profits, we federalized them and got to manage the trains and the train schedules directly. That didn't last long, though. The private industries came back and convinced Congress it was cheaper to privatize them again years ago. Now for only a small fifty percent overhead-management fee, a private train-management company is paid by the government to do all the actual operation of the trains. They get all the profits, and taxpayers pay all the costs. It is a perfect capitalist system and totally fucking stupid-ass. Like I said, people like Tammy are more like the parrot on the captain's shoulder than captains themselves. They say it is cheaper to run transportation that way."

"So Congress does this because the private companies have centuries more experience, and so they're more efficient, right?" Bob asked.

Marbles laughed. "Sure they are more efficient. They are efficient in that any delays caused by them skimping on repair costs or running older, less efficient trains are blamed on the government-oversight office and its workers. But when the trains are on time, the private companies take credit for it. Hell, if they didn't need an easy scapegoat, they'd probably have gotten fired the whole Department of Transportation by now. The government agency these days is nothing but a middleman used to launder tax money to private industry that can't survive without it. They do this, and it only places an extra twenty-to-fifty percent cost to the running of the civil rail in this country. They say it is a small price to pay for economic efficiency."

"If it costs more, then how is it cheaper?" Bob asked.

"I didn't say it was actually cheaper. I just said they get to say it is fucking cheaper. What is actual and what people get to say is actual do not have to be the same thing. Most people don't understand the concept of absolute truth like I do. Most people are fucking stupid-ass fuckwads. In this world people rarely try to be so accurate as to sort out the difference between what is actual and what people say is actual. Me—as I've said before—I'm a warehouse of knowledge and reason. They are a collective bunch of fuckwads. I know how this shit works—I know the reason they do it. I can't control what the stupid fuckwads say and think. They say life is simpler if one assumes what these idiots wish was true is true and to live in their fucking fantasy world. Fuck them! You won't find me living in a fucking fantasy world, I can tell you that." He gently placed Miss Amazing and Commander Barron von Euro back on his desk.

Bob didn't know what to say. Was this the truth or another of Marbles's fantasies? While Bob was feeling morally superior to the politicians, and not paying attention because he thought they only talked about crap, the politicians had set up the system. It was as if they publicly talked only bullshit so people like Bob wouldn't pay attention to what they were actually doing. When did they do this? Why hadn't he been paying attention? He was embarrassed that someone like Sigmund Marbles knew more about this than him. Why didn't the government talk more about this? Was it really a dishonest game like Marbles said, or was this really a better way to run the country? Why didn't Bob know more about how the country actually worked? A private company totally dependent on the government to stay afloat seemed like fantastical nonsense. These companies and politicians talked so much about how they hate socialism, and yet here they were running on profits from corporate socialism. If this really was how the world worked, how did it affect Bob's desire to get his proposal up and running in Tammy's department?

"So what happens now?" Bob asked. "I try to convince some company to take up my proposal?"

Marbles shook his head. "First thing that happens is I do my job and find out if someone who frankly isn't all that impressive to Judge Drak McNasty really has his shit together. If this fucking thing shows any fucking merit, then Tammy Usher will be in touch with you. Then you go and start getting fucking political— at least if you want this pipe dream in a folder to see the light of day." Marbles now laughed deep and hard. He picked up Judge Drak McNasty and laughed a huge belly laugh as if they were sharing their own private joke.

Bob was worried. He didn't know how to begin getting political. The whole situation seemed terrible to him. "These politicians—they will listen to me and judge my ideas as fairly as Judge Drak McNasty?"

Marbles, still recovering from his joyous romp of laughter with the judge, now tried to right himself and look more official. "Look, our political leaders are like everyone else, and you know already what I fucking think about everyone else. They're just a bunch of fuckwads. If you are a smart guy, then why the fuck should you fucking worry? If you're not, don't fucking worry—this folder won't see the fucking light of day from my desk anyways, so you'll never even have to see a fucking fuckwad politician. So relax, don't worry, and remember the old saying: Those who can, do. Those who can't do, teach. Those that can't do or teach, run for political office."

That ended the interview, and Bob left Marbles and Judge Drak McNasty to look over his proposal. It all looked pretty grim. Then again maybe it was just the dank and smelly rusting basement that made it feel grim.

Chapter 3:

Ignorance Is Like a Delicate Exotic Fruit

Money frees you from doing things you dislike.
Since I dislike doing nearly everything, money is handy.
— Groucho Marx, mustache enthusiast

M itch Boetner is an important person. He had known this at a young age because the rich are born into wealth. If he is important, it's because his great-great-grandfather had created an important process by which wealth was generated. The process was forgotten by later members of the family because the processes that generated money were not as important as the money they generated. Perhaps his long-dead relatives had sold secrets to a now-unknown enemy to start the money pile. That was not important; the process had generated a pot of money, and it was the money that was important now. There was no language that existed that did not have a word for it; if there had not been one, a rich person would have trademarked the word *money* in that language so it would eventually exist anyways.

Most people today think they could not survive without their personal portable mobile electronic device. They claim they would die without it, but you could have existed throughout most of human history without a word for a PPED that carried information in an extremely convenient digitized form. The world, on the other hand, needed money, and people had long ago spoken its name. Presumably right after words *fire, food, sex,* and *mom* were invented, the word that formed the basis for wealth was invented—*money*.

Money wasn't an abstract object meant to represent a good or service owed to you for past services rendered. Money was a living being that, when placed in large enough amounts, became one of the most powerful entities ever created. Money grew and expanded in stone, land, metals, paper, stocks, bonds, futures, derivatives, shorts, and now ones and zeros. The ones and zeros were stored in virtual banks with virtual security obtained by virtual pass codes and acquired by borrowing virtual money from other piles of virtual money. Sometimes a virtual call would ask if all the ones and zeros added up to anything tangible, and no one would know for sure. This would cause markets to temporarily crash. The money pile would virtually shrink, and laypeople with no chance to ever collect their own virtual pile would declare the world on the edge of revolution and call today's money dead. But the doomsayers were always wrong. The money pile of a rich man was among the hardiest things on Earth. These money piles of the wealthy were tough and knew how to live on eternally, it seemed, even as they ventured into negative numbers that would finish off the ordinary poor man. Money could feast on debt and generate from nothing new bodies of wealth through borrowing, bailouts, and economic bubbles.

Today money had only one major disadvantage: it was still a slave controlled by a master—like Mitch Boetner. Sure a few daft intellectuals had proposed freeing money, but other smarter ones had pointed out that these people didn't want to free money at all—they just wanted to trade slave owners. Was it better for money to be freed from enslavement by the rich only to be enslaved to some poor person? Would money be safe in the hands of the average person? Could the average person afford to feed, clothe, and shelter it as the rich did? Wealthy families had shown over the centuries that under their influence and ownership, money was able to prosper to grow. How could money be looked after properly by poor people who had never had money in the first place? I mean, would the great Lord above ever give a child to a person who'd had no child before?

Well, OK, the Lord did give women the gift of children even if they hadn't had them, but what was a child really? There were billions of worthless children around. If you lost a child or two out of inexperience, so fucking what? Children were a dime a dozen; we're talking about something actually important—rich people's money! Besides, a child's first word is usually *mama*. Though science hadn't proven it, it was obvious to the rich that *mama* was child talk for *money*. Mama, after all, was the thing that got you food, shelter, warmth, and water; that's what money got you too. Heck, money was better than mama because mama never got you a Series 4000 Big Balls self-driving electric automobile with the seat warmer built in. Money was better than your mom, and more to the point, it was your personal slave if you—like Mitch Boetner— could afford to have it.

Wealth was not necessarily a sign of greatness, but let's face the facts: unless you had money, the rich were better than you. Did you travel into space just for fun at the age of five? Did you get married in Buckingham Palace? Did you own a relic fragment of Saint Ronald Reagan? No you didn't because you were poor! You were not wealthy, and you and the wealthy both knew it. The rich had grown to not like you so much. You always wanted more of their money pile, and while you could work very hard, you could never work as hard as the rich. You might work four jobs—like a uniquely American worker—but that will not impress the wealthy one bit. Sure you scrubbed toilets, carried trash, repaired sewers, and built trinkets that kept people amused, but the rich were doing the hardest job there could ever be—they were looking after the money piles to make sure the money piles were OK. For without money, where would we all be?

Tammy was traveling today to discuss Bob's proposal with a rich man named Mitch Boetner. She was a little surprised by the glowing report from the technical-assessment office. Maybe glowing wasn't the right word; Sigmund's technical assessment consisted of "This shit don't suck much" followed by a stamp that said, "Judge Drak McNasty's personal seal of cosmic approval." Tammy wasn't exactly sure who the judge was or what cosmic approval was, but the content of the assessment didn't matter as much as the fact it had been returned to her at all. Proposals sent to them usually never saw the light of day, so actually returning something to her was high praise indeed. Even more surprising was that the report had so few pizza stains on it. When Bob's ideas were simulated on their system, they indeed produced the predicted positive scheduling impact. The results were significant enough that Tammy was encouraged to implement them if possible. They were to be rolled out slowly at first to see if the real-life results matched the simulation, and then fully implemented if the results were positive. It was the "if possible" caveat that was now her trouble. While Bob's ideas might work, in order for them to have a chance, they needed to be implemented. But such implementation by her alone was not possible. The contracts with outside private companies were handled by outside influences who made darn sure such a massive rerouting of service would require congressional approval.

Tammy knew a man who had more preferred stock in trains than any other in the country. He had named himself CEO of International Northwestern Pacific Rail. The company didn't actually exist. There were no corporate headquarters, workers, managers, or board members. The whole corporation consisted of Mitch. He was thus a very small company, and like all small businesses, he was the very foundation of what made this country great. Being such a small company, he also qualified for the government assistance reserved for small businesses because they are the backbone of our great nation's greatest gift to the world—our economy. It was because of the tax breaks that Mitch's accountants told him to create the company in the first place. Technically it was International Northwestern Pacific Rail that owned a large portion of the train business. It was a good company; the government picked up much of the cost of business, and Mitch got the profits—well, not Mitch directly. The International Northwestern Pacific Rail got most of the profits, and the company was known to be very generous to Mitch. Tammy knew if she could convince Mitch to invest in Bob's ideas, then Mitch could personally lobby the government. She thought Mitch had a lot of reasons to like the idea.

Lobbying was something Mitch could do as an outside individual who was also a corporation paid directly by the government. Tammy couldn't lobby since she was an actual part of the organizational structure of the government. There were laws to protect elected officials from having to listen to the advice of government workers. Thus she would need Mitch's help to get this proposal implemented. She had previously chastised others for not knowing how to get things done. She had always vowed if a great idea came her way she would do her civil duty and use the system to put it in place for the people. She was, after all, a planner at heart, and she loved making a good plan. Step one was to seek out Mitch and get his help.

Tammy disliked having to drive. She was driving a rental electric car toward her meeting at Mitch Boetner's estate. As a member of the Department of Transportation in charge of train scheduling, it seemed a stain on her person to have to drive somewhere. But far too often the rich simply refused to live near the train lines. No matter how much new rail the country put in service, the rich always managed to have it avoid them. She had thought of taking the bus but rejected it. The bus heading to these parts was sure to be filled only with the "help." The last message she wanted to convey was that she was one of the help. So she rented the car.

The automobile had once been a way for the poor and the middle class to show their freedom from the train robber barons. Cheap petroleum could not last forever, even if the carbon dioxide produced from burning it felt like it did. In postmodern times only the truly wealthy had the luxury of being able to afford to burn petroleum for movement. The rest of the country moved about in more expensive electric automobiles if they could afford them. Most people couldn't afford the cost of parking, maintenance, fuel, and hazardous-waste disposal on a daily travel basis. It was for them that Tammy's mass-transportation network was constructed and maintained. Not every place had embraced the change at first. There was a perceived lack of freedom that accompanied going without daily personal transportation vehicles. But people were free to walk, and they eventually voted with their feet. Mass transportation was better than not being able to afford any at all. The places that resisted the move to mass transit the most ended up being the least hospitable places to live—unless you were rich, which the train riders weren't as we already established.

Mitch was rich. His estate spread over several rolling hillsides. The main building, however, was located in a relatively flat area that had a scenic half-mile drive up from the main road. About halfway through the half-mile driveway was the guard post. Tammy pulled the automobile to a rest at the guard gate. The guard post was nicer than many apartments where Tammy was from. There was an ornate fountain in front that began running as soon as underground sensors detected an approaching visitor.

The main building had a brick facade with a clean, freshly painted white gate that at the moment was closed. A guard came out of the brick building. He looked extremely bored in his slick, official suit. He had a badge on his shirt, a rather impressive authoritative hat with another badge on it, and a black polished leather belt with various instruments of destruction. He took down the license-plate number and then walked over to the driver-side window. "License and registration, please," he said.

Tammy had planned ahead and had them waiting on the seat next to her. She pushed the electronic button that lowered the driver-side window. She reached over grabbed them and gave them to the man. She decided to smooth over the situation with a little small talk. "Such lovely weather we have today, isn't it?"

The guard was too busy tapping into his iPPED to respond immediately. Finally he responded, "Same weather as always here—hot and humid with no chance of relief. I hate it. You're on the list. Before I can let you go, I need to get a retina scan."

"Wow, you guys really go all out for Mr. Boetner. I guess he's a very special kind of guy," said Tammy.

"Not really. He's the type of guy who was born on third base and thinks he hit a single. You'd think for as much money as he has he'd be happier. He's special enough for us to take his pay-checks, but it's not like I'm going to take a bullet for the guy." The guard reach his little hand device through the open car window and flashed it into Tammy's eyes. "OK, you're all scanned in, lady. You can take that rent-a-wreck up to the main house, and good luck shaking the leaves from the tree."

Tammy still had stars in her eyes from the flash of the retina scan. Really, the nerve of that guard having said such things to her. She wasn't there to make money; she was only there on be-half of the state. To assume she was not working from noblest of intentions was one thing; to flash some stupid light in her eyes while she was unprepared was something else altogether. How rude! She decided she would complain. But then again she figured people had complained before. She didn't want seem like a whiner on her first meeting. Darn that guard. What was that third-base crap? Tammy didn't understand the entertainment value of popular sports; even worse, she could not understand archaic sports references.

The gate opened to let her pass. She cruised past the guard gate into the Boetner compound proper. It was rather beautifully landscaped. There were many exotic plants and some nice-looking European statues. Mitch could afford the best replica European statues, but why bother since people only saw them while driving by? Thus he bought statues that looked great from the road, but from the back it was obvious they were completely hollow fakes. But the backs were rarely observed, so what did it matter? Finally a large house came into view through all the foliage. It was classically styled with just a hint of postmodernism. A valet stood by the walkway. The valet stand read, *First two hours parking free with a validation; $55 every half hour thereafter up to $10,000. Please don't forget to tip.* She had to pay to park at Mitch's home?

Tammy parked the car, and the valet ran up to the driver-side window. She rolled down the window and handed over the keys. The valet opened her door, and she stepped out. He swiftly jumped into the vehicle and zoomed off to an unknown destination with her rental car. He left her standing there in front of the house with only a claim ticket in her hand. Well, thought Tammy, I guess I'll see that again when I leave. I mean if you couldn't trust a person like Mitch Boetner to not steal your car, who could you trust? She decided to consult Luke before entering the building.

She paged him on her PPED. Luke's head popped up on the screen. "Luke, it's Tammy. I need to know quickly what being born on third base and thinking you hit a single means."

Luke she knew loved being handy. "Our fearless tribal elder, I want to thank you for hailing me while on your adventure abroad. I am punching in your request now. I have been studying tribal business management intensely lately, and I'm sure the road to happiness is through proper management. Imagine you are a tribe trapped on an island. You only have your wits and your tribal-management structure to keep you alive. Where do you think I should aspire in the tribal structure?"

Tammy was always thankful when Luke abandoned one self-help strategy for another. But the new one quickly wore on you. She was already sick of hearing about tribes. And "tribal elder" made her sound old. She was only in her mid-thirties. "I'm sure you know the answer better than I do," she replied. "All I know about being stuck on island with other people is it isn't good to be the fat kid with the only pair of glasses."

Luke became excited. "I have been a good information scout, my tribal elder. It appears to be a baseball reference. One who is 'born on third base and thinks he hit a triple' is a person who is born into privilege but doesn't exactly understand it. The person was quoting incorrectly or else they were being even wittier and claiming the person was a bit of a delusional complainer despite the privilege they were born into. Looking over Mitch Boetner's personal record suggests this phrase might apply to him. Good luck, tribal elder, and I hope you bring many pelts back to the tribe."

Luke's head disappeared from the screen. Tammy rolled her eyes. Pelts? She was hardly going to slay a lion or a dragon. This was just a little negotiation with a businessman—a businessman who apparently was also a bit of a complainer. Tammy disliked complainers. But she had already planned on him not fully understanding his position in life. The guard, the valet stand, and now Luke's information confirmed she had planned correctly. She headed toward the front door.

Before she could reach the front door, the double doors opened. A butler greeted her at the door. At cheaper estates a robotic house assistant might have been expected. But a true sign of wealth was being able to afford real human servants. A wealthy man like Boetner would no doubt have a butler trained to speak in authentic, old-country English. "Greetings, Ms. Usher. We have been expecting you. Mr. Boetner is enjoying a bit of sun on the veranda." Mitch was really getting his money's worth; the butler sounded exactly like what Americans thought the English sounded like, though it was not at all how the English actually spoke. That type of training was a sign of hiring from only the best vocational or perhaps acting schools. While the postmodern world hardly had many uses for highly trained actors, it still had the typical uses: waiter, domestic servant, bartender, and prostitute.

The butler guided Tammy through several sitting rooms, a nice den, an attractive sunroom, and then what appeared to be a study. Finally they reached a set of doors that lead out onto the veranda. The butler led her through the doors. On the veranda sat a round-shaped man. He wore a tacky Hawaiian shirt, beige shorts, white socks pulled up almost to the knees, and black patent-leather shoes. While his clothes looked casual, they had the air of expensive-casual—except his poor-quality socks, which Tammy thought seemed totally out of place.

"Your Lordship," the butler said, "a Ms. Usher here to see you. I believe it is a matter of concern about your trains."

The man was tapping into his iPPED that sat on his lap. "Thank you, *Atherington*. Please get the lady a seat and perhaps a menu. As for myself I will have another glass of lemonade."

The butler motioned Tammy toward a lounge chair close to Mitch. He then slid a small glass table between the two of them and placed a menu in front of Tammy. She sat down and picked up the menu. "Mr. Boetner, I'm very glad you found time in your busy schedule to see me."

Boetner held up his hand for a second to signal Tammy to stop talking. "Just a second, please. I'm checking to see if my lottery ticket was a winner."

Tammy was shocked that a rich man would play the lottery. "You still play the lottery?"

"Of course," Boetner replied. "I find a dollar a small cost for just a dream. Most dreams cost much more than that."

Tammy believed the lottery was a tax on people bad at math. "Yes, but don't those other dreams have slightly better odds?" she said.

"I never consider the odds; I just consider the end results. You see, buying this ticket I might have won millions of dollars. I haven't yet, and I must've bought a few thousand lottery tickets this year. My accountant says I only won like one hundred dollars. You see, I might have won millions! This year I've had to settle so far for one hundred dollars, but you never know what the future could bring. I might be a millionaire tomorrow. That's not a bad return on a one-dollar dream."

"Was that one hundred dollars net or gross?"

"One hundred dollars is never gross. In fact a one-hundred-dollar bill is a beautiful sight. My father taught me that. A great man my father was. I can only hope to one day to be remembered on the same grounds as him. His death last year was a great loss to the world. I like to sit out here and think about him. Indeed he bought everything here. This was his chair, his table, his veranda, his garden with a statue he bought standing in it." Boetner sighed.

Tammy glanced out into the garden and saw a statue of former president Barack Hussein Obama. *"Oh, that's a lovely statue of the dead president. Was your father a great admirer of the president?"*

Boetner laughed a little. "I doubt it. My dad used to call it the family lawn jockey. He said he always thought of elected officials as public servants, and what white man didn't want a black servant? The president was the only thing my dad said he wanted made in America." Mitch emitted a great big belly laugh. *"Seriously, he had a great sense of humor. He wasn't racist; he just said things that sounded incredibly racist if you're a touchy type of person. He just told friendly jokes, you understand. After all we have that one black friend. We never invite him over or talk to him, but that's only because he's a really good, close friend. Close friends don't need a lot of face-of-face interaction, especially if they're black. At least that's what my dad said. I hope that erases from your mind any thought that my dad was racist, like a lot of the racist liberal people claimed after his death. I thought that was a terrible thing for them to say about my dad. My dad used to say that liberals can't say anything nice, and thus they shouldn't say anything at all."* Mitch laughed even more.

Tammy was amazed that anyone thought she would enjoy this conversation. Why did racists always assume she thought just like them and share their absolute worst thoughts with her? She didn't know; she just knew this scenario was not new to her. She was a magnet for weird racist comments told in private. The butler returned, saving Tammy from further discomfort. "Have you made up your mind, Ms. Usher?" the butler asked.

Tammy glanced down for the first time at the menu. She hadn't planned on eating. She knew it was not exactly polite to not eat lunch at a lunch meeting—it was just that munching on lunch tended to get in the way of the full impact of the pitch. She looked at the menu items—there were some rather yummy selections. Then she noticed there were prices. Prices! He expected her to pay for lunch at his house? She quickly found the cheapest option and ordered it. "I'll have the cheese sandwich and a glass of unsweetened lemonade, thank you." She closed the menu and stared at Mitch in disbelief.

Mitch was still focused on getting his lottery results. "Oh, Atherington, you know I think I'll just have the usual Tuna melt and that glass of lemonade. A person can't really enjoy a veranda in the afternoon without a glass of lemonade. After sunset a mint julep might do, but in the afternoon sun, Dad always drank lemonade. He said flavored ice tea was for queers and fags."

Tammy hoped to turn the subject from Mitch's dead, bigoted father, so she said, "I didn't see tuna on the menu. I thought it was illegal now to buy tuna; they're nearly extinct, after all."

Mitch frowned. "Crap, looks like I lost again, and I had bought ten tickets this time! With those kinds of odds, you'd have thought I would have won at least something. What did you say about the tuna? Oh yeah, tuna is still very illegal to buy and sell on the open market. That's why I don't. I bought a Puerto Rican fisherman to fish for me instead. He catches illegal fish of all kinds for me. You understand in many places while it is illegal to buy tuna, it is still legal to sport fish and catch them in small quantities as long it is for personal use. This guy gets it and then personally uses it."

Tammy asked, "How is your eating the fish this fisherman's personal usage?"

"Well, that's what I bought. I purchased from him his personal usage. His fish is illegal to buy and sell on the open market, but his personal usage of the fish is not. So that's what I bought—his personal usage of the fish he caught. That was Dad's clever idea, not mine. Dad was a genius."

Atherington returned with the sandwiches and two lemonades. He placed them in front of Tammy and Mitch. He pulled out a fresh, white cloth napkin and put it on Mitch's lap. He then placed a paper towel folded like a napkin next to Tammy. "Here you go, Ms. Usher. Would you care for a cloth napkin? They do cost extra."

Tammy replied, "While I believe a paper towel is not technically a napkin, it can be used for one, and I plan on using it just as that. I'll skip the extravagances of cloth just this once, thank you."

With that he looked to Mitch to see if he needed anything else. Mitch was now thoroughly engrossed in the tuna sandwich, so the butler took his departure.

For the first time, he was more or less facing Tammy instead of his iPPED. "Tammy Usher, when did we last meet face to face? I seem to remember it was, what, five years ago at the International Railroad Exhibition in Buffalo? I vaguely remember you trying to talk my dad into replacing a bridge of ours. Something about it being a costly hazard, and that it was bound to fail one of these days. Come to think of it, you must have been wrong because I don't remember any bridge causing any kind of disaster for this family."

Tammy had just tasted her unreasonably priced cheese sandwich and waited to swallow before she replied. "It was eight years ago, and I was only an assistant back then in charge of bridge surveillance and maintenance. I believe you are remembering incorrectly about there not being a disaster as well. I asked you to consider replacing the McConnell Transit Bridge. I had several engineering estimates of the lifetime left on the bridge and the hazards of not replacing it. Your father refused to accept the findings of the government and continued to operate over the bridge. As predicted, the bridge failed four years ago while a train was on it. I believe one hundred thirty-five people died."

Mitch sipped his lemonade. "Oh, that's good lemonade—nice and sour with just a hint of sweet. I remember that bridge thing now. But that was hardly a disaster for this family. If I remember correctly, after you told Dad you felt the bridge wasn't safe, he took out a huge insurance policy on the bridge and the trains he ran over it. I believe he made several hundred million from the insurance coverage of the failure. Bad bet for the insurance company for sure. They lobbied the government to declare it a national disaster, and they got their money back too, of course."

Tammy repeated slowly, muting her anger as much as possible, "I believe one hundred thirty-five people died."

Mitch was excited now. "Yes, but on the bright side, Dad used the overwhelming sympathy for the dead generated by the media coverage to guilt the government into paying to have the bridge rebuilt for them. The government paid all the costs, and my dad got to keep all the profits generated by the bridge. He was such a genius. He used to say government should stay out of businesses and let them sort out the bad companies themselves. If a company was truly bad, people would learn not to use its bad service. Thanks, Ms. Usher, for reminding me once again it was you who tipped my dad off to that great business transaction. I was thinking you were probably some government busybody who would just waste my time on pollution or some bullshit. Dad always told me most government workers were just leeches on our tax dollars. Instead I see you're a shrewd, business-oriented woman, even if you do unfortunately work for the government."

Tammy was a little horrified that Mitch's father had used her advice to profit from the deaths of one hundred and thirty five people! Worse, Mitch somehow thought better of Tammy because he thought that's what she had wanted them to do. She was mad. People would learn? She thought dead people tended to be particularly bad learners. She would've thrown her cheese sandwich in his face if she hadn't promised herself to do everything in her power to get a good idea implemented if she ever had the opportunity to do so. She had failed eight years ago to get that bridge repaired, but she was younger and in a less powerful position. She had in her hands a vastly more important idea. She could tolerate the Mitches of the world if it meant finally getting something worthwhile done. Still she felt the need to insult Mitch a little.

"It was luck the media didn't report how unsympathetic your father was in not preventing those one hundred thirty-five deaths," she said.

Mitch was enjoying his tuna sandwich even more. "Oh, that wasn't luck. Nah, my dad owned that particular media station. He always got good press from it. He used to say there was no better press than a few people dying, just so long as no one thought to blame you for it. Anyways, it's kind of funny if you think about it, because I didn't know them. Tragedy is when you slip on a banana peel and fall. *Comedy* is when you get to watch someone else fall down an *open manhole* and die."

Tammy thought that was not exactly how the famous quote went. It was going to be a tougher lunch than she thought. Mitch made it hard for her to keep her food down with his disgusting opinions. Hopefully Mitch wouldn't talk too much more before she could finish eating. "Perhaps," she began, "since you are keen for my business advice, we should talk about this proposal. A rather brilliant scientist came to me with a proposal for increasing efficiency in the transit line by at least ten percent!" Tammy exaggerated a little, but a little white lie never hurt a man like Mitch. She continued, "He is looking for an advocate to push through congressional approval. You see, his plan would affect the financial side of things, and thus we need Congress to approve it. I assure you it could make millions—maybe even billions—with just a small upfront cost and of course your advocacy."

Mitch made a *pft* noise with his mouth. Tammy apparently said something that annoyed him. But Mitch was not going to let such a thing ruin his sandwich. He finished his last bite before continuing the conversation. "You really should have known to order the tuna even if was off the menu. It's fantastic, and I would have offered it at a good price if the law allowed me to do so. Oh well, there is always the next visit and the hope of more fair treatment of endangered tuna sandwiches that have harmed no one and less concern for endangered tunas. Now, this scientist of yours I imagine is a young and energetic person. He probably expects life to give him everything for nothing. That's the problem with today's youth—they expect to just be given everything without working for it. Well, life doesn't work like that. Life isn't fair; you just don't get something for nothing because you want it. That's rule one by which my dad taught me to live my life. I don't just give things away because your sense of fairness says I should."

Tammy replied, "Well, we don't expect you to give us something for nothing. Like I said, the deal is actually much fairer to you than me, who gains nothing financially, for you must remember I get paid by the government. While the scientist will make a little money from his patents in the proposal, he isn't expecting the lion's share of the wealth. It is you—who did nothing to invent this proposal, spent no money to create it, and is only asked to advocate it—who stands to gain the most! Being that you are the principal owner of the companies, your benefit is bound to be huge if the proposal in enacted. In terms of fairness, I'm pretty sure you are bound to finish on top. No one expects a fair result from this proposal; we have all accepted that you will finish on top."

Mitch smiled at that answer. "Oh good—that sounds very acceptable. I see you have thought this out properly. You do always bring good business to this family. But there are other rules my dad taught me. Let's see now...oh yes, I remember: Nothing is beneath your dignity, even flipping a burger or two. Your ancestors didn't complain about doing hard work and neither should you. What today's young people complain is hard work, their ancestors called *opportunity*. So are the two of you ready to do the hard work to get the opportunity to enact this thing?"

Tammy was disgusted. When her ancestors came to this country, America had a high rate of upward mobility. But it had been years and years since that was true. The upper class had long ago rigged the system to greatly slow down the rate of upward mobility. The idea that hard work could propel you, generation after generation, to improved financial situations was a century-old truth, and today it was a pipedream—a pipedream repeated to the poor over and over so they would continue to work themselves to death while the Mitches of the world absorbed all the wealth from the work. Despite all that, they still had the nerve to charge you for a cheese sandwich at their own house! Opportunity? Heck, Tammy faced another forty years of paying off her high school, college, and apartment loans. Her children, if she were lucky enough to have them, would be lucky to have anything more than her debt to inherit.

"I can assure you," Tammy replied, "I have never expected to get something for nothing. The amount of personal debt I've accrued to get as far as I have surely will attest to that. I came here precisely because I am willing to do the hard work to get things done. I know to get this done, I will no doubt have to do the hard work of speaking to many worthless loudmouths with overly inflated opinions of themselves and very low opinions of the worth of average people."

Mitch nodded in agreement. "Oh, that is so true. Tammy, you are really a remarkable intellect. I'm sorry you chose to work in the public sector; in business no doubt you would have really got things done for people—like I do. Of course there are many idiots with big egos in Congress, and no doubt we will have to talk to them in order to get this proposal thing passed. I myself have not been particularly successful lobbying them. I believe that you, by law, can also not directly advocate them. That leaves us to use this scientist to do it for us. He might be the weak link in the deal. My dad had a rule that the real world doesn't care about your self-esteem; you're expected to accomplish something before you feel good about yourself. So is this scientist fellow one of those hippie, feel-good-accomplish-nothing types, or will he wait to celebrate until after he's worked good and hard for me?"

"I assure you," Tammy replied, "he has always worked very hard in his life. He is not living on some commune hugging trees all day while smoking God knows what. He has a normal job working at the patent office. He has excellent performance reviews that never mention happiness or joy but do mention yearly accomplishments. I believe he even works at a very low salary."

Mitch seemed a little excited by that last part. "Oh good. I hate a man who expects a huge salary up front. Now I will be expected to spend a little money to grease the political process. My dad was always willing to grease the wheels. But one of his rules was to avoid workers who expected a living wage right up front. He used to complain that today's workers expect a good living-wage salary right out of school. Totally unbelievable—I mean no one should expect a boss who is going to make you, right out of college, a vice president of a company with a corporate iPPED."

Tammy added, "I believe I read that your dad didn't wait until you were out of college even—he made you a vice president of his company at the age of ten."

Mitch replied, "Well yes, that is true. But you see, that was something to do with taxes or tax credits about something. My dad was always thinking of new ways to bleed the beast, you know. The point I was making had to do with you expecting to be made vice president—not whether you just happened to become one. At ten I totally didn't expect to be made vice president, although I was made one. You understand the difference between the purely theoretical point I was making and my actual life? People often confuse the two, my dad would say. He always told me today's people were all taught in postmodern schools to live in a fantasy world without winners and losers. But the real world has clear winners and losers, and his rule was to understand this and make sure you aren't a loser!"

Tammy thought about Mitch's comfortable life and how little he knew about reality growing up in this house with that father. The reality was that the world was a harsh place for kids without obscene family wealth. They grew up seeing their relatives die from diseases that could have been cured had they been able to afford health insurance. Then they watched their parents, if they were lucky enough to have two, work their lives away at one, two, and sometimes three jobs just to get by. In the real world, kids went to schools with incredibly large class sizes and few teaching materials for them to use. They often went to that school hungry, wearing the clothes of an elder sibling because the family couldn't afford to buy new clothes. When they came home from school, they didn't exactly walk into a pro-education environment as their parents often drank, smoked, and watched too much escapist TV. They didn't have a rich father who could pay away any mistake. They understood they got three mistakes; any more and they spent the rest of their lives in jail. They also understood the system was set up to find every mistake kids like them made and to look away from mistakes made by rich kids. It wasn't only a harsh world on the outside after you left school. Heck, most kids went to a school filled with kids who had more than them and didn't mind making you feel bad if you had less. If you wore the wrong clothes, a person like Mitch might, if you were lucky, make fun of you; if you were unlucky, he'd hold you down and beat you up or shave your head. If you acted too different at school, it only got worse. This was the life of middle-class kids. If you were poor, the reality of growing up was vastly worse. The poor grew up knowing their life options boiled down to spending the majority of life in for-profit prisons, military service, or absolute poverty with little hope of escape. If the Mitches of the world thought kids didn't understand the winners and losers in the real world by the time they left school, it was only because he had been isolated by his parents from reality since he was born.

Tammy said, "Well, that's why we have come to you, Mitch. We need a winner on our team, and everyone knows your family is on the winning side."

Mitch blushed a little in a surprising show of modesty. "Oh really, now. Like I said, I'm not actually that good at things like this. My dad was so good, and I try to be like him, but somehow things never work out as well as Dad did it. All those Congress people know me now. I think we need that fresh face in on this—like I said we need to get that scientist to pitch it to them. Now I'll arrange this thing. I'll set up a meeting with people my dad and I worked with in the past. We'll send in this guy to meet them and dazzle them with technical magic. Yes, I can see that working. We will use a little money to grease the system. A small upfront investment and boom—suddenly I pull in a big deal. Everyone will be amazed and say I am just like my father. Now I'm trusting you, Tammy, to have the real goods on this proposal thing. I don't want to read it or anything as I am a busy man, and I don't have time to learn or understand things, you understand. It's enough to know it has something to do with trains and it will make me money—like you've made me money in the past with that bridge thing. We'll trust this science guy to know stuff. My dad always told me I should be good to nerds because someday you might need to rent one for a while to extract their useful information before discarding them back to the sidelines where they belong."

Mitch stood up. "It looks like our meeting is over. Send me the science guy's contact information, and I'll have someone set up a meeting with some politicians. I'd stay and chat more, but I have to go for my afternoon swim. I have an extremely busy schedule, you know. A healthy body is a sound body, my dad always said. You can't spend all day working; you have got to recharge your batteries every once in a while. Hopefully someone will invent a way to just plug your brain into a new body over and over so you can chuck away your old body, like I do my batteries. Who really has time to recharge a battery? Oh well. I like swimming, you know. Good bye, Tammy. You'll be hearing from my organization soon."

Tammy started to get up to leave when she remembered something. "Oh silly me—I almost left without getting my validation." She pulled out her parking ticket and handed it to Mitch.

Mitch seemed disappointed that Tammy had remembered the validation. "Atherington will take care of that as he's showing you out. Anyways, you still have to pay him for the meal and the view charge."

"What is the view charge?"

"Normally my father would charge a visitor just for the privilege of seeing him. Now to charge a person in that fashion comes off a little pompous, so we changed that a little bit. These gardens don't come cheap, and we live in such expensive times, you know. I charge a flat two thousand dollars to enjoy this view with me. But seeing that we are now friends and you keep bringing in good business for this family, I'll cut you a break and give you a two-hundred-dollar discount." Mitch smiled, patted Tammy on the shoulder, and made his exit.

Atherington now came up to Tammy. "I carry change, or if you prefer I can place the charges with the credit agent of your choice."

Tammy faked a smile. She took out her wallet. She liked to carry a maximum number of credit cards not to use, but to impress on people that she was well-prepared for situations where payment was required. She handed one over to Atherington who had a handheld PPED credit scanner. Tammy said, "Oh, please thank Mr. Boetner for being so generous."

With the payment process done, she turned and followed Atherington out the door. Overall the meeting, while expensive, had been a success. She got what she planned to get. For the time being, Mitch had unfortunately placed the future in Bob's control, not hers. She was not exactly happy about that. It was her personal mission, and she wanted more control. Still, for the price of parking, a view, lunch, and horrible conversation, she had gotten Mitch to commit his advocacy and some upfront money to the proposal. He'd come out the winner today, but she'd persuaded him to commit to much greater expenses in the long run than she'd just paid. He might make money in the long term, but he'd probably lost the lottery on this part of the proposal process. Things were moving, and she felt like a winner—that was enough to keep her happy on the long drive back to town.

Chapter 4:
Live Free or Diet

Water, water everywhere, nor any drop to drink.
— Samuel Taylor Coleridge, rhymer

B ob walked up to an unassuming little DC café. Mitch had told him this meeting was important but not to oversell himself. Mitch had assured him these congressmen love nonpolitics, and the presence of Mitch would potentially sour the deal. Tammy couldn't come either since she wasn't allowed to directly lobby Congress. It was up to Bob to convince them his idea was worth investing in. Mitch had coached him that congressmen tended to have the conversations they wanted to have, but not to worry about that. But Bob did worry because he didn't yet understand what that meant. This all seemed like a lot of work to get a good idea implemented. He had not dreamed he would have to talk directly to congressmen by himself. It felt like an honor to speak with an elected official who wanted to learn more about trains.

The café had a simple green-painted front with a small front patio sectioned off by a black metal fence. The furniture outside was basic polished aluminum with plain white tablecloths. The place had been recommended to Mitch by the congressmen. In large white letters on the front of the café loomed the name of the restaurant: FOOD. A simple and overall pleasant place to meet and greet people, Bob thought. Why should he be worried? After all he understood his idea better than anyone else. He was glad the two congressmen had suggested the place now. It was much better to meet someone important in a casual setting. Mitch had told Bob to dress business-casual, and Bob as his agent had taken his business advice.

Bob walked up to the host stand in front of the gate to enter FOOD. A pleasant, smiling young woman dressed in a tight-fitting black uniform stood waiting to receive another potential FOOD costumer. "Hello, I'm Sunshine. Welcome to FOOD. We have a wide variety of low-fat, hormone-free, all-natural, homegrown, unprocessed, organic foods for your dining enjoyment. Will you be dining outside or in today, sir?"

Bob wondered if the meal would come hermetically sealed straight from the fields to his plate. The restaurant staff was clearly well trained in postmodern speaking. Modern times had only a primitive form of this called *doublespeak*. The postmodern world had elevated this to *triplespeak*, which amazingly used words to modify words in a way that actually added no universal meaning to the words modified, and yet somehow usually transformed them into something grander than before. The magic occurred in the average listener's imagination. The right word would trigger him or her to fill in the meaning of the words to fit whatever the listener wanted the words to mean. Thus the imagination would transform what might be a horrible-sounding thing into a more suitable subject for the listener's brain. For example, a rundown playground filled with drug dealers, pedophiles, and hazardous playground equipment could be transformed into a positive place not by corrective actions that required money and community interest, but by using triplespeak. Instead of calling it what it was, you might instead call it Moonbeam Pony's Magical Pedophilic Enchanted Mystery Forest. Now what parent would be afraid to send his or her kids to that?

A quick glance at other diners in the outside café area seemed to indicate the triplespeak buzzwords were more heavy-handed than the establishment's translation of them. The food at FOOD seemed normal and unintimidating, at least at this distance.

"I'm here to meet Representatives Buy and Haye for lunch," Bob responded. "I believe a Mitch Boetner reserved a table for us."

Bob looked the smiling, friendly receptionist over. She had a look of honesty about her. Bob lacked an overactive, average imagination, and thus triplespeak was not very effective on him. He decided to take her into his confidence: "Ah, can I be honest with you? I don't know exactly what all this natural and organic stuff means. Could you explain it to me?"

The simper fell slightly from her face, and she moved in closer to Bob. "Honestly, between you and me, I think it means we get to charge the customers an extra one hundred fifty percent. Heck, I myself can't tell the difference between normal food and FOOD food. On my break I prefer to go across the street to Sparky the Clown Burgers. Sparky the Clown never claimed to be good for you except in the wallet, and my wallet most days is my most vulnerable area." The smile returned to her face now as a sign of a secret told between honest strangers.

"Now as Representatives Haye and Buy are two of our best customers," Sunshine continued, "we have your party seated in the preferred congressional corner table. Follow me to your table, and good luck in your venture with the representatives." She grabbed a menu and guided Bob effortlessly through the maze of outdoor tables to the corner with the dexterity of a ballerina. She had obviously made the trip through the tables countless times before.

"Your server today will be Blessed Joy. Enjoy your dining experience with us today at FOOD," smiled Sunshine. And with that Sunshine left Bob to his own devices at the preferred corner table at FOOD.

Bob momentarily wondered to himself if her real name was Sunshine. He turned his gaze from the retreating Sunshine to the table he had been lead to. Though he was supposed to meet two men, only one man was sitting at the table. He looked clean and tidy with a nicely trimmed beard, a nice and expensive tailored suit, a polished leather jacket, and an appropriate and impressive (to Bob at least) power tie. Bob looked down at his makeshift casual department-store suit and felt perhaps he was underdressed. Mitch had assured him not to worry about his appearance with these men, but he was starting worry that Mitch's business opinions might not be totally dependable.

"Ah, you are Mitch's business associate, Bob, I believe. Yes, you are exactly as Mitch described you. I truly believe I am standing with a genius according to Mitch. Ha." The man made an unconvincing fake laugh at his own private joke about Mitch, in what appeared to have been a joke at Mitch's expense.

The man spoke again, "I'm representative Haye. Please feel free to sit down and join me. I was just trying to figure out myself what to order. You know, even with such a perfect menu of organic foods available here, I still have such trouble. In these very troubled food times, you see, the public is always eager to hear of a politician willing to stand up and identify a food issue and make it the most important food issue of our generation. You understand this, I'm sure."

Bob sat down. Dropping his guard, Bob said, "Oh, yes, I understand. Getting enough to eat to everyone is a constant worry, I am sure. It's sort of a guilty feeling to eat such fine food when so many find themselves making a choice about which child gets dinner tonight."

"Oh dear, I forget you voters don't ever clearly understand the most pressing food issue of our generation at all. That whole feeding-the-hungry thing was our fathers', or perhaps our fathers'

fathers', generation's problem to solve. I can't be caught wasting my time solving the unsolved problems of our ancestors, or I will miss the opportunity to solve the food problems of today. I would hate to think a generation from now, a future representative will curse our generation's Congress for not solving our problems today because we were too focused on our ancestors' unsolved problems. Don't get me wrong—I still support solid progressive programs like food stamps, agricultural subsidies, and the lot. It's just that if they still leave so many hungry, well that was my father's father's problem. I need to always focus on today. Do you understand?"

Bob did not understand. Bob made a face like a man who didn't understand and really hoped someone wouldn't explain it to him because he didn't want to know.

The representative went on: "My friend, today it is the 'junk food' that is killing this nation. We modern lawmakers are targeting this so-called obesity epidemic, brought on by this 'junk' food, with well-thought-out, compromised positions that target bullets of strong bipartisan support and place the cost of the solutions on the individual based on his or her ownership responsibility without overregulation of our valued free market. Now I myself—and I don't pretend to speak for the less-learned Representative Buy on this—favor placing a small excise tax on processed foods and on foods and drinks sweetened with unnatural or natural sugars. I am not in favor of efforts to remove this cheap 'junk' food from our schools, fast-food restaurants, and store shelves. In a world of illegal soda, only the criminals will have their thirst effervescently refreshed. You see, personal responsibility means if a person chooses to eat junk, then he or she simply should pay slightly extra for the pleasure. It's no different from what society has done for years to the smoker, the distilled alcohol drinker, or the gambler."

Bob glanced over the prices of the preferred healthy, hormone-free, all-natural, organic food on the FOOD menu. Three hundred forty-five dollars for all-natural, mountain-spring bottled water!

Bob was glad Mitch was footing the bill for this lunch. Not fully following the representative's train of thought, he interjected, "Isn't the difference you don't have to smoke, drink, or gamble, but people do have to eat food? Won't the effect of making this cheap junk food—the kind of food the poor can afford to eat—more expensive be an increase in the number of people who are hungry?"

Haye didn't answer right away, instead turning his attention to another smiling, attractive young woman dressed in tight-fitting black. "Ah, here comes Blessed Joy, our server. She is really a good server, you know. Buy and myself always sit in her section."

The rather nice-looking young woman came up to the table. She seemed friendly in an it-pays-to-be-friendly-if-you-want-a-good-tip way. She stood patiently with her PPED order pad. "Now, Blessed Joy, you already know I would simply love some fresh, natural, sparkling mountain-spring bottled water to drink. Bob, the spring water here is rather good, you know—shipped all the way from the natural mountain springs in the north of Holland."

Bob failed to see how a two-month boat journey from a non-existent place in a sealed plastic container would keep the water fresher than normal tap water. "I think I'll risk the regular tap water today," said Bob, noting that the tap water was free while the bottled fresh, natural mountain spring water from the north of Holland was three hundred and forty five dollars a bottle; it was five hundred dollars a bottle if you wanted BPA-free, fresh, natural, sparkling mountain spring water. The tap water did have a fifteen-dollar corkage fee, which made you wonder how the FOOD plumbing worked.

Representative Haye said, "Nonsense, my boy. Remember, this meal is on your business associate Mitch, so let's have three bottled waters all around, Blessed Joy, if you please." Blessed Joy whisked herself away, efficiently taking the drink order back into the café proper without saying a word to them. It was almost as if in months of service, she had learned conversations could quickly become complicated around a man like Representative Haye.

Haye returned to the discussion: "Well, of course I am in favor of changing our food-stamp program, you know. I don't want the starving to go from starving on cheap unhealthy food to starving on expensive unhealthy food in the future. Why the whole point is to get them to change their eating habits, and to do that they have to eat something. I need them to purchase expensive healthy food and eat it. Why in several cities we have already been able to produce bipartisan legislation that will not allow the purchase of this unhealthy junk food with food stamps. Good healthy food purchased with good healthy food stamps will lean up this darn old obesity epidemic."

"So, I imagine, would starvation," Bob replied sarcastically.

"Yes, good point. A well-planned fast here and there never hurt a person's waistline. I was thinking about introducing a food stamp for fasting, but I'm not sure where anyone could spend it. You know, it's a constant worry about perception in this elected office. I try to do what is best for the people, but people don't always appreciate it. On one hand you have people demanding action. You know—people stating the government needs to augment society to encourage good-eating habits on Americans. On the other hand there are the people who think it's their personal freedom to weigh four hundred pounds if they want to. I worry constantly of the crowd all shouting 'nanny state.' I am an elected official, not a nanny. I don't want a government that goes beyond recommending healthy eating habits and regulating food safety to now telling the people what they may and may not afford to put in their mouths—unless this recommendation comes in stamp form, and a fasting stamp might just be what this country needs."

Bob looked at the menu: $449.95 for an organic-raised turkey burger seasoned with all-natural organic sea salt dressing.

"So you have strong conservative support for this new food-stamp program?" Bob asked.

The representative sighed. "Well, no. While I'm above such petty squabbles—and while my ideas are strictly bipartisan, and

I have derived an extremely fair-handed method of working on a path toward solving this epidemic—compromise is still never easy. My food-stamp idea was originally a conservative idea that conservative think-tank lobbyists brought to me. I weighed it and decided it was an idea worth starting to compromise on. But you see, as soon as I started to compromise on the subject, conservatives had changed their mind. Suddenly they felt an additional rider at the federal level should be added, one that suggested perhaps food stamps should be forfeited by those people who refuse to lose weight while on them. There was this whole conservative legislative fear that poor people were taking advantage of the system and getting all fat and/or intoxicated on our government's largesse. Government largesse and obesity don't mix. So they introduced the concept of regular drug-and-weight testing for all those who apply for food stamps to make sure they're complying with our nations standards. I, of course, saw this as a congressional overreach of an already successful program at the state level and naturally proposed the compromise position that we only periodically drug-test them and only track the weight of the really fat ones. Demanding weight loss from people who are actually skinny and starving to begin with seems a little too extreme. Of course there is now a heated discussion of how fat is fat and what we accept as fat. I'm sure if I compromise a little more, I can reach a solid moderate position that the majority of voters will accept. As you can see, policy making is a give-and-take process."

Yes, thought Bob, it was one in which they take food from poor people to give themselves the satisfaction of feeling they are helping them out without helping them out.

Blessed Joy arrived back at the table perfectly balancing three bottles of fresh, all-natural mountain spring water and three glasses filled with ice made from tap water. She effortlessly placed the glasses down on the table, opened the bottled water, poured it into the glasses, and then left the remaining bottled water next to the glass. With her task now done and seeing Representative

Buy had still not arrived to order, she effortlessly moved back into the sea of tables.

To Bob, being a representative was starting to look like a tough picture. Bob at this point no longer felt honored to be talking to one. This Representative Haye seemed like a man eager to convince himself of something. Bob sure wished they were talking about the train scheduling, though, instead of the food issue. He wished the conversation had to do with working hard to find a compromise on getting the train proposal enacted. If only he could find an angle to work it into the conversation, then perhaps the representative would work as hard to find a compromise position on something that might help people—as opposed to whatever nonsense would likely the come of this junk-food thing. Now all he needed was a way to get out of this current conversation so he could have the conversation he was there for. Bob decided to try a dodge: Why talk about terrible unhealthy food while they were at FOOD with its very healthy and very expensive options?

"Let's try to avoid this whole junk-food thing and order from this fine menu," Bob said.

Bob pulled the menu to his face and once again scanned for a safe food to order at FOOD. They had an all-American, farm-raised Irish stew for a bargain $359.95. What could be wrong with that? thought Bob.

"I'm thinking of getting your basic meat and potatoes—Irish stew. You can't go more basic than that, can you?" Bob smiled thinking he had started the escape to safe conversational territory.

Representative Haye sighed. "Oh, we would like to think that. Let me explain how tough my job is. The question so often in these times is, 'What is junk food?' This doesn't come from my enemies, the conservatives; no, this is my fellow liberals on the attack. I need to find a comfortable middle ground between the conservatives and, worse, my own angry constituents. Take your all-American Irish meat and potatoes. That couldn't possibly be junk food, right? Well, any red-blooded liberal vegetarian will tell you meat is murder—murder in the first degree of a sentient living thing! You don't want the guilt of being a murderer, do you? Sounds bad on your record to have them shouting *murderer* at you in a town hall because you ate a little bacon. Who wants to be a murderer? Not me, because that town-hall moment wouldn't look good in my opponents' campaign attack ads. So your basic meat has to be political junk food for sure. So there goes meat from our menu options. To be safe—and I'm always safe—any vegan political advisor will quickly correct us on milk, cheese, and eggs, so out they go too. I just can't afford to be seen eating meat and animal products and be considered in favor of eliminating junk food and against the obesity epidemic."

Bob was stunned by his inability to kill the food conversation that rapidly took them farther away from the point of being there. Perhaps it was best to simply ask what to order as a matter of politically correct etiquette.

"But that potato is OK to order, right?" Bob asked.

"We'd both like to think so, but I tell you the answer is a simple no as well. The potato is made of starch. What is starch? Why it's nothing but a fancy college-schooled name for sugars that associate with each other in an aggregated fashion. We both know from first principles the answer to whether sugar is OK, right?"

Bob was pretty sure at this point they were on the verge of one of the long, logical runs the representative was fond of. What was it about this time? So many people talk and talk but never say anything worth hearing. Either way it seemed an appropriate response at this time to shake his head no in an attempt to find agreement. He was, after all, still trying to get this man to sponsor his idea and order lunch.

"Of, course not," Haye continued. "Sugar is bad, particularly sugars that hang out together in aggregated hoodie-wearing starch gangs. High-fructose corn syrup is clearly 'junk' food as any food-concerned liberal voter is likely to know. As a scientist I'm sure you're aware of that. You know, high-fructose corn syrup isn't easily identified from real cane sugar because the two can have the exact same chemical formulation. What am I supposed to do—support the facts of reality or the fantasy concerns of my voters? Ha! Foul, you cry. But to argue that would cause you to fall into those voters' trap for the representative. The difference and the trap is not what they are, but how they are made. High-fructose corn sugar is made in a chemical process by man, and natural sugar is made by a chemical process in nature. People, particularly my voters, are under the impression Mother Nature is our friend, no matter who Mother Nature kills with her earth-quakes, hurricanes, and tornadoes. Mother Nature, they know, never ever makes things we can't eat—well besides meats, eggs, cheese, and milk. This kind of stuff seems complicated no doubt, but, my friend; this is what a representative deals with on any simple daily decision."

Bob thought Representative Haye was clearly skilled in debat-ing himself out of eating anything. If this was the insanity a rep-resentative dealt with just ordering food, he was beginning to see that train-schedule green light at the end of pier drifting further away with each moment.

Bob was confused. Why did they meet at a place where noth-ing on the menu was eligible for eating? Well, certainly those $199.95 salads of pure, organic, hydroponic-grown leaves in simu-lated all-natural composted soil were OK. Perhaps if he suggested that for them to eat, he could end the conversation and start push-ing his actual train proposal.

"I can see how difficult your life must be, Representative. I was thinking of playing it safe and having a salad for lunch."

Haye once again frowned. Oh dear, thought Bob—not salad too.

The representative said, "You would think vegetables would be OK?" Hayes touched his iPPED screen a few times, and up popped an Internet site with an alarming story. Haye thrust the screen into Bob's view again. "Here, look for yourself. An Internet alarmist site about some companies putting wood product into their food as filler. Wood product! They call this wood product just another form of fiber. As a scientist I ask you, what is wood product?" In another few touches of the screen, the word *cellulose* appeared. "That's right, cellulose—another of those evil aggregates of our enemy, the sugar. That cellulose stuff is the same stuff that bulks up all those vegetables and fruit with fiber! If some random person on the Internet is alarmed about this wood product in my food, what's to stop them from finding out their vegetables and fiber are full of that wood product stuff? If they're the same people who also worried about sugar in my food, then well hell—suddenly my seat in Congress is in jeopardy if I touch a vegetable! That's good enough for me to know I need to avoid these bulked up, wood-product vegetables."

Bob's stomach made a growling sound, perhaps out of spite for the conversation taking place.

Suddenly out of the sea of tables, another voice erupted: "You're always too worried, Haye. Just order three fucking steak sandwiches, and let's get this meeting started with some meat." Bob looked over to see a fat, shaggy-bearded man with long white hair tied in a ponytail, dressed in an ill-fitting jogging suit and sandals. Representative Buy signaled to Blessed Joy—who had appeared as if by magic right next to the table—with a hand extended and three fingers up. Blessed Joy nodded her head and disappeared again into the sea of tables.

The man extended a hand to Bob. "Hi, I'm Representative Buy. I hope you guys ordered something a little stronger than spring water to drink." Buy then pulled out a chair and plopped down into it with an audible thud. "My colleague is informing you on his constant worries, no doubt. I usually arrive about the time you've been left to a nice, simple diet of nothing. Ah crap, I see we have spring water. Now, Haye, have you even asked this man yet why he's here?" Buy looked to Haye then over to Bob.

"Look, it is OK for *you* to be outrageous, but I have actual bills pending votes. I'd feel more comfortable with a salad, and I believe our visitor would too. Why he was just talking about the salad and its benefits," said Representative Haye.

Representative Buy turned to Bob and now started to explain his position on lunch. "Look, I refuse to compromise my lunch based on the fear some idiot will twist my lunch into a political, moral, and ethical statement on society. Today's pop-ecology movement is nuts. They have every moron with an Internet connection believing that plants are happy to fill their role as fodder for herbivores in a harmonious and perfectly balanced ecosystem. Screw that."

The three men were interrupted by the prompt arrival of lunch. Blessed Joy arrived at the table with three plates with three steak specials and a rum and Coke for Representative Buy. She quietly placed the plates around the three men and put the drink by Representative Buy. She then pulled out three steak knives and set them in their proper places. She then filled up Bob and Haye's water. Without a sound from her or the three men, she glanced over the table and, apparently finding it to her satisfaction, faded again into the background of the tables.

Bob was startled by the surprising silence that fell over the table. The other two men were too busy cutting and eating steak to talk, apparently. Bob wondered if they were finally waiting for him to speak. Or perhaps he should just eat like them. Bob figured the silence was more to his favor to speak since these men liked to talk a lot. He might not get another chance to see them with their faces full. Bob took a subtle deep breath and thought, OK, here I go.

"Hi, gentlemen. I see now is probably a good time to talk about Mitch Boetner and the new train proposal that he is supporting."

Representative Buy halted the pitch quickly. "Look, we all understand why Mitch has gathered this lunch together. I didn't come here to talk trains, you understand; I came to eat."

Bob nodded since he had taken the opportunity to try the steak. The steak was very good. Representative Haye was eating the steak rapidly despite being self-conscious about it just minutes earlier. Bob assumed either he was enjoying it too, or he was trying to clear the evidence of its existence before some voter noticed him eating it. Bob replied, "Yes, the steak is very good. I would say it's as good as the train proposal I have brought here today to discuss."

Representative Buy interrupted again. "Exactly. We are here to have a discussion, and let me tell you, my friend, don't let them label you a dirty carnivore just because you enjoy a steak or two. We are not dirty carnivores; we are omnivores, and don't you forget it. You have evolved to digest both animal protein and plants because you are an omnivore whether you like it or not. Me, I enjoy it especially in a fine-dining establishment like this one."

At last Representative Haye butted in: "Really, I don't think we need to bother Bob here with your mindless food phobias."

"And why not?" Buy replied. You bored the poor man before I came with your silly phobias of the perfect compromise."

Haye replied, "How could you possibly know what I said to him before you arrived? It is not like I go on and on about the same subject without any point. Anyways compromise is not a silly phobia. While you bloviate about never compromising, I do the hard work of finding common ground on a difficult subject like abortion. I started by saying to myself, the one thing both liberals and conservatives agree on is that they wish to make abortion less common. So why not make a sound proposal to meet conservatives halfway, and at least reduce the need for abortion? I have done some historical research on this subject, and there are many things we could do—such as more sex education in schools, more availability of contraception, more prenatal care for mothers, more financial support for mothers, and heck, I'd even teach perhaps sexual abstinence. I don't understand why conservatives would not meet us liberals halfway on making abortion safe and legal, but also much less needed. Don't you agree Bob?"

Representative Buy replied, "No fair bringing Bob into this like he would be on your side. Anyways he's here to talk to us about trains, not abortion. Remember? Now let me explain to you why your idea has failed in the past, will fail in the present, and will always fail. You see, that is because you believe in this thing as a physical object that happens to women. Women—who eat, breathe, and live on this planet and whose house you could visit. Women who get pregnant and due to one complication, medical or otherwise, cannot have the baby. This is a real person. Your opponent doesn't care about real people. They don't care about abortion as a historical fact; they care about it as an abstract moral idea. Is that not so, Bob?"

"Oh, trying to get my good friend Bob here on your side," Haye replied. "Well, me and Bob go much further back than you and Bob. If Bob agrees with anyone, I am sure it is me. I think you are wrong. A conservative or a liberal could have a moral failing. Sure, a person might think abortion, stealing, rape, or murder will happen only to the next guy, but these failings happen all the time to people everyone knows. So I just don't see how since a pregnancy complication is likely to happen to them or someone they know, how such rigid, abstract ideals could possibly stand. It's just pure fantasy on your part to keep you from even trying to compromise. Isn't that correct, Bob?"

Representative Buy spoke again, "I think once again you don't understand. Now Bob I can tell understands. I will explain it one more time to you. These abstract moral concepts work good on paper—they always work good on paper. They are even tolerable if they are happening to other people. But yes they do tend to be difficult to ignore when they are happening to you. Luckily almost all abstract moral dictators tend to allow themselves moral-hardship exceptions. They know their own hardships and can find excuses why they have had an absolute moral failure, but they tend to want to make sure you don't. Indeed the more they morally fail, the more ardent that tends to make them to make sure you don't follow in their path. Your life is easy for them to live in their abstract moral world. Their life and its immoral realities are easy to forgive so long as they are justifying their redemption by forcing you to live a life in their abstract moral world. After all God wants and needs them around to lecture you on their abstract perfection, which they assume is also God's. It might seem hypocritical to you to support reducing abortions and not support your bill, but to them it is not because any abortion—no matter the number—is a moral failure in Gods eyes. So trying to compromise with people who only see the world in black-and-white, abstract, religiously oriented ideals, of which they themselves are exempt, is useless. Do you get it, Bob, or is that too confusing?"

Bob at this point had given up on the conversation as an active participant. He figured out they neither wanted his input nor would care about it. For whatever reason they came here today, it was pretty clear it wasn't to talk about trains. Perhaps they just wanted a free lunch on Mitch Boetner. The steak was excellent, Bob had to admit. Not only was that true, but the side vegetables were also very well prepared. He thought the sauce might be some kind of garlic affair. He wished he had time to spend on cooking at home. Between working a full-time job, working on this proposal in his spare time, and now working on pitching this proposal, he simply had no time to spare to become a foodie. If he wasn't going to enjoy the conversation, Bob figured, what the heck—at least he should enjoy the lunch on Mitch.

Now Representative Haye seemed to be getting flustered. He was raising his voice a little more with each exchange. "Bob, did you hear that garbage that he speaks. He says they're uncompromising because they are rigid in their ideas, but all along this man is the one who never moves from his position. He speaks about useless hypocrisy; well, Bob, listen to this useless hypocrisy. Wait—better yet, I'll show you." Representative Haye started dumping the contents of his pockets onto the table. "Here it is, Bob. Take a look at this hypocrisy."

Bob looked at the picture. There in his hand was a picture of a dirty, bearded young man in unkempt jeans and a holey T-shirt that said, *Save the whales, eat a pig.* Under the clever saying on the T-shirt was a lovely picture of a man in a business suit with a pig's head. His body was pierced by a fork. Bob nodded and scratched his chin. As for hypocrisy, he didn't get it, but he was sure these men would explain it to him—even if their explanations didn't actually explain much and made for a rather dizzying experience.

Representative Haye spoke now having given Bob the time he imagined he needed to let the picture hammer home his point. "See, here he is all eating steak and telling you eating meat has no down side, and yet here he is a young man trying to save the whales. Oh, I always carry this around with me so when my esteemed colleague gets too pompous I can embarrass him."

Buy, however, did not seem embarrassed. "Bah, don't go twisting my words into what they don't mean. I have said I believe in eating meat. And yes, when there were still whales, I did favor saving them. I see no hypocrisy there. I did not want to save them for some morally abstract idea of them having some magic quality that someone would call good. I don't eat cows because I believe them to have some magical quality of bad. I did what I did, and do what I do, because I favor sustainable lifestyles. The cow simply has the overwhelming evolutionary advantage over most animals of being both yummy and being able to be domesticated. I do not slight it for its evolutionary advantage. The animals that were favorable to animal husbandry are doing great in this postmodern world, at least numbers wise. The worst animals are the ones badly off, like the whale that was yummy, but not particularly apt at being domesticated. Being capable of being domesticated by man and tasty to us humans turns out to be a huge evolutionary advantage. Why slight a cow for its great evolutionary coup? Bob being a scientist would agree, I'm sure, with the basic facts of evolution on this one. Bob and I would gladly eat our friend the cow, who having coevolved with us to be yummy, has now been fruitful and multiplied in numbers."

To Bob's relief Blessed Joy arrived to clear the table. She then refilled the drinks and set out three pieces of lemon meringue pie. This in no way changed the course of the conversation; the representatives seemed oblivious that their arguments didn't persuade Bob or anyone else in the restaurant. Bob, however, was pleased to have a little pie to eat while they fought it out.

Representative Haye replied, "Once again please do not speak for my friend Bob as I am sure he understands your failures as well as I do. You state the substance of your beliefs well enough as usual, but your choice of appearance for delivery has always been a failure. If you cared so much about saving the whales, you might have dressed the part. Can you imagine, Bob, seeing this poorly dressed bohemian arriving at your doorstep trying to get your support? People judge a man by his dress. People who don't care about their appearance probably don't care about the issue they are trying to sell you either. By looking the part of a man who doesn't care, you signaled to the world you didn't, and now there are no more whales to care about. Bob is no fool, and he can see a man of cause is a man who knows how to dress the part. Look at that picture of a dirty and argumentative young whippersnapper. No wonder no one would let you in the door, let alone sign your many petitions."

Bob knew his job here was to eat the pie and not reply. He played his part well.

Representative Buy replied for him: "With all due respect, my friend, I went for the cause of our long-gone friends, the whales. Nature was on my side. The whale was on my side, political correctness was on my side, God was on my side, and on the other side was the pointless genocide of whales for sport, industry, religion, and a few societies' unsustainable, obscure dining delicacies. A real moral man should have respected me for my ideals, not my appearance."

"True," Haye replied, "the appearance of the matter shouldn't matter to the sum worth of the substance of the matter, but we both know it does matter. Should or shouldn't in an ideal world of reason is not as important as the facts of behavior of real people in the world. You may have been right, and they might have been wrong, but when it comes to our poor whales, it might have been better had you behaved more professional and been right. In this world, as they say, the first bite is often with the eye."

Representative Buy replied bitterly, "Well, they can bite me." He then started into his pie. Representative Haye, seemly a little satisfied he got a dig in, also started working on his pie.

A silence fell over the pie eaters, and Bob once again thought perhaps now was his chance to broach the train subject. "I think now might be a good chance to start going over the details of the train proposal that I believe we came here to discuss."

Representative Buy interrupted, "Oh, Bob, it is very nice of you to try to change the subject rather than let my esteemed friend Representative Haye here continue to lose our argument. But seriously I can't just leave a subject half said. Now, Bob, did you realize when he was younger, Representative Haye here was all uncompromising and idealistic too? He used to stand in front of the shopping district and spray paint people he saw wearing a leather coat. Can you imagine that? What would be the point of such an act? To save the dead cow the person was already wearing? If they didn't want any more animals killed, why destroy a perfectly good jacket and force them to buy a new leather coat? I mean his direct action was totally counterproductive to the cause. It's almost like he was working for the leather companies trying to increase sales of leather coats. Even more hypocritical, he comes here today now wearing the same leather coat he used to hate."

"I will have you know," Haye replied, "that this is not real leather, which some of my voters would absolutely object to. Nor is it imitation leather, which other of my voters would also object to because someone might assume it is real and thus think it is

OK to wear real leather. That is why I compromise and wear only real imitation leather."

Bob, momentarily stunned, managed to get a word in edge-wise: "What is real imitation leather?"

Representative Haye replied, "Ah, that is easy to explain. Good real leather in those days of my youth, we would spray it with red paint to destroy the value. Imitation leather we would also spray with red paint, once again to show people that encouraging other people to wear what might be real leather was not OK. Now real imitation leather we could only spray with real imitation paint, which of course does not exist so must be OK to wear. Now I am sure you understand the difference and how I have reached my sound compromise position on this matter."

Bob, not understanding, asked innocently, "Why spray people at all? I mean it seems a rather mean thing to do?"

Representative Buy replied, "He has you there. See, I told you he was on my side."

Representative Haye, not feeling the least bit guilty, replied, "There you two go. I am talking about my youth. In my youth I acted like my esteemed colleague friend here, full of ideals and possibly myself. I was unable to move from the ideal to reach for the middle and find a suitable compromise. What was the result? Just a lot of stained coats, enraged people, and no real progress toward solutions for the real-world problem. Now in my advanced years, I have found the solution—the art of compromise. And progress such as my incredible coat is the result of my growth as a political person. Do you not agree, Bob?"

Bob felt like he was being played back and forth. It left him in a not-so-comfortable situation since in theory he was sup-posed to be here to woo their support; instead now they had been trying to woo him. Toward what end was this whole con-versation today? Did anything they discussed really matter? Bob was weary and full of dessert—a dangerous combination for telling the truth.

"I do agree that compromise is important at times," Bob said. "I mean, I'm here to pitch this train proposal to you, and I guess I would be happy to compromise on specific parts of it. Even if we only agreed on small parts and passed them, it would be progress. Even small improvements in transportation could make a monumental difference in people's lives. Yet I see where not compromising has its plus side too. Half a live whale is no better off than the dead one. What good is compromising toward a pointless end?"

Representative Buy now got up from the table. "I see my meal has ended. We are finally talking about the proposal. It was all in all a good meal. No doubt, Bob, you have a good proposal too. I would love to support your ideas, but alas you will likely need bipartisan support to pass it. You see, as a 'real' liberal I must be on guard against moderate and conservative ideas. I must not appear to give away my steadfast liberal idealism. There are those who call themselves liberals yet do not support the ideal liberal agenda. For the ideal liberal, any idea that falls short of the ideal, and gathers of all horrors bipartisan support, must be hated. Certainly a 'real' liberal expects another 'real' liberal to hate it; if you fail to hate it significantly, then the 'real' liberal uses it as proof you aren't a 'real' liberal. The 'real' liberals thus have a heads-they-win-tails-you-lose situation. Even if the polls show the liberals' support is with you and your proposal, I could not support it. The 'real' liberal does not believe in reality but in their idealized Platonic reality. Liberalism is a form on another plain of existence of which we only see its shadows. Stray too far into the shadow, and the 'real' liberals won't welcome me back. I'm a reality-based person, and the reality is that I need 'real' liberals to win my seat in my tiny district. Thus I will not be supporting your proposal; I never could support it. I will be praised for pointing out small imperfections in your proposal and for my steadfast rigidness not to stray even a little from some Platonic ideal. I will win a small local victory, even if the greater liberals of the national polls are really against me."

With that, Representative Buy placed his napkin on his plate and wandered into the cloud of tables. Bob now once again sat alone with Representative Haye.

Representative Haye shook his head. "I am sorry for the horrible manners of my esteemed colleague, but what can I do?"

Bob asked the obvious question: "Are you interested in the train proposal?"

Representative Haye replied, "Well, I am too busy a man to actually discuss it today. Rest assured I will take this proposal back to the appropriate interns who will read it and boil it down to me in appropriate sound bites."

Bob asked, "If they support it, will you then support it?"

Representative Haye replied, "If only politics was that easy. Have you not been listening to today's conversation? I must get bipartisan support in order to officially support this proposal. I can't give the appearance of being biased and not working with the other side. It is my job to work for universal bipartisan support; it is my esteemed colleague's job to make sure the members of his base are appeased. Support of this kind is not easy as the other side is often bigoted, ignorant, and self-interested. But if I work hard, I believe we will find areas to compromise away from."

Bob was still not getting what he was saying. "If you don't respect the other side, and they have nothing of value to add, why compromise with them? I mean, how do you compromise with those willfully ignorant?"

Haye replied, "As I've been telling you, it isn't easy. They will propose a change, then when you agree to something, they will change their mind. It is tough finding exactly the right compromise position that works for them. I promise you I will not give up. I believe if you try over and over again to work with them, perhaps over time you will simply teach them how to be more like me. I've been trying for years, and you see who has learned, don't you?"

Bob replied, "I always heard insanity was doing the same thing over and over again and expecting different results."

Representative Haye replied a little bitterly, "Well, in your case if you want this proposal to see the light of day, you better try over and over again. Find me a partisan conservative who I can find bipartisan agreement with, and I will support this proposal. If not, I am afraid it is as dead as the whales."

Representative Haye then got up and put on his real imitation-leather jacket. He then turned and headed into the maze of tables. Blessed Joy then arrived at the table with the check.

"That went well for you," she said. "You must be happy. Here's the itemized check. I gave myself a twenty percent tip as I felt Mr. Boetner would have wanted me to have it. Don't worry, I put it all on his credit. Have a good day." With that she also faded into the sea of tables, leaving Bob alone at the table. Bob picked up his check so he could give it to Mitch to write off as a business expense. He then left the preferred corner table at FOOD feeling a little bit the total failure. Clearly, lobbying for support was not his strong suit. Bob walked back toward the train station to catch the train back.

When he arrived at the platform, he pulled out his PPED to call Mitch. He was uncertain what exactly to tell Mitch. Had he failed? They were not all that open to his plan. Indeed they never really discussed it at all. Still they—well one of them—had tentatively agreed to support the plan. That was a step in the right direction. Or was it? He looked up Mitch in his contacts and called him.

Mitch answered after three beeps. "This is Mitch. Who the hell is this, and how the hell did you get my personal, private, secured number!"

Bob was taken aback. "Err, this is Bob. Mitch, you gave me this number only the other week. Don't you remember?"

Mitch's tone immediately changed. "Oh yes, Bob, of course. I forget to look at the caller ID before answering at times. Today was the big day, wasn't it? How did it go? More important—did they order the steak or not?"

Bob decided to break the news as bluntly as he could: "Well, they didn't seem all that up for our plan. Indeed we never really discussed it. We discussed—well they discussed—a lot of things that don't seem relevant to our actual train-scheduling plan. Truthfully no matter how I tried, I could never get them to talk about it. I did get sort of a commitment from one of them, though."

Mitch now sounded very excited. "Now don't worry about all the nonsense they talk about. When I go on these lunch things, Lord knows I never listen to a politician. They say nothing but nonsense. You see, they'd already made up their minds to support or not support us long before they agreed to meet us. They have interns and campaign directors and things like that to tell them what to support. The important thing for these lunches is what you eat. They always eat the steak if you got a chance at all. So did you eat the steak or not?"

Bob was now puzzled "Why didn't you tell me all this beforehand? I mean, I was worried the whole meal."

Mitch replied, "Well, I didn't want you to overthink it and turn a steak into a salad."

"But I almost ordered the salad," said Bob. "Representative Buy doesn't seem like a yes. Representative Haye seemed to neither care about the plan nor not care about it, but if we can get bipartisan support, he said he would back us. In the end we all had the steak."

Mitch was now giddy with excitement. "Three steaks! Wow, then we are nearly there, my friend. Oh yes, don't worry about Representative Buy—he never supports anything. I have no idea what his own ideas are; I guess maybe I should actually pay attention when he talks. But then since he never actually votes in favor of anything, why listen? But it doesn't matter. With Representative Haye and bipartisan support, we can easily pass the proposal. I got the perfected partisan to try to make bipartisan. Trust me—we are close to the endgame now. I'll call Tammy and tell her the good news on our progress. Your job now is to wait for a call from Luke with your next assignment."

With that Mitch hung up. Bob wondered if he really was the best man to be talking to elected leaders. Well, it was more like listening to elected leaders as he barely got a word in edgewise. Worse, they never really asked him about his plan. What was the point of talking to the expert and never asking the expert anything about his expertise? It was as if they cared more about impressing Bob with what passed for their general knowledge than actually learning what Bob knew. If entertaining congressional representatives to stroke their egos was progress, then they were indeed soaring. Bob was worried about what the term *progress* meant in this day and age.

The train arrived at the platform. Bob looked at the time on his phone—forty-five seconds late. If Bob could convince this next man to give him bipartisan support, Bob knew he could help change that. He was trying for a small step toward compromise and introducing to the world a small amount of real progress.

Chapter 5:

You Can't Take it with You

Rats, rats lay down flat we don't need you, we act like that.
— Roger Barrett, painter-piper-prisoner

O ne great aspect of the invention of hundreds, if not thousands, of television channels is that the average television viewer during the Christmas season has the privilege, if not the duty, to watch a virtual nonstop running of Frank Capra's *It's a Wonderful Life*. Watching the movie has become as traditional as buying overpriced, on-sale cheap imports to be placed in brightly wrapped boxes and placed under imported plastic Christmas trees to be enjoyed while reading e-mails of Christmas cards forwarded to you from your friends on your cheap, imported PPED. Due to the annual war on Christmas, so many people have forgotten what Christmas is all about: the presents, the television Christmas specials, the Christmas carols, and watching the relatives drink eggnog and drunkenly stumble into the Christmas tree. Just about as traditional is the seasonal complete forgetting of the content of the actual film, *It's a Wonderful Life*. As early as 1947, government officials investigated the filming of *It's a Wonderful Life* because of the belief the classic Christmas movie was filled with Communist propaganda! After all any honest, hard-working postmodern conservative knows the liberal media and Hollywood are filled with leftist insurgents hell-bent on socializing the world. How else would the Hollywood entertainment industry rise up to become one of the largest, richest for-profit capitalist industries in the world if not from the industry being filled with Socialists?

If the New Deal was signified by new government programs designed to provide positive regulations, employment opportunities, and needed services to the citizens of the country, then you'd think this film would be packed full of the government doing that. It is hard to find any of these ideas reflected in the plot of this Socialist movie! For instance, who saves you when you fall through the ice? Why a call to the local government's publicly paid 911 emergency response teams, right? No, in the movie the answer is George Bailey. Who prevents the local druggist from accidentally giving you a drug overdose? The Federal Drug Administration or the local board in charge of enacting regulations on how pharmacies operated? Nope, once again the answer is George Bailey. Who provides loans to the local poor so the community can afford to grow, expand, and prosper? The government banking regulators and HUD program? No, the answer is George Bailey. Who saves the local savings and loan from financial collapse during a Great Depression bank run? A New Deal government banking regulation? No, as you probably have figured out, the answer is always George Bailey, just a regular individual person.

So where does the government and its New Deal regulations come in? Well when the government banking investigators finally show up, it's not to provide affordable loans to the poor and help regulate the bank to prevent runs on the bank. No, when they finally show up, it is to arrest George Bailey. How is George Bailey saved? By a government investigation and arrest of the actual thief, Mr. Potter? Nope. George Bailey is saved by the very old and basically rooted conservative concept of community activism. The community finds a dollar here and a dollar there to give in charity to save George Bailey. The idea that communities will regulate and donate naturally by themselves and help each other, and thus do not need big government to do it for them, is at the very heart of conservatism. More to the point, it's the entire fucking plot of *It's a Wonderful Life.*

It's a Wonderful Life is a Republican parable about how the utopian Republican fantasy world was supposed to work. It is a world in which charity and community activism trump big-government intervention. Postmodern conservatives no longer recognize how conservatism was even supposed to work. Heck, postmodern conservatives when watching a movie about actual conservative ideals and values simply see them as foreign concepts. The postmodern conservative has long forgotten that the argument was about whether communities are better served by having a service delivered and organized by individuals in the community or by the government. A postmodern conservative doesn't expect you to need services at all, and if you want them, then you better pay for them yourself or you're a leech. A conservative who thinks the community should pay for a sick man's medical care is booed, while the conservative who thinks the sick man who can't pay for his medical care should just die rather than leech off the rest of them is cheered. It's not much of a wonderful life these days for most people.

It was just that kind of postmodern conservative Tammy was about to find herself sitting in front of today. Tammy was on vacation. Technically she was at home. Vacation to her implied a dream trip to an exotic location filled with fun. So she was in her mind only technically on vacation. Generally she wouldn't take vacations at all except she was required to by law. The law had created holidays where federal workers like her were not required to work. In theory a little time off was not bad for productivity, and certain randomly selected days were made holidays. The problem arose that there were simply became too many days considered too important for certain people to work. To accommodate them all would've required almost every day to be a holiday. The compromise solution was the floating holiday. Floating holidays were vacation time that could be used when a person wanted to use them rather than when required to use them. It was considered a huge victory, and now there would be total holiday freedom for all. No longer were you required to take a day off for someone else's religious festival for a religion you didn't practice, for the birthday of someone you didn't know, or in remembrance of an event you didn't remember. But there was a catch. Most people couldn't afford to go on holiday travel anymore. Add to that the constant pressure of the workplace that pushed people to work more to meet deadlines, and you got people who forgot to take their floating holidays. Of course there was the problem that the government was forced to pay you for those holiday hours at the end of the year even if you didn't use them. It seemed like cheating to pay you for holidays you weren't taking, so a corrective action was needed to fix this problem. The government created mandatory days where the floating holiday was required to be taken. Now a mandatory floating holiday day might seem a lot like just having holidays, but in the mind of the postmodern world it was different. Today was one of those days Tammy was required to be on mandatory floating holiday, and thus she was free to work on her train proposal instead. As luck would have it, her mandatory floating holiday day did not line up with the congressional staff's mandatory floating holiday day, so she could do what she wanted to do today. She wanted to see the senator and push the proposal.

Tammy was waiting on Luke to patch Bob into her PPED. Luke's head popped up. "Hello, tribal leader. I see you are looking a little nervous today. The thing you need to do is relax a little bit. I have the perfect relaxation technique for you. Have you ever tried acupuncture? Hundreds of needles jabbed into your skin create the perfect soothing piercings of relaxation. I tell you, nothing relaxes like a visit to almost-a-doctor's office. They also have many unknown healing powers—you'd be surprised what jabbing a needle in you can cure! I tell you, jab yourself in the right place with a needle, and I guarantee you you'll never be nervous again."

Tammy wasn't at the moment in need of special healing measures. She replied, "I'm sorry, Luke, I suffer from trypanophobia, so I don't think it is a good idea."

Luke answered, "Oh, I'll look that up in my book and see if acupuncture cures that."

Bob's head now popped up on the PPED.

Tammy said, "Luke was just giving me vital, mission-critical information. Bob, I need you on the train platform to go over the meeting information after I am done with the senator so I can share my research notes. This is what I got so far. I searched for information on conservative Internet sites; unfortunately the sites don't contain any useful information—that is to say about Senator A. J. Brown. You know, just the basics of height, weight, and where to donate to his reelection campaign. We are just going to have to rely on basic intelligence. I have decided I don't want you mucking this up like your last meeting. We need this bipartisan-support plan to work. So I am personally taking charge on this one. I need you in waiting just in case the senator wants your technical assistance."

Bob was a little worried about talking to a senator. Representatives were one thing but senators were the upper house. The office had that aura of grandness like no other in the country and who was Bob but a common man. He was glad Tammy was taking charge even if she technically wasn't supposed to directly do this. Bob replied, "Well, I'm now putting the whole weight of the proposal on you. So no pressure; I'll be five minutes away on the train platform ready and waiting to swoop in when you got him ready to hear from me." Bob had half convinced himself Tammy was going to do better than him with her years of knowledge getting yelled at by senators for their trains being late. The other half remembered how things went at FOOD.

Tammy was thinking about the meeting. She wasn't supposed to lobby directly an elected government official. She could lose her job. Still technically she was on vacation, and technically the senator was unlikely to know her from Adam and thus the risk was low. But the risk to her moral integrity was high. Still she wanted this to work. She now had high hopes of doing something. She was sure she knew more than Bob about these elected leaders. She could plan her conversation better. She went over the plan in her head: first don't go talking on and on; and make sure you let the senator have his say; second remember that a senator is an office of respect, so respect him because he expects you to; finally don't look so worried for it is only the weight of the whole proposal that is now on you. She was sure her better knowledge would lead to better results. However, *better* was a loaded word. Morally she wasn't better off at all. It was like the time when as a young girl she was yelled at for getting cookies from the cookie jar. Her mom had yelled at her. So she planned on doing it better. Next time she sent her younger brother to get the cookies for her. If he got caught, he would get yelled at; if not she got cookies. It was a better plan, but not morally a better plan. Better was a relative term. She frowned. This was better than a cookie; this was a train plan that would help people upward of 2–5 percent of the time. So maybe a little white lying was OK to better the world.

Tammy frowned and looked worried as she spoke: "I am not worried, and don't make me worry by saying the proposal is on me. It is on all of us. And be ready, for I will likely get the senator ready for your input sooner rather than later."

Luke's head popped up. "You know what cures worrying? Acupuncture."

Tammy, now angry, said, "Luke, I am having a private conversation here. If one can't have a totally secure, private conversation on the Internet, where can one have one? Now, Bob, remember—don't worry, we're not doing this for just the proposal. There is also you, me, and all those late passengers counting on you. So when we get in there and impress him, our success will mean we won't have to worry about doing this ever again."

Luke added, "And if that doesn't work, stab yourself in the chi with your pen."

The two heads popped off the screen. Tammy decided to head to the senator's office. Arriving at it Tammy opened the door and went inside. Tammy stood in the neat office of the receptionist intern of the senior senator A. J. Brown. The receptionist was a neat, tidy, smiling young boy of perhaps eighteen or nineteen. Having apparently not noticed Tammy's entrance, the young man sat slightly hunched at his desk still eagerly working over a piece of paper with a pen. It was the only noticeable piece of paper in the office. The office seemed devoid of your typical office supplies, such as file cabinets, bulletin boards, pictures, plants, and the like—just a neat and tidy metal-frame desk, a neat and tidy minicomputer assembly on the desk, a neat and tidy young man sitting at the desk, and two rather foreboding uncomfortable metal-framed chairs for, one assumed, unwanted guests. Tammy was used to bureaucracy by now and understood if she wanted attention, she would need to make an audible noise.

The young man looked up from his work at Tammy and apologized. "Sorry, sir and/or madam. I was working on this important mailer for our constituents back home to keep them informed of our most vital work this month in Washington. Would kind sir and/or madam want an esteemed advanced copy of this month's mailer?" The boy eagerly extended his hand out with the worked-over copy, apparently forgetting that he had been using it as his edit.

Tammy had no interest in this month's nor any month's mailer, either hand delivered or actually mailed to her. However, this young man was all that separated Tammy from her goal of speaking to the senator, and she felt it was best to not discourage him. Tammy perused quickly down the page:

Dear Sir and/or Madam:

We thank you once again for voting Republican. Our critical work on important conservative causes does not end with the end of the election. Vital conservative legislation is actively being voted on right now in Washington! Right now Democrat liberals are trying to create legislation that is nothing more than a free handout to fascist socialists in the guise of welfare to the lazy and the drug addicted. I urge my concerned voter to not worry. I, senior senator A. J. Brown, won't let out-of-touch Washington insiders dictate to average Americans by force acceptance of outdated, New-Age, red-tape, collectivized, atheist thinking. These progressive liberals have spent too many years feeding on the fat cow of liberal activists' money troughs, and now more than ever we need to fight back from the godless feminist homosexual humanist agenda. In my twenty-four years on Capitol Hill, I assure you, the concerned American, that I am aware of my constant need to fight against antibusiness, anti-rights regulative initiatives and for pro-life, pro-right-to-work initiatives. I'm sure you are as concerned as I in making sure we continue this nation's great tradition of keeping up classic traditional family values in the home for the greater good of our nation's helpless, God-fearing children. Please help me keep up the good fight against evil big corporate liberalism's money and possibly donate $10, $25, $50, $100, $_____, or whatever you can afford. Together we can make a difference returning America to Americans like you.

Signed Senior Senator A. J. Brown, American

Tammy looked up from the page and reluctantly reached into her purse. She was wondering what exactly she could afford. Oh well—a lot of it was Mitch's money after all, and he owed her at least a cheese sandwich worth of donations. She was told to grease the system over and over again by Mitch. Tammy smiled back at the young man and handed him a few hundred dollars.

"Oh, sorry, sir and/or madam, but we aren't allowed to take donations at this address. Please mail the money to our reelection campaign financial headquarters in the Cayman Islands. The address is on the back of the mailer," said the eager young man.

Things were suddenly looking up, thought Tammy. At least she wouldn't be asked for an upfront bribe. "I have the two thirty appointment with the senator. I'm sorry, I appear to have arrived fifteen minutes early."

"Are you with the Healthy Coal Corporation, Progress for a Better American Asbestos Company, or People for the Betterment of Better People Company?" asked the ever-eager young man.

"No, I'm working on behalf of Mitch Boetner. It was he who personally set up this appointment," said Tammy trying to sound businesslike.

"Ah yes, the senator had been waiting for you." Suddenly the eager-to-please look fell from the young man's face and was replaced with his incredulous look. "The senator is a very busy man, you know. It is very important that you come on time to help us stay on time so we can work at maximum time efficiency. You have come only fifteen minutes early, and the senator generally requires at least a thirty-minutes-early arrival for us to list you as on time for your appointment. He finds it important that you wait for him and that he never has to wait for you. As they say, 'a senator's time is money.' It is only lucky for you that Mr. Boetner himself understands the importance of the senator's time is outweighed by the importance of a senator's money. He has properly front-loaded the interview with enough donations to the senator's reelection campaign, so of course we shall overlook this serious ethical breach of time...this time." The young man smiled his empty smile again. He got up from his tidy desk and moved toward the oddly ornate wooden door behind him. He opened it and motioned Tammy through.

Tammy entered a rather spacious room filled with a smallish balding man with an unnatural aura of artificial tanning lotion. The man sat behind a desk raised on a platform above the regular floor level. The platform made visitors sitting in the guest chairs appear smaller than the senator. The walls were decorated in large posters for the Old South, energy companies, health-care companies, tobacco companies, and American flags. The man was leaned back and relaxed. Despite federal smoking bans on smoking in public places, he was smoking a cigar. The cigar smoke hung in the air of the room and made the room smell stale. A large lamp sat behind the senator and backlit the room, casting the senator's shadow over the guest chairs and toward the door. A constant hum of the air conditioner turned to maximum whined in the background. Tammy walked slowly into the room. The young man motioned Tammy to sit in the guest chair. Tammy took a seat in front of the raised desk. The young man then examined the situation, appeared to deem the situation satisfactory, and left Tammy alone in the room with the senator. The senator said nothing. He stared at Tammy while blowing smoke from the cigar.

Tammy decided he must be waiting for her to make the first move. "Hello, Senator Brown, I am here at request of Mitch Boetner to—"

Like a small balding volcano, the senator with one motion took the cigar out of his mouth, leaned toward Tammy so his backlit shadow darkened the room, and unleashed a verbal tirade on his unsuspecting visitor. "My friend, this country cannot afford to remain half slave and half free. In the old days, my God-fearing Republican party rose up to the Democrat party and its cotton-plantation owners who worked our lesser friends as if slaves from dawn to night. We can never tolerate this situation again, and yet so many today do! Back in those days, we had a nation split and bloody along the lines of the legalization of freedom for all. The country sat on the brink of revolution. Then the great emancipator broke the spirit of those who hated freedom and liberty for all.

Well, today we face a similar struggle for our liberty and freedom. I repeat: our nation cannot remain half slave and half free. In our country's past, we had the cotton-plantation owners legally keeping people as if slaves; in our country's present, we have these unions that enslave their workers. Sure, the union grants its members the security of higher wages, more vacation time, better health-care benefits, more job security, and better job safety, but at what cost? Did not the slave owners feed, clothe, and house their slaves? Unions bring security, yes, but do they still not make their members slaves? Our ancestors fought so that a person—every person—had a natural right to workplace freedom. If you work hard and want to make less than some fat, lazy comfortable union worker, then I say to you, as a natural red-blooded American, you will have the right to work, even for less, if you want to. There is a price for freedom—a nice low price, I warn you, or they might go out and find someone freer and cheaper than you. You want the freedom and the rights to work at a job as a free cheap American, don't you?"

"Ah—"

"Of course you do. I can see you are as American as Moses. And like Moses you want a senator who will stand up to the pharaoh and tell him to free his people. You're a woman who enjoys the dignity that comes from a hard day's labor, are you not? The Democrat has made a welfare nanny state that teaches people to sit back and enjoy a free couch-potato ride on the expense of the debt of big-government socialist programs—programs designed to provide houses to those without homes, food to those who are starving, and a little money to those who have none. But once again did not the plantation owner provide food, water, and shelter to his slaves? The plantation owner in one sense was kinder than today's unionized, welfare-check, big-government slave in that at least he provided his slave the dignity, self-respect, and joy that comes from a hard day's work. This country is a country divided between the doers and the don'ters. The doer goes out every day and gains the self-respect of a hard day's work. A doer understands that a hard day's work doesn't guarantee they will become rich, but a doer doesn't complain of the wealth gathered by others off the doer's hard work. No, if a doer isn't making ends meet, a doer goes and does another job after their first one. A doer might do two or three hard-working jobs, not because they expect to become wealthy, but because they have to. They're doers, and doing is what a doer does. A doer is a uniquely American ideal. Meanwhile the don'ter—with the excuse of raising the doer's children, having an injury from doing, or being just broken down in don'ter old age—says, 'Look, I've done all I can do.' But the don'ter doesn't actually do and instead stays at home and gathers a government check produced by the wealth of all the doers out there. These don'ters might have done in the past, but what I do care about are all the present doers in the world, not the don'ters. Believe me, we will have welfare reform. I don't care how hard you claim to have done in the past for a pension, unemployment benefits, or social security. I care about the rights of the doers of today, not the don'ters of today. No more free rides! All those sick, old, children, and child raisers will be forced to work for those checks so they too can experience the dignity of hard work. I believe once a person knows the self-respect of a job, no matter how small the pay for how hard the work, they will come to love it. Dignity of work is its own reward. Don't let them make you into a slave, my friend. Be a doer, not a don'ter. Hard work, my friend, will set you free."

"But—"

"Now you take this slavery of minimum wage. Oh, the unionized filth cries about the poverty of the hard worker as if hardworker work did not bring a sense of dignity that is its own reward. They demand higher and higher wages for their work. To get it they demand the right to team together in a mob to strongarm the employer into paying higher wages. I repeat: they team together in a mob against the few or the one employer. Is that fair? Me, I know what fair is. I will always stand for the few or the one and their liberty over the mob and the mob's rules any day. Should the one have any less freedom than the many just because the many do the work that generates the value that provides the few their wealth? Sure, they do the hard work, but hard work's dignity and self-respect are already its own reward. The mob refuses to allow the liberty of the few and demands payment for its services! They claim to use this payment for what I ask you? To feed themselves, and they call that process living. So they eat and eat like a herd of pigs at the trough of the few. In these post-modern times, the Democrat Party allows the many to grow to be fat-cat, unionized lazy bodies over the rewards of the wealth of their own hard labor. Do they care at all for their employer? Their employer needs the food too, you know. The company is the shelter of the few or the one to protect them from the enslavement to the many. Do the many care if the company eats? A company lives off its own kind of food—profits. A company needs profits to survive just as the many need their food, water, and shelter. The higher the profits, the greater the wealth of the corporation, and the more it can attract investors to invest to increase the wealth of the organization. And who benefits from the healthy, profited, rich corporation? Everyone, I tell you. And yet these unionized workers starve the corporation of what it needs most—profits. The mob takes the profits from the corporations' starving mouths to feed themselves instead. They, the mob, enslave the few to starve their corporations and then complain that they themselves have been wronged! Abolish the minimum wage, I say, and let freedom come to all corporations in the workplace."

Tammy seemed to be getting the gist of the conversation. Apparently slavery was wrong, but the senator's solution appeared to be some quasi state. He appeared to want not slaves, but something like a free-range slave. He seemed to want to create a place where the wealthy got all the benefits of virtually free work from their workers and none of the burden of housing, feeding, and clothing. Then again she might be mistaken because the conversation was hard to follow. She disliked the senator by now, but she needed him to get that bipartisan support. Tammy tried again to gain entrance in to the conversation: "I'm here about trains...."

The words had no effect on the senator, who was clearly not done speaking: "Trains are locomotives on the tracks riding the slaves of the socialist Democrat to freedom. How do we create free jobs in these days when all we have around us are them Democrat slave owners? The Democrats and their socialist unionists say they want to create jobs. When the times are tough and the jobs hard to find, they trick you into accepting a spot in the enslavement plantation of big-government public jobs. They claim they are creating jobs, but what they are really doing is stealing the private worker's paycheck to create tax-free, debt-ridden lazy man's work that does nothing to help society. I can't name a lazy government worker who's ever done a day's work for you or me. Name a road, school, police station, fire station, aquifer, damn, canal, drug, food, war zone, mail, or border that has been created, operated, made safe, or maintained by a lazy government worker. I can't, and I am sure you can't either. It is all a scam in the name of slavery of the working man. How would I create a real American job? I would create a job by taking all the money wasted on the government worker and use that money to give a tax incentive to a corporation to create a private-sector job. I tell you, remove the public-sector workers now so we can create new jobs for the private sector. I believe I can create almost one private-sector job for a determined, freedom-loving private sector worker for every one godless, Communist, lazy public-sector worker I remove from the taxpayer's teat. That is how in a free country I will create job growth!"

Tammy had given up trying to get a word in edgewise. The senator wanted her personally fired. If she wasn't hiding the fact she was a public sector worker, she would have told him off to his face. Sigh, she was unhappy because in her minds plan they were already calling Bob in. In the real conversation who knew where they were? She was pretty sure the oration was going to go as long as the senator's well-prepared material was going to take him. She had no idea what prompted the show, but then perhaps she should consider it getting free entertainment. Since she had no opportunity to leave, she decided she might as well enjoy it. She just wished she was getting a free steak out of the deal too though senator didn't seem to care who if anyone was listening as he was in the oratory zone.

"Don't even get me started on environmental protection. Just another device the Democrat Party uses for the many to enslave the few. You know the worst and ugliest side of them is? That somehow they claim I don't care about the environment just because I believe a corporation should have the right to self-regulate their effluence. So what do the Democrats do instead? They enslave the corporation and those in it to a bunch of namby-pamby laws designed to treat workers like schoolchildren. Sit up in the right chair, take a break for the right number of minutes, don't stand on the top rung of a ladder, eat a lunch, and don't pour that toxic waste into the drinking water. They got more rules than any plantation master ever did! How do they get away with all these rules? They claim to protect poor old mother earth. I tell you mother earth was around a lot longer than those environmental laws, and she'll be around a long time after we make them and us all gone. I think it is arrogant to believe a few simple creations of God could ever affect the inner workings of God's creation—Earth. So in a false claim of protecting that which we can't harm anyways, the Democrat enslaves the worker, forcing him to work extra hard to do the work in a safe and environmentally friendly way. His workday would be a lot faster, easier, and cheaper with just a little touch of sunshine-unicorn-friendly pollution. And who benefits from the higher cost of safety? Not the worker who loses his job due to the higher costs it creates. Sure, a few less workers might lose an arm due to worker safety, but at what stake? You can only lose two arms, my friend, but it shouldn't cost you all your freedom. The stakes, I repeat, are higher costs—a cost the company would gladly pay anyways if the effect was real. Everyone claims that only the worker wants to protect the environment, but why wouldn't the company want to protect the environment too? Does not the company suffer the same exposure to the pollution as the worker? Does not the company suffer pains and heartbreaks of illness from diseases spread by the pollution? Of course it does. Why every company can't escape its own pollution, thus it is only natural a company would try to be as clean as possible already. So why protect the worker? Why? I'll tell you why—because they want to enslave the worker under the disguise of environmental protections meant to make them more likely to remain not dead."

Since Tammy realized she was also still not dead, she tried once again to say something: "I am representing a scientist sent by Mitch Boetner...."

The senator wanted no part in a two-sided conversation—not now while he was still feeling the hot streak. "Science isn't what it used to be in the old days. Today science is nothing more than a collective bunch of nonsensical myths and legends. No greater falsehood was ever spread across this nation than the alarmist noise of big science and its lies of climate change. The climate-change agenda is nothing but a bunch of store-bought liberals with their Ivy League diplomas and need for public money to feed their thirst for million-dollar mythmaking grants who are trying to force the American worker into slavery on the plantation of alternative energy. I went to Brown, and let me tell you the Ivy League is filled with pussy-footed, feel-good professors with too much tenure, too little original ideas, and too many connections to the Democrat party don'ters trying to funnel your paycheck into big science's pocket. It is a simple fact they claim that man is putting carbon dioxide into the air, and this carbon dioxide is changing the global climate. They are a bunch of grant-generating falsehoods that looks good on paper, but doesn't measure up to the facts. Remember, it has been scientifically proven that it is impossible for man to place anything into Mother Nature that would change the environment. The whole effects they claim to measure are just computer-generated falsehoods and lies. It isn't real. I do not approve of a weather-based theory for climate. Go out in the dead of winter and tell me the globe has gotten all warm. Anyways even if it was real, which it isn't, global warming is totally and completely beneficial to us. Why who doesn't want a warmer winter? Hell, in a popsicle stick, global warming if it were real would be great with a winter of less snow, less cold, and more time for you to enjoy those warm-loving flowers, provided there's still enough water in the spring runoff to grow them. Who doesn't like flowers? Commie-loving, Ivy-Leaguer Democrat Party members and their global-warming, alarmist fantasies, that's who. Anyways, even if it were real, which it isn't, and it wasn't totally good for the world, which it is, we could totally mitigate any of the effects. So why worry about it? I mean, which is cheaper: preventing a person from cutting off their arm or growing a new one back? Everyone knows the answer to that. The thing is, most of the time you don't cut off your arm, so why be all arm-cut-off worried? In the same vein, why get all climate-change worried? Sure it might be cheaper to prevent it rather than mitigate the effects—if it is even possible to do so—but why waste all that upfront money for something that might not happen? I say save a dime and wait to see if it happens; if it happens, then spend that stack of dimes to fix it afterward. Global warming is just a bunch of easily mitigated, totally beneficial, totally nonsensical myth that isn't happening, has never happened, and will never happen. And you can take that dime you'd save not worrying about it to the bank if banks still allowed you to give them dimes. And seriously, why don't they have those change-rolling machines anymore? Now you might say, 'Senator, what if you are wrong and the liberal Democrat's big-science lobby is right on this global-warming thing?' Well, I'll tell you back I'm not afraid. This is an ownership society, and if I'm wrong I expect them liberals to take ownership of their mistake and apologize to us all. For theirs would have been the greatest mistake of all—being right."

The senator now in one motion leaned back, put his cigar in his mouth, and sat back down in his chair. He mumbled through his cigar-filled mouth: "Was that ten minutes yet? I always like to treat my guests to a stunning ten-minute oration. I figure if they're still here by the time I'm done, they actually need to talk to me. Well, never mind all that shit. Since you are here, I guess I should see who you are." The senator looked into his iPPED appointment schedule on his desk. "I see you are here to discuss grains on behalf of Mitch Boetner. Good old Mitch. I knew his dad. Never cared for Mitch, but he's a loyal donor, and that counts for something."

Tammy attempted to correct him: "Not exactly. I am here to discuss trains for Mitch Boetner."

The senator pulled his cigar out of his mouth again. He blew a large cloud of smoke into the room. "Why the heck is Mitch Boetner talking to me about grains and trains? He isn't trying to get into the alcohol business? Use to be America made the greatest grains in the world, and with it we made the greatest beers in the world. Incredibly beautiful, mass-produced, pale, watery beers without any distinct flavor or aroma. The best were stored in aluminum cans with color sensors that told you when they were iced cold. You could pop the top and guzzle them down fast to numb the throat to prevent you from tasting anything. While there were many companies, there were no true differences in style. Just interchangeable pale ales with no worry that the cheap beer you bought in Wisconsin was any better than the one you bought in Texas. That was before the European-style microbrews and their collectivist thoughts and their feel-good, New-Age variety invaded the market. It has totally pussified our young men and is turning their tastes into the tastes of a bunch of women. No offense. I thought better of Mitch Boetner than to get on the feel-good variety, taste, and aroma bandwagon of actual good beer.

Well, he can't count on my support. I like my beer plain, flavorless, from a can, pale, and as attractive as that feeling you get when waiting in line at the DMV."

Tammy's respect for the senator wasn't increasing. She tried again. "No, I think there was a miscommunication here as Mitch has no interest in grain or beer. I am here to talk about our proposal to transform America's train system."

The senator took his cigar back out of his mouth. He suddenly was looking a little long in the face. "That's too bad. I was hoping you were here to discuss something about that idiot Senator Washington's ideas on funding of the National Endowment of the Arts again. I could really use some help fighting that crap. It is just what we don't need—a lot of hippy, drug-smoking, feel-good artists doing circle jerks on Uncle Sam's dollar instead of painting. There is nothing worse for creativity and originality than the government giving these people a free handout. It will kill originality in this country. The free market is where you find originality and creativity. The artist in the free market is a happy productive artist. Just think of architecture in the free market. When I go to an American city, I know just where each fast-food and shopping store is because they look the same everywhere I go. That's the creativity of the artist in the free market. You start issuing out handouts, and suddenly you starve to death because you don't know where to buy a burger. Let the free market determine what a burger joint should look like, not some feel-good government handout program. You couldn't name one artist who was state sponsored who ever did anything worth seeing, I can you promise you that."

Tammy could name many. She threw her mental plan out the window and tried to correct the senator: "Well, I believe Leonardo da Vinci was state sponsored by the Duke of Milan."

The senator got very animated. He took his cigar and pointed it at Tammy. "Smart girl, you are. I can see why Mitch sent you to represent him. I agree that Leonardo was such a hack. I took a state-sponsored trip to Europe as a feel-good diplomacy campaign on behalf of the American citizens. I saw that hack's work up close. No greater false advertisement was ever placed on a work of art as the *Mona Lisa*. I paid twenty ringos [after the fall of the European Union's common currency, the euro, the union needed a new name. While attempts were made to introduce the bono, it was not universally accepted as a quality currency. The ringo, though, everyone seemed to like, even though no one seemed to know why] to see that *Mona Lisa* crap. Moaning? Hell no, that bitch wasn't moaning at all—she was smiling. What a rip off to all those visitors. Here's an artist promising moaning and delivering some half-baked smile. Any art student could have painted a more convincing moan than that. Real artists don't need government funding. Your Leonardo da Vinci was a great example of the kind of hack artist work state sponsorship produces."

Tammy was in disbelief. She asked, "So the best course for a person who doesn't want to conform to what corporations or government want, and what the public desires at the moment, is to sit around starving until someone decides they do want to accept these artists' new and creative ideas? Without a little government fallback money to keep the private, inspiring, new creative artists going, aren't they likely to either give up or starve to death before someone discovers them? Almost any of them who don't give up will lose precious creative time because they'll breakdown and conform to do part-time work that actually brings in a paycheck. Wouldn't it be better to have a safety-net system in place to help them out so they won't have to either conform to the popular and the bland or, better yet, a small amount of grant money to perhaps help the artists popularize their new styles and creativity expressions? I mean, you wouldn't just be giving them a handout; there would be a rather loose peer-review process and annual audit to make sure the vast majority of the money went to actually generating art and not, say, pot-induced circle jerks. Sure, without them a few people will persevere the hard times to create new art, but most people will either spend their creative artist years working other jobs to make ends meet, or simply sell out making the world a less creative, more cookie-cutter society."

Suddenly it occurred to Tammy what she said might apply to her as well. Who knows what Tammy could have done had she not wasted her working life on train schedules. Then again she must've secretly loved it, or why would she have done it? Still it bugged her that with a little government funding, Tammy might have actually created something grander. Maybe she would have the time to work on her dreams too. Still, she had an opportunity now, a good idea, and she didn't want to let this senator ruin it.

The senator, on the other hand, seemed very pleased. He puffed happily on his cigar as Tammy talked. When Tammy was done, he replied back, "Wow, Mitch must be a lot like his dad. I would never have imagined it since he always came off as an idiot. His dad always knew the right guys to send me to grease me up. You're right, that's just what that coward Senator Washington will say to me. You even had the thin, reedy voice going. You delivered pure sarcasm that would do a comedian proud. Man, you captured Senator Washington's weak lameness excuse for a rationale perfectly. It was almost like you meant it."

The senator frowned now. "Looks like I puffed this guy out. I need a new soldier. You want one too?" he asked Tammy. The senator pushed his cigar into an ashtray and rubbed it out.

Tammy didn't smoke and disliked being a room filled with smoke. She disliked the senator. She disliked compromising her morals to be there. She disliked the windbag senator ruining her plan. Still, she needed his help. Her lungs were aching by now, and while the air conditioner was working hard to cover the signs of global climate change that was going on outside, it wasn't pumping in enough fresh cool air to mask the odor. It was odd for a man who didn't want flavor in his beer; he sure wanted it in his cigar. Even odder to Tammy was for a man so afraid of being enslaved to another man, that this person should freely enslave himself to a corporation's highly addictive product. Should she admit she didn't smoke, or would it hurt her chances? Then again, what were the chances this man actually cared why Tammy was there to see him? Tammy replied, "I don't smoke," and then forced a smile.

The senator nodded. "Few people do these days. It hurts my tobacco friends' feelings terribly. I try everything I can to help them out through these troubled times, but too few in the Congress favor cartoons for children, product placement, and just free handouts in our schools. You'd think smoking was bad for you or something. They push for sex education in our schools, and they push to get tobacco out. The worst thing I ever did was trust sex education and get married to a woman; the best thing I ever did was start smoking, so one way or another I wouldn't stay married to that woman too long. No offense. Today's child-raising values just don't make sense. I bet you've been told over and over not to smoke since you were thigh-high. Don't worry, though, because we're all friends here. I won't judge you poorly if you open your mind to the pleasure and joy of tobacco. These are the best; everyone knows America makes the best cigars in the world!"

The senator pulled a cigar out of his desk. He unwrapped the plastic wrapper that was around it. He clipped off the end and placed it in his mouth. He then pulled out a fancy, ornate lighter that was decorated with a confederate flag and puffed until it was lit. He then handed it to Tammy as a sign of friendship. Tammy took it with as much spirit as a nonsmoker who wasn't really keen on the joys of nicotine addiction could muster. The senator then went to work on one for himself.

Tammy thought that now with the senator pacified with tobacco goodness, there was an actual opportunity to talk. She wasted no time, and while holding the cigar in her hand, she started to pitch the train proposal. "Ah, Senator, while you have a moment, I would just like to interject that I am here once again because Mitch Boetner is looking for support for a new and incredibly innovative idea that will transform the transportation industry. It was an idea that I guarantee you wasn't developed using a dime of government funding. This is a hot idea, and Mitch wants to bring it to you to get you in early before everyone else jumps on board."

The senator was too fast to let Tammy get too much in edgewise. "That is good to hear. Like I always said, the most creative people are those that are creative in their spare time. Nothing feeds the brain of ideas like a little starvation. I could never support an idea that was supported by money from my government. America needs that money to support the Mitch Boetners of the world so they can produce creative ideas and bring them to me to make sure they get enacted. It's not these sucking-on-the-government-dime hippies who create the jobs; it is the people like Mitch Boetner who do. Hell, Mitch is small-time compared to the giants of job creation among us, like Peter McKinnon. I am glad you brought this totally privatized opportunity to me to give public funding too."

Tammy was finding it hard to ignore the fact Mitch had nothing to do with the idea other than sponsoring it after she brought it to him. And he was the guy who was likely to make the most money from it—with a lot of that money coming from the actual government. Tammy had always wondered what it was about people like Senator Brown that they felt giving more money to rich people gave them the desire to work harder and to create more, but the same money given to a poor person gave them the desire to not work at all. She debated again walking out on the senator in disgust. She could demand this senator think about the people he represented. She thought of Bob counting on her and she thought she just had to try to close the deal.

Tammy said, "So we can count on your support then?"

The senator frowned. "I would love to give you my support, you know. But you see I cannot act without official support from my spiritual guidance. These days that comes mainly from the Eternal Missionary to the Lord. I give you and Mitch my personal promise, if you get their support and possibly donate a little more to my reelection, I can't see how I couldn't support this fine idea about grain or trains or whatever. Who gives a fuck really, right? Now let's not worry too much more about this. Sit back and relax a little with me. Enjoy that fine American cigar with me, and don't worry too much. I won't tell Mitch you smoked a little and possibly drank a little Kentucky Bourbon on his dime. It will be our little secret."

With that the senator laughed and started pouring some bourbon that apparently he also stored in his desk. Tammy realized she had come to the end of the road in this office. She had two choices: she could either not drink, not smoke, and blow the deal, or she could drink, smoke, and not actually make a deal but possibly leave it open to a deal in the future if these missionary people agreed. Well, would she transform into Tom Joad and tell the senator what she really thought of him? Sigh, she wouldn't. She took the bourbon and tried to enjoy smoking; she had come too far getting to Mount Doom just head back to the shire now.

Tammy walked back toward the train station to meet Bob. The mid-afternoon sun beat down on her. The senator might not have believed in climate change, but it turned out climate change wasn't Tinkerbelle and didn't require his beliefs to be real. Worse than the heat of the day was that instead of a great meal like Bob got, she got stuck drinking cheap whisky and smoking. Her lungs hadn't felt this bad since that year she tried breathing in Houston. She wheezed her way up the train platform steps. She was disappointed as they had once again failed to gather any real support—just another vague promise of support with a rider attached to it. When she arrived at the platform, she pulled out her PPED to call Mitch again and advise him of the current situation.

Mitch answered after three beeps. Mitch once again yelled back out of the PPED, "This is Mitch Boetner. Who the hell is this, and how the hell did you get my personal, private, secured number!"

Tammy calmly replied back, "This is Tammy. Remember me? We are working on that train proposal together. Mitch, you gave me this number weeks ago. Don't you ever remember anything?"

Mitch's tone immediately changed. "Oh, yes. Is Bob there? We need a three-way conversation. I don't mind three ways, but you know without the two-guy part. Get it? I was joking. Did you get the joke I made about three-way sex? Damn, I was thinking that one up all week. Nearly pissed myself now thinking about how funny it was going to be. While you recover, I'll patch him in."

Then followed five minutes of clicking and Mitch rambling to his PPED about why it couldn't understand simple verbal commands. Bob walked over to Tammy on the train platform. She gave him a wait sign with her hands. Bob shrugged and waited. Finally Mitch was able to patch Bob into the conversation.

Mitch replied, "What is going on with you two? I haven't heard a word about progress. I've been waiting to get updates from this Luke, but then again I have a hard time translating his e-mails. All he talks about is quantum tribalism e-mailing, which he insists is a mixed-media merger of two self-help philosophies and texting. He says it will change the world. However, these e-mails sent to me don't register as words used by any actual communicating language. So what is going on?"

Tammy decided to break the news as bluntly as she could: "Well, we aren't making as much progress as we would hope. We got approval from the technical office. Then we got you to back us and lay out a small amount of working capital. Then you set up a meeting with some liberal-like representatives. Bob ate steak, which it turns out was a good thing. It doesn't sound perhaps good, but it was. But they didn't agree to help us unless we could find someone from the opposite party to make the proposal bipartisan. Well we found one, but he apparently has moral objections to the proposal that need smoothing over. So we need further moral convincing."

Mitch asked a very serious question: "Did he make you smoke a cigar?"

Tammy replied, "Yes, I still feel ill from it."

Mitch replied, "Oh, then he used the good stuff on you. He must really like us. I told you people were going to love us. We are nearly there now. What is the next step?"

Tammy was puzzled. "Poisoning me with cigars is good and a sign of progress?"

Mitch replied, "He only poisons the people he really likes. If he hated you he would have smoked one of those horrible Cuban cigars. Feel lucky he spared you from the cheap foreign imported crap."

Tammy, who was now getting a little impatient, spoke: "What the hell are you talking about? We are supposed to be passing a very monumental transportation bill. We are not supposed to be eating steak and smoking cigars with our elected officials. I see I am going to have to personally take over the planning from here on out. If it is one thing I know how to do, it is how to plan. My last plan didn't work but my new plan will!"

Bob said, "Well, as far as I can tell the next phase of the plan is someone goes talk to something called The Eternal Missionary to the Lord."

Mitch got excited. "Oh, I know them. They're Washington's premier think tank. I've met their founder, Reverend Davies, many times. He loved my dad's donations. He told me to keep up my dad's good work. I think he will clearly be on our side. Now we will need to send someone to talk to him."

Tammy, working on a new plan, answered, "Well, shouldn't you go since you know him?"

Mitch said, "Well, I would. But you see, I've got to travel to Europe for a little bit to work on this little project I've been working on."

Tammy said, "Couldn't you put it off as it only should take a few hours to talk to these people?"

Mitch said, "I'd love to put it off, but it has been threatening to tell my wife unless I visit with my money right away. You can see how this little project is an urgent matter."

Tammy said, "Well then I'll go."

Mitch said, "Terrible idea. The reverend hates women in any type of authority situation. Nope, it looks like is up to Bob again."

Bob said, "Really, I haven't made any progress at all on this. Perhaps Tammy should go."

Tammy replied reluctantly, "I know these religious types spend a lot time around other men. They might be more comfortable talking to you, but you better get results we are counting on you."

The train arrived at the platform. They looked at the time on their PPEDs. Four minutes and thirty-four seconds late. They frowned.

Bob said, "OK, I'll do it for the proposal."

Tammy said, "Mitch, you set up the appointment with this reverend. I'll dig up what I can on this agency and have Luke send it to Bob. Bob, when the time comes, you don't say anything antireligious and offensive because we need these people. OK, team, let's get to work."

Bob and Tammy hung up their PPEDs and found themselves standing next to each other on the platform. Communication was easier using a PPED while standing next to each other than actually talking to someone face to face. After today's meeting, Tammy felt she needed no further verbal face-to-face communication. Bob wasn't good at starting conversation. So they stood awkward and silent next to each other until their respective trains came to take them home.

Chapter 6:
Magnesium, Proverbs, and Sobs

Einstein, don't tell God what to do.
— Niels Bohr, discrete thinker

Tammy knew today was the day Bob was supposed to go to the mission. She was unhappy she hadn't found good information to help move the plan forward. All she found out was what they already expected: the head of the organization was a Reverend Davies, and he was very opinionated. He had spoken very strongly on matters of the church and seemed to not like women, as Tammy had suspected. His writings online seemed to indicate someone who thought women should not work, have opinions, be strong, or—most insulting—be educated. Then he would complain that women weren't intelligent. Really, how did one become intelligent without being educated? She thought people like that treated women like pets; even worse, she needed their help.

They didn't even treat women like good pets—not like Chester A. Arthur who had his own drink bowl, bed, and door. She thought her dog was very sensible and a completely independent

dependent. Tammy learned no matter how interesting her dog was to her she found thirty-minute stories about her dog were not nearly as interesting to other people. Even Chester A. Arthur refused to sit and listen to them, so she could hardly expect someone less central to the story to care. She thus wisely refrained from telling too long a cute animal story. She would tell other people to refrain as well, but then she could only do so by violating her whole dog storytelling rule. So she didn't. Either way her dog was more interesting than the type of woman the reverend claimed society needed.

She called Bob to see if he was ready to go. She decided not to use Luke as he had a tendency to distract from her central plan of a solid pep talk to boost Bob's spirit.

Bob's head popped up on Tammy's PPED. "Hello, this is Bob. I am set to go. Any words of advice before the next meeting?"

Tammy replied, "Hi, Bob. This one is critical. We could close the deal here today. Just remember these aren't politicians per say, so don't get too political, and whatever you do don't listen to any of Mitch's advice. Remember, the people today believe things and try to not *not* believe things that may not be the things they want you to not believe in. If you can't think of nothing to say, then say nothing. Now go get in there, and make the proposal happen. We all believe in you, unless not believing in you is what they wanted us to believe in. If not, good luck." With that Tammy felt she had successfully prepped Bob for the day's critical mission. Tammy signed off and left Bob to get at it.

Bob arrived at a large box building. The building at one point had housed a large supermarket of a dull brand. It had unfortunately lost out on the food wars as larger and larger box stores in the suburbs had been able to replace its function in the community. In the world of postmodern food delivery, the most calories for the buck was the key. A warehouse superstore was the in thing provided it could deliver mass quantities of a food made with at least six different ways to say *sugar mixed with artificial flavorings and coloring thrown in.* This maximum yummy food was what the commercials pushed on the masses. Sugar was prime to sales, but fat was a good second too if you could force it in there. Sure there was that small middle class that could afford to purchase healthier foods that were fresh grown, but as a rule they headed to the snobbier trendy "whole" grocer. They were trained to shop away from the masses if you could afford to. Even better were those local farmers' markets that were available in the best places. The core of the country, though, couldn't afford the cost of fresh-grown foods, and even when they could, the commercialized high-calorie food was what they were pushed to like. Maximized yummy food had high-priced marketing campaigns, and fresh food didn't. This box store was large, but too small to compete with the larger superstores, and was too big to convert into a trendy artisan food store. Thus it failed as it was originally designed, and now it had been repurposed as a religious think tank headquarters. It actually made sense if you think about it as a superstore selling the maximized yummy food of everlasting life, if you were the type who was prone to be cynical.

It was, however, the perfect size for the current organization. The Eternal Missionary to the Lord had purchased it. The store had a good location in the Washington area, and it was large enough to hold congregational meetings and parties while at the same time allow partitioning of the building into smaller meeting rooms and office space. Next to the converted supermarket was a tall apartment complex that housed the missionary's holy order and a few select congressional members when in town. A large sign that once housed the name of the supermarket now housed a large, bright-pink glowing cross. The sign read, *The Eternal Missionary to the Lord,* and under that in smaller letters, *other positions welcomed.* A space below that was reserved for the daily inspirational quote. In bright red letters was written the inspirational quote, "Accept into your heart all denominations and donations to the Lord."

Bob was heading toward the nicer business-office side of the complex. A sign on the front door read, *Welcome and bless all visitors. Please remove shoes while in the house of the Lord*. Bob entered into a smallish inner room. A metal-framed rack in the main hall was filled with all types of shoes. A small dispenser was next to the rack. It read, *Insert credit card to receive holy slippers for forty dollars*. Bob inserted his card, and a pair of white slippers wrapped in plastic came out. The slippers had a gold-yellow colored cross-stitch in them. A tag on the strap lip read, *Proudly made in Somalia*. Bob unwrapped the slippers and inserted the plastic wrapper into a waste container placed conveniently next to the dispenser. Bob slid on the slippers and headed through the front door proper.

A large woman sitting behind a sleek, metallic table was the only thing to see in the inner entrance room. The large room had very nice polished-metal padded chairs that Bob assumed were for visitors to wait in. The large woman motioned him forward.

"I saw you comin' from de cameras, sugar. Our security system identified you all good and proper as de Bob we have scheduled for ahs meeting with de organization. Please, you all sit down, and de good and proper Father McNally will be out to meetcha." The lady then smiled and pointed toward the metallic seats to sit down.

Bob paused a second to admire the desk now that he was closer. The desk projected three-dimensional pictures up to a pair of glasses the lady was wearing. She was apparently typing on a virtual keyboard with the aid of small attachments on each of her fingers. Apparently this place had big bucks for the latest technology could offer. Bob had a general dislike for organized religion. Not that he considered himself an atheist. He felt himself more of a confirmed agnostic. Like a good scientist, he believed in anything he could prove with facts and experimental observation. If God did pop down from the magic land in the sky and say hello, Bob wasn't going to disbelieve him because God's appearance disagreed with his preconceived notion of his nonexistence. Still,

Bob was placing the chances of that event on the rather low scale as probabilities go. Bob started to shuffle for his seat not sure how such a nonbeliever would be accepted. Before Bob could reach his seat, a voice called out.

A rather thin older man with a Catholic collar on was calling his name. "Hello, Bob," greeted the man. "I am Father McNally. Our computer-control system alerted me you had arrived." He looked down at Bob's feet. "I'm sorry to see you weren't alerted ahead of time not to buy the slippers. Those were not my idea. I generally wave those for *my* invited guests. We have a mutual friend I believe in Mitch Boetner?"

The man was leading Bob out of the inner welcoming room and down a hall toward his office. Bob replied to him, "Yes, Mitch contacted this organization because we need your help with Senator A. J. Brown. The senator apparently needs divine inspiration to do anything besides complain about the poor and the unionized working class." Bob paused a second. Darn, he shouldn't have said that this man was probably the senator's acquaintance. "Why didn't Mitch do these things himself," thought Bob. Seriously, Bob felt he was too honest with his feelings on people who seemed a little less than worth respecting. Before Bob could continue, the father responded. Bob felt a pain in his stomach. Darn, too late—here it comes.

Father McNally said, "Yes, I understand. There are many in this organization that feel the plight of the poor, disabled, old, young, and the working man are ultimately a distraction from the mission of God. A man like the senator would argue that faith and belief in God was more important than these 'trivial things.' Sure they may occasionally lose sight of that, but in the end their pursuit of God in their vision of his word is never put off long. They always in the end urged the congregation or voters to always turn back to their version of the faith. Those trivial things interest me more. I belong to this organization because it has the power to change people's lives and do good works. If people like us, Bob, have to tolerate the senators of the world and run through their hoops to get it done, than that's what I do. It is my belief these hoops are only temporary anyways, and people like the senator won't be joining me in my ultimate destination. If I can get them to listen to me, on the other hand, perhaps I can save them. One has to try, and here is the place for a trying type of man because you'll find a lot of people in need of saving."

Bob and the father finally arrived at the father's private sanctuary in the organization. The father now leaned toward Bob, and in a hushed tone asked the all-important question Bob knew was coming: "Are you a firm believer in the Lord, my son?" The question of was or wasn't was not at present on Bob's mind. The question of is or isn't the father, and would or wouldn't he see through Bob's answer no matter what answer Bob gave, was more at the front of his mind. The father's initial statement was not what Bob expected; still he assumed the father was more religious than Bob could ever pretend to be. He decided the safe answer was to believe but not to profess too much. "I'm not exactly an atheist. Like most people, I have a belief in the Lord."

Father McNally replied, "So you are a believer, but not one of those who forces God into everyday conversation. You perhaps only see God as our prime mover. The view is a popular and archaic term, but it is acceptable. I approve of such ideas. Much safer a believer and not a doer than one who thinks they must act too much to prove their faith. I often wonder why people simply assume a person is moral just because they are outwardly outrageously religious. It is altogether a most unbecoming of traits. A sports figure can spout the most hateful saying against women, other religions, and homosexuals in the name of God, but then score a point and send prayer of thanks to God in front of thousands, and everyone assumes the perplexing assumption of 'what a good guy.' What's so good about him? He hates other humans based on his own religious belief. Is that good? Another ninety percent of people in the locker room believe in a God too. They don't spout off in the press or worse in infomercials about their vast belief in God and his dislike of women and/or gays. But hey, they don't pray on TV every time they score, tape God's voice on his body, or thank God every time they get a microphone in front of their face. Why is it open and over-the-top worship of God is considered a sign of consistent decent morality? Aren't the people that live their lives in silence and obedience of any value? Why does the public hero worship the profane just because it professes, like Lady Macbeth, too much?"

"I'm pretty sure that was Queen Gertrude," added Bob, a little perplexed at the conversation. Father McNally wasn't at all what Bob thought he would be.

Father McNally sat down on the plain wooden benches that sat in his very modestly decorated office. He motioned Bob to take a seat. "Oh, I am sorry. I am only a preacher of the Lord, you know. While I am expected to quote continuously due to this state of occupation, I am thankfully glad the public never insists that I quote accurately. As I was saying, people who make vows too openly and affirm their belief in God so incessantly are always, I fear, too presently phony. I do not wish to do business with them, but when I must for the greater good, I reluctantly do so. It is best to work with those who do not, but best is not always an option."

Bob was very perplexed. The organization didn't seem very much like he thought it was going to be at all. This person seemed both honest and actually interested in helping people. Bob sat down next him. "You see, Father, I have found a way to make our train system run better. I have solicited the Department of Transportation in an effort to use my ideas, but they need congressional approval. The department can't solicit Congress directly, so we went to Mitch to help us. Mitch doesn't want to handle this personally; he thinks I should be the face of this effort. I will be honest: I have no idea how to talk to congressmen. Either way, they seldom seemed interested in talking to me, even when they were actually talking to me. Even less were they not interested in the idea I brought them. Yet despite this disinterest, somehow nearly everyone I've talked with, at the end of whatever conversation we actually ended up having, said that they were interested in my project—even though they had no idea what it was because they never had me explain it to them. However, they were all willing to act with a 'but.' It is the 'but' that has led me eventually to you. I need your organization's support in order to get Senator A. J. Brown's support in order to get Representative Haye's support in order to allow Mitch Boetner's company that supports Tammy Usher's department to enact these ideas. Apparently Brown needs moral approval from God to take action on this. You would think God would have granted those in power the vision to see good from evil so they could take action themselves."

Father McNally laughed a good-natured laugh. "No doubt it is frustrating, I assure you. I fear far too many people are morally religious these days. I personally long for the old days when morality was decoupled from religious institutions and the fabric of religion. I enjoy reading the old philosophers: the Stoics, the Platonists, and the Epicureans. The gods then were many, and not a particularly moral in deeds and nature. People worshipped them because they were powerful, they might grant you a gift and they might not make your life worse that day. Not because they granted you some seed called morality. The philosophers were argumentative and better at tearing down pompous assumptions of morality than they were at building them up. Today too many people worship religion because of the magic aura of morality they think it gives them. Me, I think morality comes from inside. People just place their own internal morality into their religious beliefs and then reflected them back at the world as sanctified morality. At one time this way produced a God that thought it was moral to kill Jews, punish homosexuals, enslave blacks, and subjugate women. Most think the Lord wants them to be rich, because they themselves want some external ultimate sanctification for their good fortune so they don't need to feel guilty for those with nothing. But was it the Lord who thought these things or the men who reflected those words into the holiest of holies mouth? The God I read about in the Bible told me to follow the commandments and above all love one and all and to treat them like I want to be treated. Other than those ideas, I don't look much for ultimate morality etched into stone from the infinite in power. The philosophers seem more interesting to me and more refutable than God."

Bob was taken into the conversation now. "Which was your favorite?"

Father McNally sighed a little. He scratched at his chin in search of divine inspiration. "Oh, I don't know that off the top of my head. I guess I'm an idea thief at heart. I steal a little idea here, a little idea there. As I said I don't just hold to anyone's final idea or belief. Since God didn't make them, I don't feel as guilty when I borrow the bits I think I'd enjoy and ignore the advice I think ought not to be indulged upon. A philosopher is a man that considers himself an authority but most others do not. A prophet is man that considers God the only moral authority and claims God speaks through him and demands others recognize his authority. I'll take philosophers any day. For me, Jesus was the ultimate philosopher, or else why would I wear this outfit?" Father McNally tugged a little at his collar and laughed again.

Bob appreciated that. Father McNally was ultimately a man of faith, but his faith was not blind faith. Bob respected that even if he didn't share that faith so deeply. Bob agreed with him for the most part. He always thought religious morality was a logical constructed. Religious morality was the poor man's excuse to pass an idea onto society that they could not convincingly argue for. He asked Father McNally a question: "So what is your best philosophical advice then?"

Father McNally once again scratched at his chin a little. "Well now, let's see. My favorite advice that I live my life by is this:

For I was hungry, and you gave me something to eat;

I was thirsty, and you gave me something to drink;

I was a stranger, and you invited me in;

naked, and you clothed me;

I was sick, and you visited me;

I was in prison, and you came to me.

Then the righteous will answer Him, 'Lord, when did we see you hungry, and feed you, or thirsty, and give you something to drink?

And when did we see you a stranger, and invite you in, or naked, and clothe you?

When did we see you sick, or in prison, and come to you?'

The King will answer and say to them, 'Truly I say to you, to the extent that you did it to one of these brothers of mine, even the least of them, you did it to me.'

Then he will also say to those on his left,

'Depart from me, accursed ones, into the eternal fire that has been prepared for the devil and his angels;

for I was hungry, and you gave me nothing to eat;

I was thirsty, and you gave me nothing to drink;

I was a stranger, and you did not invite me in;

naked, and you did not clothe me; sick, and in prison, and you did not visit me.'

Then they themselves also will answer, 'Lord, when did we see You hungry, or thirsty, or a stranger, or naked, or sick, or in prison, and did not take care of you?'

Then he will answer them, 'Truly I say to you, to the extent that you did not do it to one of the least of these, you did not do it to me. These will go away into eternal punishment, but the righteous into eternal life.'

"See, I can quote fairly accurately when I have to. It troubles me that in this world so many have such absolute faith in an invisible Lord in the sky and yet so little faith in each other. Following the Lord is easy, most people think. You kneel at the right time, tithe at the right time, vote the right way, and profess to everyone your faith. It's actually even easier than that. Simply give yourself into service to other people, and work for their good here on Earth. Yet so few people seem to be able to work for each other and not think of what is in it for them. Well, what is in it for them is right there in Matthew. A person who lives in comfort while others live in misery should be worried. They'd rather get to heaven on faith alone. That makes life a hell on Earth, and there will certainly be hell waiting for those people after death who made it that way. We could try to make it as heaven-like as possible here on Earth if we tried. Not to be so melodramatic, of course." Father McNally once again laughed.

Bob now was feeling a little guilty. "Well, while my train-scheduling program will no doubt help a lot of people, I have to be a little honest here. Sure, I started working on it because it was interesting. I thought I could improve it, and I figured out that beyond a doubt I could. I started out working on it because, well, it was fun. But ultimately I also was hoping to make a little money from that patent. I guess I am a little short of your crusader for equality. I doubt ultimately that most people can give up every-thing and sacrifice their whole being into service of the good of others. I mean, I'm happy society will benefit from my ideas, but I'm also happy I might benefit a little too. I doubt that is exactly what the writer of Matthew had in mind."

Father McNally got up from his seat and moved over to his desk. He opened a few drawers and pulled something out. He handed Bob a set of rosaries. Father McNally said, "Now, now, there is no need to be so hard on yourself. Most people are bound to fail from time to time. That's why the Lord allows us to confess our failures. As Paul stated many times, people are not likely to be able to keep up the Lord's ideals and laws. I'd rather meet someone with a little sin of doubt every once in a while. The problem they say is that the intelligent man has too much self-doubt and the idiot nothing but confidence. The intelligent man is supposed to fear he can always be wrong. You just have to accept it. I might be wrong. You might be wrong. I'm a man of the cloth, so to speak. I've spent my life reading and searching for answers to life's greatest questions. I've weighed all the facts and tested them against all the theories. I've done the best I can with within the confines of what are the limits of what I can possibly know and do. If I'm wrong after doing that then so be it. I'd rather be wrong for the right reasons than right because of some idiot's blind confidence. We all fail sometimes. We all have a self, and we no doubt always think of ourselves first to some extent. I don't think we can possibly live up to the ideals of Matthew, but I think we can from time to time try. Trying and failing, being a little selfish from time to time, and hopefully having a little confidence from your self-doubt beats blindly going by as if faith alone makes it heaven here on Earth for everyone."

Bob thanked him for the gift. He said, "I'm not Catholic, but I guess asking a little forgiveness doesn't hurt. It's easier to ask for forgiveness than seek permission sometimes. Particularly in this case as the forgiveness comes from someone unseen and unheard and is the ultimate decider, whereas the permission comes from people I keep seeing. They talk on and on forever and yet never decide on anything. I wish there was just some place I could go in public and say, 'Here is my idea, here is why it benefits you, let's do this.' I guess that is what the government is supposed to be, but so many times it feels like it is not of the people, and agencies have purposely tied the government's hands until it doesn't work. Ironically they did this under the claim it didn't work and they were making it work better. Better? It doesn't seem to work at all. Why can't intelligent people just fix it to actually work? I mean it feels like the system almost set up so it is easier for the idiot to get heard than for intelligent men and women."

Father McNally scratched his chin again. He nodded his head in agreement. "I know a lot of intelligent people, and they are just as confident as the idiots. Their confidence comes from their self-doubt, not in spite of it. Why do we hear so little from the intelligent and so much from the idiot? Why is it that every opinion is allowed in the market place of ideas but the intelligent informed view? Why is intelligence simply frozen out of the market place of ideas? I am an intelligent man, and I do have fear. I fear that we are all the idiots that elect idiots that ignore the obvious to explore the absurd and pretend that's progress. I'm afraid you will find the system was not set up by the idiots, but other intelligent people. People that have a self-interest greater than that is good for them and the wealth to game the system in their favor. They desire useful idiots and do not desire intelligent opposition. To truly get intelligent ideas through in this system you need to be as persistent as I have. I have learned to work with those in the machinery and use their system to occasionally do what I can here on Earth for those that can't do for themselves. Not every selfish man is evil and from time to time you can work the system to a positive goal."

Bob seem relieved. Perhaps finally progress would be made. Here was a man who could help him. He was a man who could somehow cut through all the red tape and get his ideas into the market place. Bob said, "You know, I was reluctant to come here, and yet you seem like the first truly helpful person I met. You're also one of the few genuine people I've met so far in DC. Washington seems like a place where being genuine is unnatural."

Father McNally thanked Bob for the compliment. "Well, if I am unnatural for this town, then I can honestly say I came about it naturally. Unfortunately I can't say I will be much use to you. My job here was just to greet you while the organization's top leader was busy. As I said, I use this organization to do what I can. I am, like you, a person who needs the aid of this organization. But I can't do much more than put in a good word for you with Reverend Davies. I'm afraid it is him you will need to impress service on, not me. It's about time; I will bring you to him."

Father McNally took Bob down a small hallway carpeted by a rare imported Persian rug. On the walls were expensive religiously oriented paintings. At the end of the hall was a large doorway made of stone. The door had Mark 16:3 written on it. Father McNally opened the stone door to the offices of Reverend Davies. They entered the office. "This man is here to speak to us on a matter of trains," said Father McNally.

The Reverend Davies was an elderly man wearing a fancy, vaguely religious suit with nice tailored cuffs with gold buttons and trims. He reached out and shook Bob's hand vigorously. The office was impressive. A beautiful desk sat in the room with the 3-D technology built in. Had Bob been wearing 3-D glasses, he could have seen the virtual Bible it was displaying. Then he would have known the room virtually had the Bible in it. Also a nice marble pedestal sat in the room with a cross etched in the top. The room's walls had crosses made from all over the world. A giant fireplace occupied one wall. Despite it being rather warm outside, a fire blazed in the fireplace, and cool air flowed in as the AC churned from the vents.

Reverend Davies spoke: "A pleasure to meet you. Now, trains... trains? I do not approve of these trains. Full of sin, trains are. Always coming into tunnels and coming out of tunnels then blowing a full stack of hot sticky white smoke. Trains are always used as symbolism for sex. I dislike symbolism almost as much as I dislike sex. You can't spell trains without *sin*, I tell you. I wrote a full ten-page pamphlet on the hidden sexual sins involving train symbolism for my Sunday church reader. I charge only twenty dollars for it. It's all in there—the trains, the sin, and the symbolism. Twenty bucks is a bargain for that kind of soul-saving information. The pamphlet has several suggestions on proper and improper use of symbolism and trains in case you find yourself on the tracks to sinning. The pamphlet is just a condensed version of my full tome on symbolism. I find symbolism of sex in movies rather tiresome and bored. Trains, fireworks, and small boys eating ice cream cones. The work of the devil, I tell you. Or I would have told you had you come to the sermon, bought the pamphlet, or purchased the easily downloadable full tome. Don't wait until my next compilation 'best-of' books to read it. I collect my best thoughts on sin, ideas on salvation and place them in a condensed easy to read book. Many people like to learn of their sin in short, concise aids to prayer and faith. There's also a building wealth through prayer section for the sinful minded entrepreneur. All this is modestly priced I might add too. The e-book version is fully illustrated in case you like your identification of sexual sin graphically represented. Have you read or purchased any of them yet?"

Bob looked around for Father McNally but found in the time of the delivery of that pitch, the father had quietly took his leave. Bob suddenly longed for his previous conversation with Father McNally. Bob said, "I really never considered the sexual aspects of trains. I'm here to discuss the business of train scheduling. You see—"

Reverend Davies spoke quickly "But one must consider the aspect of sex in everything. Particularly in business! Some people say that their sex is none of your business, but sex is a business and thus your sex is part of everyone's business because it is a part of the business world. I find sex without the thought of business a terrible prospect. People claim they are for sexual freedom. I think of free sex for just pleasure of each other a disgusting idea indeed! I see contraception as a device to allow people to engage in free pleasure for pleasure's sake. It makes sex just another free sinful transaction, like skipping out on a check or your call girl. It is truly disgusting, the concept of people using each other for free pleasure. What are we, godless Communists? When it comes to sex, always think of the business aspect of it, and if you must seek free sex pleasure, remember the Lord wants us to seek the content in the simple pleasures of pleasuring oneself."

Suddenly Bob was beginning to regret shaking the reverend's hand. This was in some way more successful than other adventures to date since at least they were talking about trains—sort of. Bob spoke, "Well, my idea, you see, would I guess lead to less sexual sin. You see, it is a plan to control the schedule of trains more accurately. You see, by precise planning there will be less wasted time on trains and thus less time in theory for sinning on these trains."

The reverend scratched his chin and nodded his head in agreement. He replied, "Planning is a good idea so long as it isn't that artificial family planning. I find all forms of birth control with the exception of natural family planning a sin. Abortion is a locomotive running off the tracks chugging toward a tunnel of damnation, if you catch my train of thought. Condoms aren't much better. I have no use for them myself. Now I have a six-week abstinence-only life class that is only three hundred dollars. You'll love it. It has the power to change your life. Remember, you might want to consider registering early as classes tend to book up—you know, lots of mothers signing up their daughters. The best part of our church offering abstinence-only life classes is the repeat business."

Bob was getting a little worried once again as the conversation was drifting away from him. Either way he had no intention of signing up for any classes or buying any literature. The stupid slippers were bad enough. Bob said, "Yes, I'm beginning to see how sex is good business for the church. Now this train idea is also a great business idea—"

Bob was interrupted again: "Well, my son, the Lord works in mysterious ways, particularly when it comes to the ways of business. For instance, we accept many different ways here. Ways like cash, credit cards, food stamps, student loans, and even online payment service. Heck we even accept bartering for our services. If you got some sin and only a chicken to your name, we will take your only chicken to save your soul. We are that kind of kind and faithful organization. Your eternal soul is important for us, and there is no amount of wealth worth your immortal soul. I mean it is one of those things you can't put a price on. I mean if you stuck a price tag on it, it would be invisible too. I mean there are some people who can view your soul. Spiritual faith healers, touch healers, and New-Age chakra viewers all claim to be able to touch and move your soul. If you are interested in your soul being stroked, touched, or appraised, we provide the service, and it is discounted this month at three hundred ninety-nine dollars. And don't worry about the cost, because when we massage your inner soul, we guarantee you get a happy ending."

Bob had decided on a new idea. He would claim poverty, and thus perhaps the man would stop trying to sell him things and listen to the train proposal. Bob said, "I'm sorry. I just bought a new iPPED, and it tapped me out. I just won't be able to purchase anything today."

Reverend Davies looked very grim on Bob. He picked up his limited-edition, illustrated, leather-bound edition of the Bible from a drawer in the desk. The reverend reserved it for when he needed a tangible Bible for thumping purposes. He then placed it on the pedestal made of fine Vermont marble. He spoke, "Come here, my son, and pray over this good book. I am glad you have decided to confess your sins to me and the Lord. Now beg forgiveness so that our savior may forgive you. To have no money is not a sin, but to have no money because you spent it unwisely is. I forgive you for this grave sin in the eyes of the Lord, and he will too."

Bob was confused. He went over to the pedestal and put his hands on the rather nice book. Bob said, "I need to ask one question before I can ask forgiveness. What exactly did I do wrong again? I'd hate to not be forgiven because I didn't one hundred percent get what it was I had done wrong."

Reverend Davies replied, "Well, my son, it is wise to fully understand the nature of sin before you can understand if God has forgiven you for it. To have traded something for nothing, the nothing better have been worth it. You have traded the greatest gift the Lord has ever given a man—money. You have received for it not the word of God, modestly priced from many of my fine products, we have a website too, so be sure to check it out the next time you get paid. Where was I? Oh yes, I remember. You chose not the word of God but an electronic device full of sin instead."

"PPEDs are full of sin?", asked Bob.

Reverend Davies replied, "These devices are the source of the vilest of all sinful acts known to man or woman—masturbation. The Internet is filled with nothing but it. Trust me I have searched hour upon hour on this electronic net, and nothing but porn and sin did I find. I remain ever vigilant for it. No night passes that I do not search and find it. I do this not for my own enjoyment but as to know of it and so I may remind my parish of the sin that is lurking on this Internet. It is bad enough that the sin of porn feels to be everywhere these days. Now with these PPEDs you have a source of masturbation right in your hands to squeeze, press, touch, and stroke! Is it not written in the Bible that those that deny the Lord their essence here on Earth will be denied feeling the Lord's ever-flowing spiritual effluence in heaven?"

Bob was pretty sure if such a notion was written in the Bible, it was only due to a most careless scribe. Bob said, "I don't really use that for masturbation, so perhaps it would be wrong to ask forgiveness for something I didn't do."

Reverend Davies said, "That is just what Senator Robertson used to tell me. He was a deeply troubled man, you know. Rich and successful, and his life was full of sexual desire. He finally broke down to me and the Lord and confessed that he was addicted to the stuff. Sex can ruin a man, but luckily man has the Lord, and the Lord has created a weekend class that can cure you of this sexual desire. It is only nine hundred ninety-five dollars with an additional four hundred thirty-five dollars if you want the take-home sexual desire material that once again comes fully illustrated. I tell you it can change your life. Yesterday Senator Robertson was a lonely man with a horrible sex addiction; today, thanks to my class, he is a happily married man with thirty-two lovely kids."

The room fell oddly quiet for a minute. Finally Bob broke the silence, "I really don't think I need forgiveness. I am here, after all, to help people just like you help people. I am here to free people by providing a modest boost to the train-travel experience."

Reverend Davies replied, "Freedom, you say. Have you not listened to me at all? Freedom is what is crushing this country. They claim I have freedom of religion, but every place I turn the government is oppressing me. This word freedom is used today as the greatest source of sin the world has ever known. I want the freedom to prevent women from having access to God-draining contraceptives and abortions. But on this issue where is the precious freedom of religion? Nowhere because the government crushes my freedom at every turn! They claim it is right and good that I not pay for abortions for myself. But I'm a man, I don't need them. I need to prevent women from having them, but they rob me of my right to force other people to do things I don't want them to do in the name of the Lord. They claim my freedom does not equal you having less freedom. I tell you if those women don't agree to have less freedom, then how can I truly be free? Freedom is the greatest source of sin in the world because it prevents God from forcing you to do what I tell you to do. I hope your idea will do nothing to support such an authoritative nonsense concept like freedom."

Bob thought about all that had been said and decided on one last idea to get to the point of his mission here. "Well, I guess you will not like this idea then. It is too bad to because Mitch Boetner had thought you'd like it. Mitch himself is in love with the business side of the deal. He said you were a man who understood a good business idea when he heard it. He thought for sure trains and the huge profits were right up your alley."

The reverend scratched at his chin a little. He remained surprisingly quiet for a good minute as he appeared to be mulling over the train scheduling. Bob had used the word profits. His eyes appeared to be envisioning the word and the trains arriving and going from some phantom station in his mind. Perhaps the station was at some religious pilgrimage site. Perhaps it was at some site of sin made more convenient a target now that it was more likely to be visited. Bob couldn't tell for sure, but he was rather sure dollar signs rolled on the tracks of the reverend's mind just now.

Finally the reverend broke his silence: "Trains, huh? I never really thought of transportation in relationship to the Lord. Moving people around on trains can be big money. Big, big money if it were done right. It would matter who controlled that money— whether the money went to our good, God-fearing, church-tithe-paying men or our lazy, spendthrift government. I have never known a government based on separation from our Lord to be anything but a godless and non-profit agent in society. Trains have rather good marketing opportunities for the Lord. I would love to give you my consent, but if we freeze government out this thing, I fear it could be huge. But it might be perhaps too big. I'm afraid this thing might be even too big for my organization to handle."

"Too big for the Lord to handle?" asked Bob.

The reverend had slid back into his more casual, pulpit-preaching animated form. "Exactly! I think we will need to bring in Philip Flip. Phil is the greatest Christian and the greatest lobbyist the world has ever known. He is on par with no one here on Earth. I would compare him to a marketing angel brought here by the Lord's only son to further his work and bring profits to the believers and economic ruin to the nonbelievers. He has the ear of the real movers and shakers in this country. He is beyond the binds of Earthly morality that hold the honest government politicians and instead goes right to the heart of democracy—capital. Capital has the miraculous ability to transform any issue into a hot topic that can be used to sway and profit from the capitalistic democracy's lifeblood—the voters. He tears at the heartstrings of the people with an onslaught of corporate, private, nonprofit, and public capital like no man I have ever seen before. He is truly the evangelist of capital. A true modern-day John the Baptist that declares the good news and without ever losing his head or needing to eat a locust. The man has truly taught me everything I know about marketing in the Lord's name. Yes, we need Phil Flip on our side if we are going to do this thing right in the eyes of the Lord. Lucky for you, Phil is coming to a party at our group's collective interaction, mass marketing, and prayer center tomorrow night. Yes I believe we can get Philip Flip on our side there. I'll do the groundwork, but I need you there tomorrow night. And for God's sake, bring a date. I don't want Phil thinking you're some momma's-boy small-time queer."

With that the reverend shook Bob's hand with a hardy handshake. He took out a few flyers on a religious camp on the evils of freemasonry's influence on fitness programs and birth control, a pamphlet for an after-school work group on conversion from a sex-driven humanist to abstinence-only-driven spiritualism, and a pamphlet on a lecture on biblical capitalism and the Gospels' support for the belief that helping the poor via public services robbed them of their dignity. He hand them over to Bob as it never hurt to try to drum up a little business whenever the chance presented itself. He then took his leave of Bob with a final promise to contact Bob with the party information and another stress that Bob not come alone.

Chapter 7:

Did You Think Money Was Heaven Sent?

We tried to speak between lines of oration,
You could only repeat what we told you.
Your axe belongs to a dying nation,
They don't know that we own you.
You're watching movies trying to find the feelers,
You only see what we show you.
We're the slaves of the phony fucking leaders,
Breathe the air we have blown you.
— Pete Townshend (expletive added by Roger Daltry in
concert), rock 'n' rollers

Tammy was at the moment planning her outfit for the night. She did not want to appear too casual because this was not a social date. There was no romance here—although one never one hundred percent knew that there would not be romance. Still Bob did not give the impression of a person one had a passionate affair with. Still a person needed to keep up her prospectus at all times. Her mother had always wanted her to marry, but Tammy had planned ahead for a career first and romance later. The fact that romance was often overrated and filled with nights out with prospects that failed to meet her plan for the ideal man tended to underscore the romance-later idea. The children's books made Prince Charming appear to last forever after. In the real world, Prince Charming rarely made it a month before his cracks showed through. Perhaps Tammy's standards were too high. But there was a reason for that as Tammy never understood why real movies about real adults in real romantic situations were reserved for art houses and given ratings as to embarrass the average viewer away from watching. However, one was free to watch childhood fantasy romance or worse, horrific violence in place of romance. The entertainment industry hired the most attractive people on Earth, but the only thing they could think to do with them was to have them dance around fantasy landscapes dressed in impractical clothing singing to animals, or grinding them to death slowly into small little bits in full graphic 3-D animation for your entertainment. Only it didn't entertain Tammy because she was an adult. If Tammy was not going to get the romance she wanted and planned for, then she could wait. There were not that many eligible Prince Charmings out there, and Tammy felt she was still too young to settle for something less. So the goal was an outfit that stressed business but gave a hint that possibly more could occur—but almost certainly wouldn't.

Tammy's wardrobe was carefully planned to allow her maximum flexibility. She exercised the process of sophisticated shopping as popularized in the famous fashion book *Sophisticated Shopping* by Huo Chen. Chen had been born in the Communist Socialist utopia of postmodern China, which was why she was such a great capitalistic shopper! She was an expert sophisticated shopper and had written a book to teach the world how to also be a sophisticated shopper. It turned out, Tammy thought, to be such a simple thing. To become a sophisticated shopper you needed to do three simple things: maximize your savings by maximizing your spending, understand the importance of the logo, and understand the importance of appearing like you spent a lot of money on your clothes by actually spending a lot of money on your clothes. With that easy-to-follow advice, Tammy obtained the true perks of being a sophisticated shopper.

Tammy pulled a sweater down from her closet. The sweater had been a real bargain! Sure it had cost Tammy $500, sure it was neon lime-green, and gave her the appearance of a frog, but it had been on sale. Tammy pulled out a more practical and flattering navy-blue sweater that her cost her only twenty-five dollars on sale. The blue sweater was a much better choice for the evening, but the other sweater had been the more sophisticated purchase. The ultimate secret was that the green sweater had been half off. Five hundred dollars might not sound like a deal for a sweater, but this had been a $1000 sweater. That navy-blue sweater at full price was only what, fifty bucks? She only saved twenty-five dollars on that sweater. With the other sweater she had saved $500! Did the average shopper understand how many more navy-blue sweaters they'd have to buy to get the same $500 in savings she got! What would they do with all those sweaters anyways? Thanks to global warming, sweater weather wasn't exactly a long season. Tammy held up the neon lime-green sweater to her body. She looked at the mirror carefully. She then put it back into the closet. It had only cost her $500 to save $500, which was a virtual bargain. That was maximizing her savings by maximizing her spending. Too bad it wasn't the sweater right for tonight's party. She would save it for a more sophisticated occasion where looking like a frog was more appropriate. She felt like she had failed at being a good sophisticated shopper, but shopping was one thing, wearing was another, and the book really wasn't very helpful for planning what to actually wear after sophisticatedly buying it.

Tammy looked at her watch. She would have to head out soon to pick up Bob. Mitch had rented them an electric vehicle for the evening. Bob did not know how to drive. Really, she thought, this was a major strike against him. Men were supposed to do manly things: kill spiders, move heavy objects, pay for meals when dining out, and drive. She seriously doubted Bob's prospects, not that it mattered. It was after all a business affair not a romantic affair. It was Philip Flip and his skills they were really after.

They arrived at the Eternal Missionary to the Lord. It had been an awkward drive over. Bob wished he had bothered to learn to drive. But really, what was the point? He never thought it would be needed. He had thought they might just take the train over—it's not like the missionary wasn't on the train line. Mitch insisted they take a car. Really, it seemed totally inappropriate to drive to a meeting where you were going to pitch the incredible importance of mass transportation. Tammy on the other hand looked rather nice. Bob's attempts at casual conversation did not go anywhere. He had brought up important subjects that he thought she might be interested in. He inquired about the weather, that local sports team, that recent entertainment feature people had watched, and that popular celebrity that has the two different-colored eyes. None of the conversation had gone very far, and somehow Bob ended up telling a long story about the time as a kid he went away to summer camp and got diarrhea. Now in retrospect he was thinking that perhaps that wasn't a very good topic of car conversation, and he wondered now how they even got on the subject. Too late now—they had arrived, and it was time to find out why this Phil Flip would fail to resolve the situation. Bob had developed a natural tendency toward pessimism by this point. Tammy on the other hand looked rather optimistic and prepared. Really, she looked rather fancy and sophisticated in her clothes. Bob was in general not very good at dating. In the back of his mind, he felt he had been scared by all those romance books he was forced to read in high school.

Secretly he was always worried the date was going to end in a tragic sledding accident, like *Ethan Frome*.

The Eternal Missionary to the Lord looked different by night. The missionary was all lit up and glowing—sort of like a shining beacon on a hill. This time Bob was not heading for the main office but into the large worshiping chamber that was serving tonight as the main party gathering center. A valet was at the door and took their car keys leaving them with a ticket stub. He handed them to Bob who awkwardly had to hand them over to Tammy. A bright, well-lit red carpet lead the couple into the insides of the Eternal Missionary to the Lord where they assumed Phil Flip would be.

Bob was not used to being on dates—even dates of the purely business variety. Upon entering the room, Bob quickly looked around. He was looking for other people who looked somewhat young and businesslike. He noticed various older men in various vaguely religious outfits—people who were clearly priests, preachers, elders, and rabbis. But he also saw people who were harder to define. There were women around as well—none, however, who looked like they were someone's date, which did not help make Bob feel any more comfortable. There were just a few extremely dedicated wives of elder religious gentlemen—not young, unattached singles. He did notice a few younger women, but they were rather oddly dressed in robes that Bob figured must be religiously oriented in some fashion. On the far side of the room, Bob spied Reverend Davies at the minibar apparently ordering a few drinks. Bob motioned to Tammy to see if she might be interested in a drink while they waited. Drinks, he thought, were totally businesslike and not at all romantic, so she wouldn't get the wrong idea.

Tammy nodded in agreement that Bob should go get drinks. She was scanning the room for Philip Flip, whom she knew from photographs. Bob went toward the minibar. It had not occurred to him that leaving Tammy alone in a room filled with lonely male religious figures might not be a great idea. As Bob walked away, an elderly man in a nicely tailored suit quickly moved to engage Tammy in conversation. Tammy was more interested in watching the room than having conversation, but she was too polite to not engage in casual conversation lest she make a bad impression.

In front of the minibar stood Reverend Davies who, although the evening was young, had already gathered an impressive pile of empty glasses. The reverend appeared to be lightly nursing a white Russian as Bob moved toward the minibar. The minibar was designed to be portable—a small thing that could be rolled from location to location as the functions desired. It was one of five located in the room. On the minibar top sat a glass with a card taped to the side that read *Tips*. It was empty.

The reverend noticed Bob and tried to straighten himself up from his slightly tipsy state. The reverend greeted Bob: "Ah, Bob, my friend, thanks for coming. I tell you tonight's the night. Phil is the goods. We need support and Phil brings it balls out. Did you bring the eye candy? Phil measures a man by the eye candy he keeps, you know? He isn't all deep and sophisticated like most in his field. He figures if you aren't good enough to attract attractive women, you aren't worth his time. A smart man, he excludes us men of the cloth obviously."

Bob reluctantly turned over to the direction of Tammy. He wasn't sure he was comfortable calling Tammy exactly eye candy; she was, after all, the person who would be in charge of the day-to-day management of the plan everyone was working on. That was not exactly vacant candy in a display case. Still he was told to go along with these people by Mitch. These were the people you needed to go along with to get a proposal ahead. Bob pointed Tammy out from the crowd of older men that seemed to be despite the large space disproportionally standing nearer and nearer to her. At the moment she was now surrounded by three celibate, yet rather eager-looking aging clergy men. "That's Tammy Usher. She is in charge of managing the trains for the Department of

Transportation. She's the one that basically set this whole thing in motion for us."

The reverend seemed to lack the same celibate eager look as the other men around Tammy. He turned and stared at her. A little bit of scorn showed through, yet he seemed happy enough. The reverend pontificated, "Oh, good job, Bob. She's such a lovely dish to bring to our party. No doubt Phil will be impressed. Brains and she looks good in a skirt. Nice logos—you can judge the quality of a woman by the quality of the logos she wears, my friend. The only young ones we get like that here are usually dykes. Damn shame we don't get too many heterosexual young women to these things. Tons in the congregation always chasing after you, but you know a formal party like this you can't have the common congregation around. Tonight we have mostly the celibates who have given themselves to service the God, or worse, New-Age, fish-eating lesbians. You know, I could use some more refreshments. It's not a good thing drinking on an empty stomach when there's expensive food around."

The reverend's bony hand tugged on Bob's shoulder and directed him off from the minibar over a few feet to the smorgasbord. Bob seemed reluctant to go as his original mission was to get some drinks for himself and Tammy. However, the bony grip of the reverend was too much for him.

Reverend Davies pulled out a paper plate and start piling items on it. Just as Bob was getting comfortable and thinking of grabbing a plate himself, the reverend returned to his pontificating: "What were you just mentioning? Oh yes, I remember now—you mentioned 'the gay.' The gay is a bane to a religion, I tell you. If you ask me Moses got it right in Leviticus when he wrote that 'Thou shalt not lie with mankind, as with womankind for it is abomination.' Homosexuality is such a plague on society since the dawn of religious enlightened parishes. The lesbian is just as horrible. The great apostle Paul stated correctly that when 'leaving the natural use of the woman, burned in their lust one toward another; men with men working that which is unseemly.' So you got to make sure you fill the pews with lots of attractive young girls, or the parish will go all queer on you. The fuel of a parish is plenty of young, believing parishioners with loose feelings about donations. Young, lustful parishioners generate new young, lustful parishioners with each other. A God without plenty of young followers is an angry God in danger of being forgotten. The gay denies God what he needs most: the young people needed to carry the God from generation to generation. You get too many of those lesbian types of women who prefer women, and suddenly you end up with a bunch of lonely, lustful guys who will turn all gay on each other in a minute. It was this biblical idea that in the absence of women a man will be turned on by other men that inspired me to turn my life to studying the Lord in an all-male seminary, I can tell you. There I learned a thing or two I could show you about ah...preaching the good word. I promise you if you get too many of the 'gays' in a parish, suddenly our children will all be worshiping a flying ball-of-spaghetti instead of our Lord and savior. I, I can assure you, am as straight and as unbending as the flight of an arrow and a big Leviticus believer."

The reverend paused to eat a little more from his plate. He then added, "Here, have you tried these shrimp? They are absolutely to die for." The reverend speared a shrimp with a toothpick and handed it to Bob. Bob picked up a shrimp on a toothpick. He dipped it into the cocktail sauce. Reverend Davies was correct—the food was very good. Perhaps, thought Bob, not good enough to die for, but still perhaps good enough to defy the laws of Moses just once. Since the reverend was offering advice, Bob thought he'd have a go at having such a biblical expert answer a clarifying question. "You know, Reverend Davies, you were just talking about Paul and his thoughts on women. There was always one question I never understood, which I thought you might be able to answer. Did Paul want women actively involved in religious matters or not? In Corinthians he states, 'Let your women keep silence in the churches: for it is not permitted unto them to speak; but they are commanded to be under obedience as also saith the law.' Yet not too before that, he stated that every 'woman that pray-eth or prophesieth' which implies women can speak on religious matters. Which is it? Did he want women to speak on religious matters or not? It seems so confusing."

There, thought Bob, that ought to get him going. While the reverend went on, Bob thought he would be free to eat up the rather tasty spread here. Bob started busying himself with a rather delicious-looking cheese-and-ham spread. Since he figured Reverend Davies was likely to do a lot more talking, he might as well help himself.

Much to Bob's satisfaction the reverend did indeed have an opinion on the subject. The reverend finished up the frog legs he was sinfully enjoying and began to speak, "Ah yes, an interesting conundrum but not a difficult one to sort out I assure you. Women, of course, may speak about the good works and deeds of our Lord at the proper time and place. Indeed it is about the only thing I and the Lord prefer to hear women speak about. Day after day the men of my parish come to me seeking guidance about what to do with their women having opinions, suggestions, corrections, advice, ideas, and thoughts. Let me tell you, a woman is never unwilling to not share these things with a man at a moment's notice. Women do tend to rattle on and on as a bunch of noisy busybodies. Not like men who like myself are the soul of brevity. The men of my parish assure me they have important things to do, you understand. Men do not have time for endless prattling about gossip about individuals you never have heard of or if you had, never cared about. The men of my parish cry out, 'why must a woman go on and on about my relationship?' In exacerbation they blurt out to me, 'Can't the Lord tell that bitch to just shut the fuck up?' I reply back to them that he did. The Bible states clearly a woman can talk about the Lord, but it reserves the man's natu-ral right as the first created to tell her to shut her fat lip when she talks too much. God doesn't care any more about analyzing your relationship than you do when there's college football on TV. So the Lord reserved the right for a man to silence a woman lest she feed you the forbidden apple of her pointless, useless knowledge you never freaking asked to hear in the first place. Bah, women. Let me tell you, Bob, I never cared for them personally."

The reverend paused a moment to eye Bob over. He reached over and helped himself to a slice of ham and cheese. He then finished off his White Russian and casually left the glass near some rabbit pâté. Bob was equally impressed by the reverend's blatant sexism that seemed to match his over-the-top homophobia. Bob was pretty sure he couldn't think less of the reverend. Bob filled up his plate a little more.

The reverend then started on again, "Women, I tell you. I just could never stand them at all. You know, another thing I can't stand is a hypocrite. You know, one of those holier-than-thou atheist men who shout about how much he hates the organized religions in public. No doubt, though, when the shit hits the fan and he finds himself on a downturn toward oblivion, he wanders into my church seeking forgiveness. When times are good, he ignores the Lord's word but as soon as things go bad, he shows up and converts. Like the Bible condones that type of thing! If the Lord wanted a better-late-than-never convert, he would have said so. I mean there goes forty-plus years of alms out the door with you late converting. You think the Lord will let you get away with forty years of ignoring your financial duty to the Lord? Sure, some of them give it all away to the church in death, but if God wanted you to give all your money away, he would have said so! God can't survive on random unscheduled deaths to pay the bills. He needs the weekly dues coming in to make a proper budget and get the compound interest. God has bills to pay, and most people won't take the Lord's word when it comes to credit! Even worse than the Johnny-come-lately atheist is the religious snob that thinks they are too good for the organized church. They never come to mass, but they claim to be ever so involved in a more intimate personal relationship with the Lord. Like the Bible tells you to pray to the Lord in private? The Lord likes a mass, I tell you. Not just any mass. A grand display on TV and with a live feed for the Internet with the rafters filled to the brim for the whole world to see. A grand show filled with silver coins and good, high-angle camera shots of my good side. The world needs less hypocrites, more men, and a few attractive women who are not afraid to stand up to make a full display to the world that they are believers. And if you are not, it matters not because we shall make such a grand show and raise so much hell that the laws will force you to follow our beliefs anyways. That is what this organization is all about. As for the coward hypocrites who take our Lord's name in vain, God damn the lot of them."

They moved away from the table spread. Bob said, "Oh darn, I never got the drinks I was going to get."

"Don't worry. The minibars are portable; eventually one will travel near us."

Bob and the reverend now arrived back to Tammy. Bob hoped the passage of time had made her forget about the whole drinks thing. The presence of the reverend seemed to open a path in the elderly men surrounding Tammy.

Tammy seemed relieved for them to depart. "Thank the Lord you two have arrived when you did to rescue me from that man. You would not believe what he was saying to me. That one man was trying to get me to baptize my parents. I told them there was no need, for you see they were baptized as little children, and most important of all, they were passed on, deceased." Tammy stopped and looked for a glass from Bob. The best Bob could do was shrug and hope there weren't too many crumbs on him.

Tammy seemed a little frustrated at yet more failure and inadequacy on Bob's part. However, she turned to the religious man Bob was with. She recognized him from the celebrity pages as Reverend Davies, the founder of the Eternal Missionary to the

Lord. She continued speaking, "The oddest thing was he said it was not too late to baptize them. Too late, can you believe it? Even though they were dead. Apparently death is no big matter to him, for he said he could baptize the dead! I told him there was no need to dig them all up just for baptism that they already had, but he assured me there was no need for the digging either. It was all easy enough. Well, really, have you ever heard such nonsense in your life? What will people think up next?"

Reverend Davies replied, "Ah, yes, that would be our organization's Mormon friend. The Mormons do like to baptize the dead. A good racket if you ask me. I wish my church had thought of it first. Big moneymaker, baptizing the dead. And it does tend to overinflate the worshiping numbers when you can increase the faithful by backfill from the already dead. Do not worry your poor little fragile female head, though. Lucky for you, my dear, I sell a holy pendant to be placed with a deceased loved one in their casket that is guaranteed to warn off baptism from beyond the grave. I call it the Christian anti-Mormon baptism holy talisman. Think of the horror an unwanted baptism from the grave could bring your dead relatives. One minute you are seated at the right bosom of the Lord, and the next you are whisked away to the satanic Garden of Eden surrounded by a boiling pit of lava, somewhere below Missouri. The pendant is only ninety-nine ninety-five with a special e-discount if you order at my church's electronic online gift shop. Ah, I see the minibar has moved within reach. Let us order and drink up heavily the nectar of God's bounty. Drink up, my young lady friend. I assure you booze will help release any shock. You know I hate seeing good alcohol go to waste." The last bit seemed the most sincere.

"Does this device work?"

The reverend was distracted now getting another glass of smooth alcohol. "What did you say, work? Oh, Lord yes it works. We sold ten thousand units last month. That's the Lord's work in action," answered the reverend.

"Are you enjoying the party, Ms. Usher?" asked Father McNally who had suddenly appeared behind the three while they were busy getting drinks.

"Oh, it is very nice. I do love a good party, and I get invited to so few. I do wish there were more women, though. Why are there so few religions with solid female leadership? It does get to make a woman feel uncomfortable," said Tammy.

Reverend Davies replied to her, "Oh, do not suffer your pretty head to think such difficult thoughts. God has a proper and righteous place for you. But I suffer not a woman to teach, nor to usurp authority over the man, but to be in silence. For Adam was first formed, then Eve. And Adam was not deceived, but the woman being deceived was in the transgression. Notwithstanding she shall be saved in childbearing, if they continue in faith and charity and holiness with sobriety. You see, God did not save enough clay to make both your curvaceous and tempting body and give you mind to think too. But God did give you the simple joys of childbearing and charity."

Tammy thought this was for the best that God had given her the gift of charity, or she might with less charity have kneed the reverend in his pompous groin. Sobriety was another gift Tammy had that this holy superior man lacked. Tammy replied, "I thought Paul said it was OK for women to preach as long they wore a sensible hat."

Tammy, who previously had scanned the room trying to find Philip Flip, then turned in the direction of some young ladies standing in a group. She pointed to them with her drink, "Oh, and those women there have the most sensible of hats on. I do love that basic flat color they are wearing too. They have such spring feel to them. I just can't believe a group as lovely as those women are damned to subservience, or else why would they be here as part of your organization? If they, like Eve, will trick us all into eating forbidden fruit, I'm sure you would not even let them in your front door."

Bob, giggling a little now, asked, "Father McNally, what religion are those women here lobbying for?"

"Oh those are the Wiccans, I do believe," replied Father McNally.

"I don't believe I heard of such a thing. What's a Wiccan?," questionedTammy.

Reverend Davies replied a little acidly, "They're like witches with a better marketing department. They're good at selling merchandise like candles, cat food, and incense but not at saving a man's soul from sin. Still money is money." He trailed off as the thought of money seemed to distract him. He started drinking a fresh drink from the minibar.

Tammy was feeling perhaps she should not have asked about women. Men were so nonsensical when it came to the simple subject of women, she thought. She didn't want to get on these men's bad side, but still she would not be subservient to anyone. She worked too hard her whole life to naturally give an inch to someone just because they thought they were her natural superior. Best to change the subject before Reverend Davies said something offensive about women again. Tammy spoke in general about an easy subject: "It certainly seems like you have all your religious bases covered. I feel any person could feel comfortable under this roof. Look like even that funny little man over there is having a good time."

They all now turned in the opposite direction. A thin bearded man with no hair on top of his head stood. He wore a T-shirt with a mass of noodles with arms on it. Tammy spoke, "What is his religion anyways?"

Reverend Davies spoke half slurred and half disgusted, "Oh, that's our atheist. Not that good for business. Hard to sell nothing—so many people got it already."

Tammy ignored the reverend and spoke to the still-not-formally introduced father: "An atheist here?"

Father McNally replied, "Yes, we do try to cover all religions. There are common causes that atheists and those who believe in a higher power share. So why should they not seek to have representation in our midst? After all, the believers far outnumber those who don't believe. Once again this organization is about collecting likeminded people who do works in the common good."

Tammy was still trying to absorb why an atheist was there. "I still don't understand totally. I get that an atheist might want a street paved as much as a God-fearing Christian, but are atheists really a religion? I thought you only had religions here."

Reverend Davies answered now, totally baked with alcohol: "Bunch of faggots and religious-bigoted queers they are. I should never have allowed them. My mistake because I thought they would attract more of that sweet gay-agenda money. Turns out not a lick of them are gay, and trust me, I asked them more than once. Would anyone else care for another drink?"

Father McNally ignored the reverend and replied, "Well, many people assume that believing in nothing is just as hard as believing in something. I've always considered believing in nothing much harder work. Now judging by my colleagues, like the reverend here, preaching this nothing that the atheist believes in is exactly what we are told God calls upon people to do each and every day. They tell us God justifies us by faith and faith alone. If people are Christian by faith alone, and not by their actions toward each other, then I fail to see the difference between having faith in nothing and having faith in something and doing nothing about it."

The reverend tipped his glass very dangerously close to spilling. He balanced his hands on Father McNally. "Oh, Father McNally, you always expect too much from our Lord. Don't get these good people all upset and thinking about good works. We're about to do some good work, or at least some good business, in the name of the Lord. Commit to the Lord whatever you do, and your plans will succeed. For the plans of the diligent lead to profit as surely as haste leads to poverty. The blessing of the Lord, it maketh rich, and he addeth no sorrow with it. I don't look too much for helping the poor and needy. I live by faith, not by sight. I close my eyes to all those but the Lord and the money the Lord made for me."

Tammy looked on the bright side. "Sounds like God at least was proplanning, and if there is one thing I'm good at, it is planning."

The reverend replied, "Speaking about good planning, how about that whole marketing campaign with the John 3:16. Man that was great planning and marketing. Most people don't give a crap what it means. I've read the passage and it's not really that all inspiring to turn me toward God. But oh that slogan itself—'John 3:16'—well it just rolls off the tongue. Much more quotable than, 'For God so loved the world, that he gave his only begotten Son, that whosoever believeth in him should not perish, but have everlasting life.' Too wordy. People need simple marketing phrases like 'John 3:16,' not the promise of everlasting life. The guy who thought of marketing religion like it was a shoe, soda, or aftershave lotion was a genius. Wish it was me."

Father McNally spoke, "I always liked John; he had Jesus turnover the money tables right from the beginning and not wait until the end. Made it clear up front that business in the temple was not going to be tolerated."

"Sure, but what did John know? He kills Jesus on the wrong day," replied the reverend.

Reverend Davies suddenly seemed to sober up. His face brightened, his posture straightened, and his eyes opened wide like he had just gazed upon the divine presence of the Lord.

Father McNally turned around to look at what he was looking at. "I see your man Philip Flip has arrived."

Tammy and Bob turned together to get a sight of the man of lobbying legend. Phil Flip was a man who looked much younger than his actual age. His plastic surgery was top of the line. All the right scars were hidden in all the right places. His hairline was nicely done by the best professionals. His present state allowed him to dye his hair back to its original natural color or, if needed, show some gray depending on the age he wanted to show. This no doubt depended on the situation. Tonight for the party his hair radiated auburn, and long bangs fell over the forehead. The look gave him the chance to pull off a dazzling youthfulness. Phil knew that good, youthful, boastful looks had advantages against the shallow people who often occupied big religious think tank gatherings.

Reverend Davies tried to walk the group straight up to Phil. But try as he might, his legs refused to work in a straight manner. He chugged along the floor trying hard to get his body to reestablish a suitable equilibrium balance. Arriving in front of Phil, he reached out and pawed Phil's shoulders. With a smile of the Cheshire cat, the reverend greeted Phil. For Bob, Phil Flip's appearance seemed as obviously phony as so many others in the room. To Reverend Davies, Phil seemed to represent a sort of Second Coming.

The reverend as expected started the conversation: "Oh, Phil, my friend, you are truly an inspiration. How do you stay so young? These are the people I was telling you about. Bob, meet Phil Flip. Big money, Phil, I'm telling you. These people are the real deal, keys to the kingdom ideas people."

He then turned to Bob. "Bob, this is Phil Flip. The man taught me everything I know about marketing. To him marketing is as holy as the grail and much easier to find. Huh, Phil?" Phil with effortless ease walked out from the reverend's hand on his shoulder and toward Tammy and Bob. He ignored Father McNally. Phil spoke swiftly. "You two are the goods, huh? We'll see. You two follow me into here. Father, Reverend, get lost."

Phil effortlessly moved away from the two religious leaders who like good dogs did as they were told. Bob and Tammy looked at each other, then at the two religious figures. They excused themselves and went in Phil's rapidly fading direction. Phil had made it the outskirts of the large main party room he opened a well-hidden door in a niche in the main room. With a smooth motion, he ushered the two inside. He then turned to the room and glanced over the crowd. He rolled his eyes, smiled to himself, and entered the room.

The room was beautifully decorated. Ornate religious statues of the Christian faith lined the walls. A large crucifix made of gold stood on the east wall. On the west wall was an equally impressive silver cross. On the north wall was an inspirational reading from the Bible that read, "Unto a stranger thou mayest lend upon usury; but unto thy brother thou shalt not lend upon usury: that the Lord thy God may bless thee in all that thou settest thine hand to in the land whither thou goest to possess it." The floor had a Persian carpet. Several marbled leather chairs sat around an ornate metallic coffee table with a polished top. Phil motioned for them to sit down.

A man in a white tuxedo came out from behind a recess in the room with a pot of coffee. Phil quietly sat down in a chair himself. The man poured the coffee out into three cups. He motioned first to Tammy for cream and sugar. Then he motioned to Bob, who refused. Finally he made Phil's cup. There apparently was no need to ask him if he required cream in sugar. Phil sat smiling at his guests, his hand extended. The hot cup was placed by the man into his hand. The man then silently whisked himself away from them.

Properly equipped, Phil began the association: "It is a pleasure to meet you both. Do either of you smoke?" Tammy and Bob stared at each other. Neither of them knowing the other well enough to know for sure the answer. Both apparently did not smoke and finally admitted as much to Phil.

Phil seemed even more pleased. "Good. I hate the stuff myself. Who wants to be a nicotine customer to some tobacco company? I'd rather make the money lobbying for them than be one of the customers. Too bad too many of their executives don't agree. Oh well, a fool and their money eventually comes to me. Now the next import question is do you two understand what it is I do? I help facilitate a compromise between politicians that I assure you really want to compromise; it's just that no one has told them they do." He turned to Tammy, smiled even greater than seemed humanly possible, and asked her, "Tammy, for instance, do you know how to correctly compromise?"

Tammy seemed very pleased with herself. Why yes, she appeared very certain she did know how. She replied, "Well yes, that is what I do for a living. I'm a planner, you know. One train-line manager may want a certain time line, and another train-line manager may want another. It is my job to sort it all out. Trains are always breaking down and running late, and it is my job to make sure everything at the end of the day is ready for the next day. Many, many meetings, as I'm sure you can understand. There are often a lot of pie charts to analyze. I have to sort out which time line is the cleanest based on existing scheduling problems and at the same time I needed to keep in mind which option produces the least probability of future delays. I talk to my line manager, consult the computer schedule operations, and then I make a decision based on the best information available to me. Indeed I am very hopeful that Bob's scheduling programs will greatly aid my compromising process. That is why we have come to you in fact. We need Congress to agree to allow the system to incorporate these changes."

Phil nodded in a conforming, understanding fashion. His smile never seemed to fade from his face. He now explained to the two of them better what he did. "I can feel you two are very rational people—very willing to use the facts and let them be your guide to make the world the best place possible. That is of course my job too: to make the world the best place possible for a certain price. What you described to me is rational reasoning between parties and decision making. A solid negotiation may also be what you expect from me too, but that's not the kind of compromising a lobbyist does. Let Phil Flip explain to you how a Washington artisan lobbyist produces a compromise between two parties for the benefit of Phil, and of course you as Phil's clients. Let's say we want to tear down a certain upper neighborhood preschool and turn it into a lowlife porn shop. This is a silly and reprehensible idea no doubt, huh?" The two nodded in agreement. "Yes, of course, but you will see that I'm actually doing it for the betterment of mankind and my mutual clients—the porn industry and this organization."

Tammy could not believe what she was hearing and interrupted him. "How can this fine institution ever come in league with the porn industry, particularly to close schools? I simply can't believe it. You are putting me on."

Phil smiled since it appeared to be the only thing he could do. "Good, good, a natural response. I knew you two were thinkers. Let me fill you in on the details, and then you should clearly understand it. First, the porn industry comes to me because they know high schools are a natural source of clients. They know my association with the religious institutions in this country. They understand, no doubt, that angry parents will turn to places like this one for support to prevent this from happening. The porn industry thinks a good word from me will smooth over a rough fight with certain energetic Christians, you see. They want me to lobby. Me, I want money. I smell money in this process at once. Now the problem with schools is they are often not surrounded with too much free private land. However, preschools are often private and often located nearby other schools. Why should my porn client have to negotiate to buy occupied land when with some good work I can free some up for them? Are you following me so far?"

Bob and Tammy nodded in agreement. Phil smiled in maybe-approval since he apparently could not *not* smile. He took a sip of his coffee and continued, "How do I go about my work now that I know my path? Now I would first introduce a bill to ban all preschools in the whole cities. This no doubt causes alarm with the community. They head off to this organization to complain, but the trick is before anything is started, I've already got the church leaders such as this institution secretly going to lobby the city councilmen about the preschools leading children from God. Why would they do it? Because of the money we're about to make. No man comes sooner to church to pay alms than the man who's sinned. How can a man sin without opportunity? We need the porn industry to give them an opportunity to sin so they can come and get saved. On the way to being saved, they're likely to drop a gift in the collection basket equal to their guilt. That's one source of money, but not the only one. So the churches pay me to lobby the city council to remove these preschools with the assurance that the church will not speak out against them when they do it."

Phil took a break and sipped his coffee. He waved his hand, and as if by magic the man appeared again carrying some coffee cakes and cookies. He motioned to Bob and Tammy to help themselves to a snack. Bob appeared to still be a little full from the buffet table as he frowned at the sight of more food, but Tammy, not having gotten the opportunity to get to the buffet table, started to help herself.

After everyone seemed properly snacked, Phil continued his story: "Now we are clearing this place for the porn industry. I don't want the church being too eager to get in league with the porn industry. No, we demand a little greasing from them, you understand, in the form of cold cash. The church and you have a common enemy—these preschools—and with a little Uncle-Sam greenbacks I think we can compromise: you know, some for this organization here to help it do its good works, and some for me too so I can continue to do my good works. The porn industry hands me money, and then we agree to help. No one but me knows who is on whose side and how much money is changing hands and for what."

Bob replied, "So let me get this straight—you get paid by the porn industry to lobby the church to not complain and lobby the politicians to pass this crazy idea? The religious think tanks are already on your side, but you haven't told the porn industry you already have them in your pocket. The church is in your pocket because they are paying you to lobby the elected officials because secretly they want a little sin. So you are getting paid on both sides of the deal?"

Tammy gasped a little. "Now, Mr. Flip, this all sounds awfully unethical."

Phil's smile grew wider. He explained further: "Well, yes it might. To the man who equates morality and ethics to religious absolutes, I'm sure we in this room aren't among those types. What is more ethical than pure capitalism? Did not Jesus himself accept aid from the wealthy women and tax collectors? Should not the religious institutions also accept money from modern sinners? Sinners I find tend to have the most money for donating. Now me, since I don't equate morality and ethics with anything written down thousands a year ago in the name of God, am more than happy to place more than my share of that cash in untraceable bank accounts."

Now Bob became a little animated and stopped thinking about the cookies in front of him. He interjected his opposition: "By more than your share, does this mean you will be stealing from us as well?"

Phil smiled, of course. He explained, "Don't be so worried, my friends. I think we all understand to some people I sound dishonest. I'm dishonest, but I go about my dishonesty in an honorable fashion. I promise you if I managed to get a party to offer up cash up front to help keep things all honest, I may take more than my share, but in an honest fashion I tell you that up front. Remember you will get some butter for your bread too. I'm not a greedy man. I've never left a client without any of a share, just not a fair one. That's a better deal than many in this town will give you. That's why the best come to me."

Phil paused a moment. He took up a cookie and ate it with satisfaction. "They make a good cookie here, you should try one.

Now where were we? Ah yes, we still haven't got our porn store next to the high school yet. Let's see now. Next I'd get the state legislature to pressure the school districts with a bill written by myself that inserts prayer into all preschool curriculums or face elimination of their head-start grants. If that doesn't work, I bring out the big guns and a bill that threatens the elimination of deducting child dependents from the parents taxes if the parent sends their children to one of these godless un-American preschool programs. In other words, I stir up the shit, the panic, and hopefully the anger. The shit, in this case is the usual shit for brains that occupy so many city council and state legislatures. The idiots my fellow lobbyists scout out from the many vocal in the maddening crowd that often finds itself on local PTA boards trying to ban books and forbid the teaching evolution, or the NIMBYs that show up at every city council meeting to protest any public expenditure and lastly our friend the pathetic moron that comes to our corporate made protest and is willing to hold a corporate made-and-paid-for sign declaring this idiot's supposed support for my store-bought grassroots movement. I love these people. They actually think my beliefs are their personal beliefs and hold my signs up high for the TV cameras at one of my manufactured fake grassroots rallies—the rally that I made damn sure the press knew about before any of these grassroots idiot participants. We scout them, and then we help place them into these political positions so we can use them later on. The honest ones are stupid, religious zombies who need a few hours of institutionalizing; the dishonest ones are grifters without any moral compass. Some are both as these aren't mutually exclusive personalities. Either way they are all useful idiots to me and you. It's a game rigged by us, for us. In the end the proponents of my porn shops are lucky if I only get the original porn shop I wanted. I bribe them with porn money, I bribe them with church money, and I get the politicians to bribe me to keep it all quiet. I could get all of the preschools thrown out and turned into the porn shops, even though I didn't even want that to begin with. Compromise, fuck that. I play only to win. I kill them all and sweep the field. If you two want to win, then stick with me."

Tammy seemed unsure of Phil. She wanted to win, but she wanted to win fairly, and she didn't want to hurt people. She then asked him, "But what if you lose? I mean, so many people will object to this. The church can't pacify them all. You can't own all the city council, can you? Plus there are organized people on the other side, surely."

Phil smile grew as wide as Bob had ever seen a man smile. "You see, Tammy, I can't lose. The lay people might object, but I own all the gatekeepers. The more people object to any sides of the argument, the more money I can loosen from all sides for me. In the end it doesn't matter. Going in, I owned enough of the people who matter on all sides of the argument, and most important, enough of the politicians who judge it. I play sides off each other, and it doesn't matter. I was always going to win anyways. I play to win. You play with me, you win too. Politics is for winners."

Now Tammy felt a little guilty. "What about the people who actually care about these issues? I mean the people who actually care about the cause on either side? You know, people who want four-year-olds to have a school to go to?"

Phil nodded. "Well, don't worry too much about them. The true believers get what they want too. Politics is for winners, causes are for losers. The more the people of a cause lose in the political arena, the happier the people in the cause actually are. This is because the people in the cause will get even more devoted to the cause. The worst thing for a cause is too much victory and too much general popularity. Once a cause wins, there isn't any more cause to be passionate about. People start to become complacent. It can leave a people empty inside. I give these people meaning, even if ultimately they are fighting for the meaningless because their voice simply doesn't matter. In my world money talks and causes walk. If possible they walk in one of my manufactured causes with one of my personally thought-of signs."

Bob now added, "I guess causes are pointless unless the cause has you and your money sources behind it. How do you know you aren't just part of someone else's cause?" Bob gave in and took a cookie. They were good, but Phil seemed to Bob as a rather bad person no matter how good a lobbyist Phil thought Phil was.

Phil smiled his usual smile. "Yes, you could call what I do a cause I guess. The self-interest of a few or the one extremely rich over the general welfare of the many or the one, is a cause in its own way. Not every few has only greedy moneymaking causes. Many of them are interested in forcing their religious morality on people as well. Heck, not every one of these ideas is necessarily a bad and harmful idea. It's not like those on the bottom always lose when I win. It's just that I have gamed them on the bottom like children to get the most bang for the buck in your deal. Do you understand? Now I say up front I'm for a cause that is on the side of money. Money for me, for you, money for our mutual friends; but hey, if the wealth trickles down to the bottom, I am more than willing to piss wealth on whoever is down below me. I'm not evil by nature, you understand. I believe no cause I support is inherently evil. Good and evil are artificial constructs the poor and the stupid are taught to label things to prevent them from rationally and objectively thinking about them. For instance sure these people in this community won't have a preschool anymore; however, they will now be slightly stupider and have a much more conveniently placed porn store. As we know only the stupid buy their porn as the smart person can just download it free on the Internet. So see, society wins. More porn sales mean I've improved commerce and created more jobs for the bottom of the community. If the rich tend to support things that help them maintain their wealth, am I to blame? The rich also support many other causes. Some of them probably do some good to society. The rich, after all, live in society too from time to time."

Tammy seemed more relaxed. "I'm glad to hear that. Our cause could potentially be both beneficial to society and I guess make some people more money. Not for myself, of course. I make my paycheck from the government. I am simply here doing my job trying to improve the country's train-transportation system. I was a little uncomfortable coming here because I am not by law supposed to lobby. It is ultimately Mitch Boetner who will gain anything if Bob and I are successful. Well, and Bob will benefit a little too, I guess, since he owns some of the patents. My only benefit is peace of mind. Right now I'm not sure I have it. I am worried you only worked on both sides of the principles of saving the holy from the sinful. I never saw transportation in any type of religious terms."

Bob laughed, spitting out part of the cookie he was eating. "Oh, our Reverend Davies would disagree. He sees sin everywhere— even in trains."

Phil Flip dismissed this. "Don't worry about that. Our good Reverend Davies tends to see sin everywhere, particularly in the activities he enjoys participating in personally. While I am generally known for my Christian think tank connections, I do work in other areas. I feel this train thing has certain potentials."

Tammy was relieved. She had read up on Philip Flip before coming to the meeting. He apparently was good friends with professional opinionist Clapton Armstrong. Tammy didn't know how people became professional opinion writers and personalities, but she had determined it was not due to their carefully thought out, accurate opinions. A stopped clock was right twice a day; the typical professional opinionist would be envious if he or she were right more than twice a decade. Amazingly no matter how often they were inaccurate, lying, or just plain obviously wrong in a prediction, their opinion was always sought out and publicized when something new came up. If a typical employee made as many mistakes as an opinionist, he or she would be fired; opinionists instead generally got promoted the more comically entertaining their horrifically inaccurate opinions were.

Tammy replied, "I'm glad to hear that. I know you are good friends with radio personality and bestselling author Clapton Armstrong, so I read one of his books before coming to meet you. He has the most appalling things to say. Particularly about government workers like me. He calls us leeches on society. He says that government workers have high pay, paid holidays, paid vacations, health benefits, dental benefits, and pregnancy leave, and yet they still claim to need a union! Can you imagine writing something so stupid? Does he understand the union helped us get and maintain those items? But worse and most troubling to me was that he simply hates public transportation. He claims people would be freer if everyone could just buy a car and personally drive wherever they wanted like the good old days. Does he know how few people can afford personal transportation these days? Then he wants to privatize the roads on top of that! Why should a person pay for roads they may never drive on? Roads should be up to the individual to supply and the individual to maintain. He goes as far as to privatize the side walk. Really, does he know how hard it is to maintain good scheduling with public transportation systems? Can you imagine the chaos if everyone was in it for themselves?"

Phil laughed and of course smiled. He also sipped some coffee. His routine was actually pretty simple. It didn't take long to figure it out. A sip of coffee and a smile was all he needed to pull out of his brain whatever talking point he was going to throw out next. "Yes, Clapton Armstrong is an important ally of mine, but I'd say rather a free nonthinker. I've tried to get him the most excellent ghostwriter to write his books for him, but he insists on writing them himself. I've honestly never heard of such a thing. I said to him that the least he could do is dictate something into a recording machine, and I'll give it to my best spin artists to clear it up and punch it up. I got this great sixteen-year-old Malaysian kid that writes just killer propaganda, and he works cheap. Not him, though—Clayton insists on typing it out by hand and having final cut. The result is the pointless drivel you read. I really apologize for you having to read the whole thing. Clayton thinks he is an original thinker, but he's just a lot of hot air. Without my words in his mouth he fumbles the message every time."

Tammy was puzzled now. "But the book went to number one on the best-seller list for ten straight weeks. Why the back cover has quote from you saying, 'Mr. Armstrong was one of America's truest original thinkers of our era. I enjoyed this book cover to cover!' I can understand a few white lies here and there to Congress. After all it is my experience an American expects a good member of Congress to be as loyal as their spouse and an even better liar. Lying to a liar for most is seen as just fair game, but I hope you don't lie to Americans on the back cover of books. If we can't trust a random excerpt quote on the back cover of a book, what can Americans trust, Mr. Flip?"

Phil naturally smiled his very unnatural smile. "Oh, not a word of that is a lie I can assure you. I do find Clayton Armstrong an original thinker. Why most of us lobbyists think the man has the brains of a jellyfish; we just wish he'd use the jellyfish's brain to write his books instead of his own as the jellyfish often outwits him and never thinks it is America's leading humorist. A person that is lacking in interesting things to write about is a form of true originality as most writers are at least not lacking in interest. See, not a lie. And as for enjoying it cover to cover, why that is also true. I use all one hundred copies this organization personally bought for me in lieu of toilet paper."

"How is that a form of enjoyment?"

Phil replied, "Well, I enjoy a clean backside as much as the next person, Mrs. Usher. Once again I hope that assures you I am hardly the enemy of either you our hard-working public employee or our beautiful railway system. Indeed I have often suspected Clayton Armstrong was a secret Communist. He claims to have won two Sherman awards that he has never actually won. One can understand why a person would lie about winning one Sherman award. I mean lying about winning one award is a sign of accomplishment and excellence. Claiming to win two means you weren't satisfied with just one self-determining award. No, he needed a collection of them. The need for collectivism is the surest sign of a Communist."

Bob had determined Phil was now putting them on. Bob was pretty sure that had things been different and Tammy said she loved the book, Phil would have told them how much he respected Clayton Armstrong. With Phil, even when he told you he was lying, you had to be worried as to what the truth was. Probably Phil was so use to shoveling bullshit for a living he did know when he was doing it and when he wasn't. But he probably thought he did. Phil was the type of person that thought he created a new reality for you out of thin air, but deep inside Phil thought Phil new the real reality from the lies. The lies were a show for you but the liar always believes they can remember the truth from the lies. But that's the lie they tell themselves. Every artisan bullshitter throws so much bullshit around them that it stacks so high around them that eventually all they can see is the bullshit. When you live in a world of bullshit, it's impossible to know reality from the bullshit because it's all bullshit. Bob admitted to himself that Phil was so honestly good at bullshit, it was an actually enjoyable show he put on—as good as those cookie crumbs that now ran down Bob's shirt. But Bob remembered the bullshit was going to come at a cost. The world had taken a lot time to build, but the bullshit artists in it can smash it down for everyone in just seconds.

Phil now spoke again, "Now I am interested in this train thing, but I need an angle if I'm going to tap into Mitch's money and work more money out of Congress and other prospective parties. You see, we got a lot of pigs to grease. You have representatives, senators, vaguely religious think tanks, and lobbyists to pay off. That takes a lot of money, and you guys still need to make a profit. So we will need an awfully good angle...." Phil stopped talking. Phil was suddenly lost in thought. Phil did best when thinking on his feet. He smiled, sipped his coffee, and ate the last cookie. He needed to stall for a second or two, then an angle would come to him, they always came to him. "I respect you two amateurs tapping Mitch as you have. The last time I tapped him was for a casino."

Bob felt guilty about poor Mitch. Apparently he thought the world of Phil, and Phil thought Mitch would buy him the world if he schmoozed him just right. Phil had that you-scratch-his-back-and-he'll-charge-you-for-the-privilege aspect about him that Bob disliked. Bob just wished he thought Phil was the end of it. But he knew the way this was going Phil wasn't the end of anything. Phil was a starter for chaos and dishonesty. Still Phil did get results before, and it was Mitch who was likely to be in the short term the loser. The whole situation left Bob unhappy with himself for even letting any of these people anywhere near his ideas. He thought to himself, he should just leave now. Leave and go back to the patent office and his work. His ideas would work, but really—were the Phil Flips of the world necessary and the only way to get things done?

While Bob was contemplating if he could still get out of this, Tammy asked, "How did the casino deal go?"

Phil answered, "Well. Well, well for me. Mitch didn't seem to mind that it never got built. He enjoyed that Singapore sock factory we built instead with some of the money. In only five more years, Mitch will actually turn a profit on the deal too. See, I am not a horrible person. And just think, as one of the principal owners I set it up so Mitch gets his socks from them for almost half price."

"Well, I hope this time things go more according to how our proposal plans it to go. I will not accept a socks factory as a suitable result for a train-management proposal. If you are planning to remove our plans from your plans, then I am planning on walking out that door this very minute," said Tammy who was good at planning.

Phil replied, "You have nothing to worry about. I respect both of you deeply as individuals, trust me. I got it!" Phil now jumped out of his seat and strolled rapidly around the room. "That's it— the perfect angle. And I know who to work it on. I mean we want real money. There is only one target in the world if you want real money poured into your vision: Peter McKinnon."

Bob replied, "You mean the crazy trillionaire? I heard he ended up flying to Mars to live in some nudist colony or something."

Phil smiled slyly. "That is not exactly how things worked out. Now it is true Peter McKinnon loves space and is in love with the idea of leaving us imperfect people behind to live a utopian life in his own world founded by him, for him, and of him. But his space partners sort of dicked him on the deal, and he instead had to settle for the time being living on his own manmade island out in international waters. They call the place 'Déjacque.'"

Tammy spoke, "Oh, I remember reading about that. A group of incredibly rich men built that together. I believe they all live there tax-free because there is no state that governs them. It must be a fascinating place to live."

Phil Flip said, "I'm glad you think that way because I'm going to arrange it so you guys go there to pitch to Peter McKinnon personally."

Bob said, "What? I thought the whole point of going here was to get you to lobby for us?"

Phil Flip said, "Now, don't worry. I'm on board. I'll do the heavily lifting. I will do the ass kissing to Peter that will get you in his front door. When Peter agrees to help you, I'll be there to grease the fat pig through the halls of Congress. I've got the angle, and it fits in perfectly with the whole train plan. The man loves space so you guys will be building a space train."

Tammy and Bob said together, "What?"

Phil said, "I know it sounds impossible, but don't worry about the details. The real details you care about—this Earthly train-management crap—will get tacked on. Think of it this way. With really big impossible ideas, the actual idea never works, but all that extra pork tacked on almost always gets funded. Stick with me. I've done this a hundred times if I've done it once. We sell them on your brilliant space-train idea and tack on that extra crap you care about, and Peter McKinnon will come running to your door. Peter is the closest thing to God this Earth ever created out of a pile of wealth. If we get that ungodly wealth on our side, everything will pass very quickly."

Tammy and Bob had got their lobbyist. He was going to send them to do his lobbying for him. They were paying for that service. Well, Mitch was paying, probably. Tammy frowned. Bob frowned. Philip Flip smiled, which could have meant anything.

Chapter 8:

To See Nothing and From So Far Away

There can only be one.
— Highlander, best movie ever

It had all started as just an idea. The idea was inspiring, and Peter McKinnon worked hard and long on it. The idea was transformed into a product produced in the garage of a house. The product he created turned out to be popular, and the product began to sell. Soon the garage could not hold the demand for the product, so he bought a small storefront. The storefront was too busy for just him to work, so he hired help. The idea had grown and become something more than a product, for now it had become a company.

The company had demands for new ideas and new products. Companies needed growth and continuous expansion of space and people to gain fulfillment. This did not come without a cost as new ideas and space created a new need. The company needed capital. So the company went to search for the capital investors. The capital investors needed returns on their risk, so they issued shares of the company to each other. Soon the shares grew too profitable to keep amongst themselves. The company needed more capital to satisfy its demand for growth. So they moved the company into the public domain. The company acquired public stockholders, and the shares floated on the free market. The stockholders needed black-line profits, growth, EPS, P/E, target estimates, dividends, and yields to keep the shares up. The company had become a corporation.

Corporations, we are told, are just people—people gathered together for the common good of the idea. Taken together, the corporation is more than the sum of its parts. The corporation needed a vast and cheap workforce. To keep the workers focused on the prize, the corporation had branch managers whose job it was to keep the workers working hard by reminding them they were the most important part of the corporation. The corporation needed directors to manage the managers in the many branches of the corporation. The director's job was to keep the managers working hard by reminding them the managers were the most important part of the corporation. The corporation was large and had too many directors, and thus it needed vice presidents to manage the directors. The vice president's job was to keep the directors working hard by reminding them the directors were the most important part of the corporation. The corporation of course had a chief executive officer. The CEO's job was to keep the vice presidents working hard by reminding them the vice presidents were the most important part of the corporation. The corporation of course needed to attract a good CEO, so it had bonuses. The job of the bonuses was to keep the CEO working hard by reminding the CEO that the CEO was the most important part of the corporation.

Now the corporate world is tough, and when things went well, people might expect good times; when things went wrong, people might expect bad times. Corporations in such times just do what is best for the corporation. As for the hard workers, well they had to understand when it came to the short-term good of the corporation, the corporation always came first. The corporation always needs to remain healthy, and a measure of a corporation's health is its profits. Naturally when profits went down, things were bad, and the corporation needed to cut its size to get back into profits. This was OK because people knew that when profits rose, so might the dividends to the investors and stockholders, and maybe a few more workers would get hired and their salaries would rise. Bonuses might increase as well for the CEO, directors, vice presidents, and managers. But corporations are a tricky thing, and sometimes even when things were good, the corporation still cut jobs and benefits because that could also raise short-term profits.

A corporation doesn't fire people or cut benefits because it's mean; it does these things to fit into the greater world of corporation. The corporation needed to keep up with the corporate average. When one corporation cuts, they all cut; no thinking was needed to decide whether the corporation's cutting was good, bad, well managed, or an intelligent idea. The corporate average had gone down, and thus the corporations' benefits needed to fit the new corporate average. Margins needed to be maintained, and when all the cutting was done the corporation would hold a vast victory celebration for the milestone of mediocrity reached. Each level in the chain of the corporation had always told each other they were the corporation's biggest asset. The corporation's people would tell one another how much the corporation meant to them and how the corporation cared for them. But surely these people were all fooling themselves. To the corporation, the corporation always came first. They were just cogs in its machine. The founder, the investor, the stockholder, the CEO, the vice president, the directors, the managers, and the workers were all just cogs fooling themselves into thinking that while the other cogs might not matter, they were different because the corporation needed them. A corporation is a special, privileged type of person as it has no emotions. Corporations don't laugh, they don't cry, and if you prick them, they do not bleed. They feel no joy in good times, they don't worry about regulations, they don't hate people based on logical constructs, they do not fear the president or any man on Earth, and they certainly never feel sorrow in the coming or leaving of any person. So when the corporation thought it was time for Peter McKinnon, the founder of the corporation, to go, the corporation just let him go. To the corporation, the corporation always came first.

Peter McKinnon was not a broken man by any means. He had grown bored with the limitations of corporations. The challenge was gone. He had bought lobbyists to buy and create the politicians he needed so his corporation could set up phony corporations that allowed him to embezzle money from the company directly into his bank accounts. He had the local police in pocket to make sure organized labor and protests stayed clear of his corporation's business assets, or else the police were free to use what violence he told them was necessary to keep commerce flowing. He had made sure to keep employee wages low and his taxes low to keep income where it belonged—with him. He made sure the courts stayed divided in order to keep angry voices focused away from corporations and toward the part of the federal government the people had the least say in. He made sure there were voter-ID laws, proof-of-citizenship laws, poll taxes, literacy tests, and threats of violence to keep the wrong people from voting. The wrong people were whoever might possibly disagree with him as determined by him. He had made sure the people were too busy arguing over race, color, creed, immigration status, sex, and sexual orientation to notice or care about what he really wanted. The era was not unlike the gilded age of James J. Hill and was complete with that era's negatives—well, negatives if you weren't a self-made man like Peter McKinnon. Hill believed in manifest destiny and American *exceptionalism*, and that's what Peter McKinnon believed in. Hill wanted to own his own future for the country, and that's what Peter McKinnon wanted too. Only there was no place left here worth going except out there among the stars.

It had grown all too easy for him, and he had grown bored. He wanted his own world away from shareholders and financial systems dependent on the rules and whims of governments. He wanted a world without money, the need for other investors, the paying of dividends, the constant worry about bottom lines, and the fear of the system collapsing under the weight of other people's dishonesty. He worked hard to stymie government, but try as he might governments still existed, and one could break its systems, but one couldn't kill it dead once and for all without people noticing. In the old days, the wealthy could hide in remote corners of countries on estates away from the worthless, but the world was now a crowded place, and it was getting more and more impractical to do that. He dreamed of his own world run for him and by him. He dreamed of the future taught to him in online infomercials, comic books, and movies. The future as it should be, not as it was likely to be. The problem was that government was in the way of his brave new world. They designed and built the vehicles he needed to reach these new worlds. Unfortunately his robbing and stymieing of the government had severely slowed its pace in getting him to his new world. He would have to change that. So he left his corporation behind and chased his new dream of private space exploration full time. He worked hard to produce the technology to realize this dream. In the meantime he had built his own little world for himself. A private island paradise was constructed for him and a few other self-made enlightened men in international waters away from governments and their chains of enslavement. Tammy, Mitch, and Bob were flying there to meet Peter McKinnon. The meeting was arranged by the skilled Phil Flip who assured them everything they ever wanted was about to come true. They trusted Phil—well sort of.

The pilot landed the helicopter on a large platform erected in a lush green garden of laurel, bamboo, Malabar, chestnut, and ivy. The helicopter came to a halt with a rather jerky motion. The pilot turned toward his three guests in the back seat. The pilot spoke softly and apologetically to the three of them: "I am sorry for the rough landing. The copter is feeling a little sluggish today. I'll be sure to look at it before I take you to your journey home. Mr. McKinnon is down below waiting for you. I will see you later to fly you home unless, of course, Mr. McKinnon decides to take you back himself. He does love to fly, you know." With that, the friendly pilot waved them out onto the platform.

The three of them had a terrific full view of the island's grounds from high on the platform. The island was separated into great houses with each island resident having his own garden, power source, freshwater source, communication satellite dish, and roads. Not every great house connected its roads to its neighbor, hence the need for helicopters to pop you around the island to reach some places. The island was lush, green, extravagant, and amazingly inefficient. An electric elevator on the platform stood at one end. The three slowly moved toward it.

"Guys, I can feel it. This is it. We are close now to finally getting everything we wanted. I guess we take ourselves down on this?" said Mitch.

The elevator slowly rode them down from the platform into the lush greenery below. As they arrived on the bottom, a truly tremendous figure stood to greet them at the bottom of the elevator. The figure was a well-built man of at least six two with well-groomed blond hair and a slightly graying mustache. He wore a striking tailored gray business suit and a sharp pink power tie with little red spaceships decorating the front. The three stepped out of the elevator to meet with the man who was clearly Peter McKinnon.

"Hello, I am Peter McKinnon, formerly of McKinnon and Sons Enterprises. As you know I have no sons, but what is in a name? You must be the two geniuses—and Mitch—that Philip Flip told me about. He believes you have greatness about you. According to Philip with you and me together, great financial things will soon be ours." He looked over the three guests and picked out the roundest of them. "I believe you are Mitch Boetner, aren't you?" He turned toward Mitch and greeted him with a powerful handshake.

Mitch seemed at ease now with a fellow man of wealth. Mitch wasn't in Peter McKinnon's league, but still the rich naturally like the rich in Mitch's experience. Mitch replied, "Of course you know why we are here. We have been lobbying—and very successfully lobbying I might add—several key politicians toward a totally novel idea in train transportation. As holder of a substantial portfolio of train-transportation companies whose money comes directly from government services, I personally stand to gain rather a lot from this move. But you see, I am just a man of investing—not a self-made man like yourself. Politicians tend to drag their feet on these issues. They don't have the luxury that comes with a self-made island that governs itself through the will of self-made men. Thus they dither on support of this project. I feel in many ways those politicians are totally incompetent. Phil Flip felt if we could solicit a self-made man like you, your sheer will and influence would help sway the weak. These politicians cannot make up their minds for themselves, but a man like you can make it up for them. Heck, I find so many of them are afraid to make a decision out of fear of not knowing the financial benefit to themselves first, or worse that they might not get any financial benefits at all. I, however, like to think beyond their financial benefits to mainly the financial benefits to society's best and brightest members like me."

"Oh, Mr. Boetner, you make our bureaucrats seem so dishonest. Really, many are just looking out for the public good. I'm sure Mr. McKinnon understands that," said Tammy in hopes of smoothing out what she thought was Mitch's coarseness. They were, after all, trying to attract Peter to the idea of lobbying Congress on their behalf, and the thought of lobbying a bunch of seedless corrupt men seemed less than appealing.

Peter said, "Trust me, I know how to keep a politician honest. An honest politician is one who, when he is bought, will stay bought. If you want to keep them keen and honest, be the highest bidder. Mitch, I knew your father. He was in many ways as great a man as me. He was a self-made man who like me deserved the power to control his own destiny. I know it must have been a great disappointment to him when he died."

Mitch replied, "I believe you mean it was a great disappointment to me that he died."

Peter replied, "Yes, I gather you were a great disappointment to him too. Death can only end a great man's life; a son can end a great man's dreams. Now come, let us move from these gardens to my dining halls." Peter motioned his guests toward the grand building in the distance.

They moved through the gardens toward a huge mountain of a building. While above the gardens on the helicopter pad the gardens seemed bright, warm, and rather inviting to the guests, now down on the ground the gardens seemed dark and overgrown. The garden was patterned after a grand European garden with fountains, flowers, hedge mazes, and a flowing freshwater stream with several beautiful swans in it. Large stands of trees stood in the far distance that stretched high into the sky and blocked too much sun from penetrating the ground level.

Peter spoke to them, "I am very excited to have you here. When Phil first talked about space trains, I thought he must be crazy. But he convinced me it wasn't as crazy as it sounds. People have been talking about space elevators for years. You know, of course, a space elevator is a long cord that goes from the ground to outer space that things ride up to get into orbit. Now if you have one cord in your space-lifting device, it's a space elevator. And here is your genius part, as Phil told me. If you add a second cord to the space-lifting device, one that is parallel to the other cord, what you really have is a track. If you build a vehicle to ride that track, what you have is not a space elevator but a space train! Sure, people have been talking about building one here on Earth for years. But they never built it because they are weak of thought and will. But you two geniuses and Mitch have come up with the truly bold plan to build them not only here, but everywhere. Imagine a space train to Mars. A track placed into orbit between Earth and Mars. When Earth's orbit and your space-train tracks' orbit come close to each other, you set the train in motion. The train moves on the track until it reaches the end of the line. If you schedule this time right, and I see a lot of this proposal is about train time-scheduling accuracy, the end of the tracks' orbit will be close to the planet Mars. Sure, you can't rapidly day-to-day move things back and forth as Mars, the end of this track, Earth, and the start of the track will only line up every so often, but think of the ease and savings. Hell, since the whole thing is in space, you can even use solar panels on it to power the tracks and have an all-electric space train. No pollution, which should keep those environmentalist in line. I love this idea! It will work—I know it will. I can't wait for you to fill me in on all the little details."

Bob, having no clue what he was talking about and was wishing Phil consulted them first before spinning yarns to Peter, tried to think of something to say. "Ah, that space-train idea is rather good, but what did you think about the rest of the proposal? You know, the stuff about trains here on Earth."

Peter replied, "Oh, don't worry, Phil already told me that was the fluffy crap he added to your proposal to keep the political pork flowing. What a genius that Philip Flip is in his own way. Not exactly up to the measure of accomplishment of the great men of this island, but not many are. But then here I am talking about genius when I stand with two fellow geniuses…and you, Mitch."

Tammy looked over at Bob and mouthed to him, "Any idea what a space train is?" Bob shrugged and gave the stretch motion. It was as she expected—their hired lobbyist had sold a totally different proposal to Peter McKinnon, one that none of the geniuses here understood. No doubt even Phil had no idea beyond his five-minute warm-up pitch. They needed to get off the subject and allow them some time to think. Tammy noticed that the garden was less dramatic on the ground than when seeing it from the helicopter pad. She said, "It really is such lovely grounds you had crafted here. The flowers are just right for that endless midsummer feel. You almost expect Oberon and Titania to pop out at any minute. I wish there was a little more sun, though. It seemed so cheery from up above, but down here it gets a bit dark. Not good for the flowers, I imagine. You should really consider a plan between you and your neighbor to cut back those trees edging the garden and let more sunlight in."

Just then the whole island shock violently and they fell off their feet into the grass. The shaking lasted only a few seconds, but its violent nature caused alarm throughout the party—all except Peter McKinnon. Peter got up first and dusted himself off.

"What the hell was that?" Bob asked.

"There is no need to worry," Peter answered. "It is just a small island quake. They happen all the time. They have become so common, I have come to not even notice them."

Tammy asked, "What causes them?"

Peter laughed, "Oh, it is a funny story you will all enjoy. You see, on the other end of the island one of the many pillars holding the island up has started sinking into the ocean floor. Now Rostislov Demyanvich insists that the whole island repair this pillar, but you see it is under his property. We are a free island. Everyone is responsible for themselves. It is his pillar under his land, and he is responsible to repair it. Now here is the funny part. He hired an engineer who insisted that if this pillar fails, the whole island would collapse. He insisted for the greater good we all pitch in and pay to repair his pillar. Can you imagine such a violation of the whole principles this island was founded on?"

Tammy asked, "So these island quakes—what was your solution?"

Peter replied, "Don't worry. I hired my own engineer who I paid quite a lot of money to tell me that indeed the island is totally safe. That shut Rostislov's engineer right up. Money talks, my friends. In fact his engineer refuses to come back to this island and speak to any of us at all again after I paid him not to."

"That was just genius," Mitch said. "I bet that Rostislov was just fuming when he had to pay to fix his own faulty personal pillar."

Peter said, "Well, not exactly. He sent a nasty tweet that he refused to live in a place on the verge of total collapse. So he simply moved to Detroit rather than fix the pillar. Big Lions fan, I believe. Well, that solved the problem once and for all."

Tammy frowned and looked over to Bob. Bob crossed his fingers back at her. Not exactly a sign of reassurance. She frowned more. Peter spoke again, "You asked about the lack of sun in my garden. Yes, it is a burden, but as I've said, we are a free people on this island. My neighbor has every right to grow his high trees that block out the sun from my garden. I would never dream of impinging on his natural-born rights and complain. I am working right now with some engineers to create an artificial sun to place into orbit that will beam light back into my yard and keep this area better lit. I don't want this area cluttered with obvious lamps and nonsense. I want it to retain that natural outdoor feel. So they are working hard to incorporate lighting in a way that makes this area feel natural while piping into it artificial light from a man-made sun."

Bob said, "You'd think it would be cheaper just to get your neighbor to trim his trees."

Peter said, "Good point, Bob. I forget I am standing with other geniuses. Bob, you are totally correct—totalitarianism is always cheaper than freedom. Nice social point, but I don't want this conversation to become a college campus sit-in, Bob."

Mitch asked, "Who is your neighbor?"

Peter replied, "Yoruba Smith."

Mitch said, "Wow he is the biggest man in entertainment today. I personally try to watch as much entertainment as possible. I am thinking of investing in plan to create a twenty-fifth hour just so I can squeeze an extra hour of viewing each day. It must be amazing to live next to the magical world of entertainment."

Peter replied, "Well, yes it is in a way. You all know how he made his money don't you? He pioneered computer-animation entertainment. Thanks to the rapid advances in computer technology, his company was able to reproduce actual lifelike humans. He then founded the computer-animated reality digital entertainment network in which computer-animated real people simulate real people behaving on old-fashioned reality television. It's far cheaper than hiring real people and has the advantage that the real animated people tend not to behave so fake like real people do when placed on reality-entertainment programming. Yes, modern technology is truly amazing. But we must stay grounded. Remember: the real testimonials for products on those programs' commercials are, after all, just simulated fantasy. A self-made man has to keep his eye out for fantasy disguised as reality. I have been burned before."

Tammy asked, "What happened?"

Peter said, "It is well known I love space. People use this love against me. People have tried to scam me before. My other neighbor, Nigel Lancaster, once got me into a space-mining operation. The whole project never went anywhere. I had dreams of being a space miner. The romantic vision of watching poor minorities in silver shiny space suits with coal-blackened faces ferrying space ore from my orbited space asteroid always touched me. I could almost see it: Those space ferries arriving at my moon-base processing space plant to be used to supply the moon-base pioneers. Those pioneers space-smelting the space ore in the space-smelting factories and space-buying and space-selling it in the space-commodities market in space. It would be my moon base built for me just like I built this island—I felt the object of my reality was nearly there. Unfortunately my other investors were more interested in the self-interests of their bank accounts and not a vision of making a true, lasting society of equality."

"So they just took your money and ran?" Mitch asked. "That's happened to me countless times. Usually you get nothing out of it but a broken heart or some discount socks. People can be so greedy and untrustworthy with all these made-up ideas that make money for them but none for you."

Peter laughed, "Oh, we made money. I'm not an idiot. We made it hand over foot. The people, the politicians, and the venture capitalists all handed us money. We were a private company, you understand. The best source of money for a private company is the government. We had NASA handing us billions in no-bid contracts to construct private launch vehicles, private space-mining robots, and private moon-base facilities. It was the perfect kind of private company. We could build my moon base with their tax money for a profit and yet still ensure the social feminists' Communist-liberal-homosexual agenda didn't fill my moon base with postcolonial Kenyan technology. We would stick their NASA logo on it as product placement. NASA is a trusted brand name for the people. The American people love a futuristic American *exceptionalistic* vision. I find the bolder the vision, the better you can profit. Everyone assumes if it sounds like the technology they were taught is our future, then it must be science. Americans are trained from an early age to love technology and science. Their lives are surrounded by it from their first toy that beeps and bops as an infant to their latest PPED. The problem is they love their science and technology, but no one ever bothers to teach them the scientific method. Thus things that sound like science but are total science fantasy are so easy to fund. Hell, at the height this space-mining company had ten billion in government contracts a year and rolled out an IPO that tripled in value in one week. Rest assured we made money. When at last the bottom fell out of that canteen, we moved from space mining and my dreams of a moon base to this island. An island is cheaper and easier to convince people to invest in and live on. I've found people are very reluctant to live on a moon base built by the lowest bidder. So I sit here biding my time until I have enough money to make my Martian colony free from the doubtful and greedy. "

"Isn't Nigel Lancaster now dead?" Bob asked. "Yes, I am sure he is. I read that he was in the news last year. How can he be dead and your neighbor?"

Peter spoke, "Yes, it is true he died last year. But Nigel was a truly great man. He hated the idea of giving to the worthless all his life's work. Can you believe after a life of achieving and crafting to have the idiots and leeches of the world taking your things? The worthless in life are never taxed in death, and do you know why? It is because their death is their own gift to the world. They had no value in life, and removing themselves from society is the only benefit society can derive from their death. Death tax is just another word for leeching from the hard work of the dead self-made man. Leeches of society only tax from those that create value. Worse than having to support the worthless citizen sponges of this world with the duties of death is the thought of having to leave your life's work to other humans in the form of inheritance. What have these relatives done to deserve it but share a few splices of your DNA sequences? Would a self-made man leave his legacy in the hands of random-chance genetic inheritance? Nigel was a true genius—he created a supercomputer that he programmed with as much knowledge of himself as he could enter. He then left all his worldly possessions to this computer like some idiots might leave them to their pets named Mitch. He has achieved a computer-animated life after death so he doesn't have to pay death taxes or rely on the generally disappointing performances of often-overrated children."

Tammy asked, "Really, is computer technology so advanced these days that a computer can simulate you in every detail to achieve another computer-sentient you?"

Peter replied, "Well not yet, but his supercomputer has been programmed with a large artificial desire to produce one. So as artificial intelligence increases in sophistication, someday it may be possible that Nigel does truly live again. Until that day there is still tons of things Nigel can get done being dead."

"What?" Tammy and Bob said in unison.

Peter said, "It is true. In these postmodern times, your death can be the fastest, most effective means of turning your unproductive, valueless life into a life that had value. Or if you were productive like Nigel, death is a great means for expanding your productivity matrix and cementing your influence on others. Today as in no time in history, it's the dead who truly inspire and influence society and the dead who captivate our lives while the living simply bore us and so often get ignored by us. Take Henrietta Lacks, for example."

Mitch asked, "Who is Henrietta Lacks? I never heard of her."

Peter answered, "She was nobody—that's the whole point, Mitch. In life Henrietta was a worthless child breeder who did nothing of value and lived a life that was totally worthless. She was a true nobody among the countless nobodies who occupy the world. Then fate happened to her, and she truly changed the world and how we think of cancer."

Mitch said, "You mean she found the cure for cancer!"

"Well no, she was diagnosed with cancer and died. But her death was not an end. No, her death was the true beginning of the incredible life of Henrietta Lacks! Before her death some doctors sampled her cancer cells. Unlike many human cells, Henrietta Lacks's cancer cells were easier to culture and grow in a laboratory environment. Soon parts of Henrietta were in laboratories around the country and the world. In life Henrietta never wrote a science paper and never created a cure for any disease. In death Henrietta Lacks contributed to research in cures for countless diseases and over twenty thousand patents! Truly an amazing and productive death that eluded the poor soul in life, wouldn't you say?"

Mitch replied, "Wow, I can't wait until I'm dead too, the way you make it sound."

Peter said, "Mitch, trust me, I can't wait for your death either."

Tammy looked over to Bob to see if she was the only one who thought the conversation didn't make any sense. Bob made the circular motion of his finger around his ear to signal *he's crazy*. Then Bob shrugged.

Tammy asked, "What is the point of building islands, moon bases, and such with the goal of a perfect society if we're all better off dead? Dead people don't need any of those things!"

Peter replied, "Of course we all aren't all better off dead. Certainly it would be better for the truly great self-made man to live forever. But until that is possible, we must do what we can with the time we have and hope after our time has run out that fortune gives us the opportunity to prevent the leeches from sucking out all the value we added to this world."

Tammy shivered, "I suddenly find this whole subject of death a bit chilly."

Peter said, "Yes, the afternoon winds are starting to blow in off the ocean. Let us move inside the main house."

The main house was truly titanic in size. Modeled after a European estate house, it was composed mainly of stone, not wood. Wood rots and does not generally last long, but this house was built to last generations. Indeed if artificial-intelligence immortality was possible, Peter seemed prepared to have it last forever.

Bob spoke, "I have to say your place is truly amazing. It is almost like something you would see in a fantasy movie. It's hard to imagine just one man living here. So this is Déjacque, then?"

Peter laughed, "Oh no. The island is called Déjacque. I call my house Xanadu, of course."

Bob said, "After the great palace of Kublai Khan. It makes sense to me."

"Well, not exactly. I named it after the famous movie, I must admit."

"*Citizen Kane*?," Tammy asked.

"Well, now I am embarrassed. No, I named it after the movie *Xanadu*. I was always a big Olivia Newton-John fan. Not much for acting or singing, but what a great ass she had."A rather well-toned male servant held an oversized door with beautiful endangered rosewood inlay. The four of them stepped inside Xanadu. After they were all inside, the servant closed the door.

The group was shown to their respective rooms to freshen up before the big presentation. Tammy was shown into a vast chamber that was three times the size of her actual apartment. The central figure of the room was a large, ornate ivory double-king-sized bed that overwhelmed the other expensive handmade furnishings. Tammy laughed to herself as she figured it must take at least two people to make the big impractical bed, and thus a self-made man didn't and couldn't even make his own bed. She moved around the room to investigate. She loved the floors. They were bare, natural hardwood floors, just as she always wanted but her apartment complex refused to allow. She went over to look out the window, but upon closer inspection she discovered the windows were not really windows at all but holographic projections of windows that turned into mirrors when you moved closer to them. Apparently the most important attraction on an island of self-made men wasn't looking outside at the other self-made men, but looking at your reflection in the mirror. Tammy rolled her eyes at the apparent narcissism and went to the bathroom to freshen up.

The bathroom was more stylized, yet typical of any high-end hotel bathroom. A large medicine cabinet caught Tammy's eye. She was always told it was impolite to look in other people's medicine cabinets, but she figured it was OK since it was technically her room. Inside were various illegal drugs (well, illegal in countries with actual laws). Then again they weren't exactly illegal if you were rich enough. They were the rich sort of legal drugs of choice—prescription synthetic narcotics that came with their own personal doctor's prescription already made out for Tammy. Then there was a medical-marijuana stash that came with its own personal medical card already filled out for Tammy. There was also homeopathic cocaine that came with a straw, apparently to sip it as it was in water form. Indeed being homeopathic you couldn't tell it from water anyways. Tammy frowned at the thought that someone else had thought she might use or need these on her visit. She wondered why the rich would need these drugs at all. For many poorer people, illegal drugs were a form of destructive escapism. Did the incredibly wealthy need to escape, and from what? she wondered. She had no interest in self-destruction and she left the bathroom.

She decided to open the closet. The inside stunned her. The closet wasn't really a closet at all but more of its own small boutique shop. Inside were all the latest fashions, all with very sophisticated subtle labels. Why? Because the self-made men didn't need to tell people with logos they bought the best, like the book told Tammy. Still in one corner was a pile of sophisticated oversized logo bags from all the best stores. They were stores Tammy had dreamed of one day being able to afford to shop in. Now in a way she could because her closet was like a mini sophisticated store all for her. She opened the jewelry cabinet and lost herself trying on the contents in front of one of the closet's many mirrors. She chose a pair and decided she would wear them. While she didn't like to wear earrings in a business environment, she had to admit these went with her shoes, so it was OK. But of course for that really to be true, it meant she needed to find new shoes. She dug into the shoe rack in the closet. Soon she had placed the shoes into four piles. The first pile was shoes that were cute and looked good with her earrings. The second pile was shoes that were cute and didn't go with the earrings. The third pile she reserved for shoes that weren't cute but went with the earrings. And the final pile was for ugly shoes that did not go with her earrings. She debated for a while over pile one, and then finally chose a good pair to wear. While she loved the feel and texture of the clothes, she decided not to completely change outfits. She still wanted to look businesslike, and Peter seemed to like women in the type of clothes women wear in those childhood fantasies set in mythical and medieval times. That was very impractical for a business meeting, so she decided it was time to leave her dream closet behind. She took a glance back over her shoulder and thought it really was kind of a sad place. It was dazzling to be in there, but on leaving she realized most of the clothing was destined to sit on hangers, shelves, and boxes, never to be used or cared about. Somewhere there was someone without who would cherish these clothes, and here were clothes left to be unloved. The vast room had a cold, unfriendly feeling and an odd, unwanted quality. Here was everything Tammy could ever ask for, but upon getting everything, you wanted and more; it now felt a complete waste. Maybe she understood why the rich needed all those drugs. Things for the sake of things had very little permanent meaning. A knock on her door distracted her from the cold and shallow room. She was suddenly glad to be leaving. She was hoping to see Bob at the door, but unfortunately it was Mitch collecting her for the big presentation. She thought Bob needed to be manlier and should have known to beat Mitch to her door. Bob really was very inadequate. Sigh. He better at least have come up with some good space-train ideas, she thought, since he clearly wasn't thinking about her. She left the room.

The four of them soon found themselves in an enormous dining hall. The walls were lined with mirrors so that it appeared that infinite sets of diners were seated at infinite tables. Peter, like all rich people, had an affinity for English-styled servants. The hall was attended by rather attractive servants dressed in what people of the postmodern world thought servants in the world of

Victorian England dressed like based on movies made in Holly-wood during the 1930s. Plenty of legs and bosoms showed on the various girls at the table. On the table was a virtual cornucopia of delights from which one could eat breakfast, lunch, or dinner depending on your actual meal desired. Mitch chose the lobster, Tammy took a salad, Bob got a steak, and Peter took whatever he wanted. The four seemed occupied at gathering their feasts and sorting out exactly where at the impossibly long table they should all sit. Since it was a business meeting, Tammy managed to arrange them all on one side of the table so they could all hear each other properly.

Mitch was the first to speak: "You have some amazingly attractive servants. My wife would kill me if she found out I had servants like these."

Peter replied, "Yes, I do enjoy the beauty of youth. But all in all, I dislike the young. I only hire them because visitors expect the rich to be surrounded by beauty as well. It is hard to find young who are willing to work hard and expect the pay I want to pay them, not what they think they deserve. The terrible thing about the young is they are filled with the energy and desires of youth. They are too simplistic and idealistic and believe they can make the world as they believe it should be, and not accept the world for what I need it to be for myself. Too many want to change things. I do not desire my world changed. I built it to benefit me because above all I matter! I built this island as a small taste of the utopia I want to create for myself to benefit myself. I will not let the young try to make my world into what they desire. So I search hard in the poor areas of the world for eager, beautiful, young people who see my island as a true utopia compared to the harsh reality of their youthful poverty. As for the rest of the young, well the great thing about them is that with enough propaganda and time, you change them into the older people I require them to be."

Tammy thought it was a very distasteful thing to say—par-ticularly since the servants were within earshot. She hoped she wasn't as pompous as this man in front of her. Truly, the next time she talked to Luke, she would be kinder and pretend to be more interested in his self-improvement ideas. She looked over at Bob, but he appeared to be ignoring Peter and eating his meal. Really, how had he developed such ability to ignore such people like Peter, she wondered?

Mitch spoke, "Wow, that sounds great. How do you exactly transform the young?"

Peter replied, "A good question Mitch, for once. I will tell you. We live in the real world that exists all around us. We search through that reality with the tools evolution has granted us to do so. We can touch, feel, smell, taste, and hear. We use reason as our guide to tell the reality in this world we have detected from the fantasy authority tells us is reality. When we do this, we learn certain inalienable facts about the world as truth. The world is a reasonable place where reason alone can discover absolute truths. In this reasonable place, happiness comes from satisfying personal desire for oneself. You and you alone are what matters. Thus the needs of the many do not outweigh the few or the one, if you are the few or the one. Do not think of this as a cruel world of *nature, red in tooth and claw.* If you are truly a self-made man who uses reason to sort out and craft this totally reasonable world for the better of yourself, naturally you will make the world better for other people too. A rising tide will lift all boats, provided you are on something that can float. There is only one possible system that can allow such a reality to happen, and that is a totally free-market interchange, which people refer to as laissez-faire capitalism. However, we need not think of it as a system of money. No, for in a truly perfect world there need be no money. For the perfect, self-interested person like myself would simply give you what I think you need to have, and take from you what I need to take from you. You would have no use for money because there would be no way to use it in my world."

Tammy then spoke, "But wouldn't we all be at each other's greedy little throats? Each one of us thinking the world exists for us and us alone, and not caring for the greater good?"

Peter replied, "Ah yes, it does sound like a little flaw, doesn't it? But remember, not everyone has the ability to reason and transform themselves into self-made men. Many people think the world a very unreasonable place. We self-made men may understand notions like ethics and integrity are absolute moral truths discovered by reason like I just mentioned. But like the character Socrates in Plato's play, we fall into a conundrum. We find we must lie to the rest of society for the greater good of that society. The unreasonable and the stupid must be told a totally false set of ethics and integrity, or else they will try to change us with their unreasonable attitudes and failures. The important thing to understand about ethics and integrity is that they are empty, dead words. Dead words that like clay from the ground you or them can breathe life into and give them meaning. I tell you this: never let the thems of the world define your ethics. You should give meaning to those words and not let them do it. Be your own creator. For them are the worthless of society who will be greedy and cover their laziness with outdated modes of ethics and integrity. Instead you will define them to mean what you want them to mean. Predict what it is you want and need to do for your self-interest, and then define your personal ethics and integrity as the process of doing them. Then use propaganda and the big lie of absolute and outdated moral ethics and integrity of authoritarianism to force your opponent to stand by the old rules of ethics and integrity. I tell you to weigh down your opponents with the boat anchor of impossible standards of ethics and integrity that you never expect or demand for yourself, because those ethics and integrity mean nothing to you. You have defined new ethics and integrity that suit your needs and self-interest, not theirs. So while you triumph in the success of not being weighed down by other people's outdated unreasonable ethics and integrity, you at the same time have stymied your opponents with those very same words they call ethics and integrity."

Tammy thought the whole thing sounded rather unethical. She looked over to Bob who noticed her glance. Bob shrugged again. She was a little cross at him. Really, to say nothing at all to this man seemed unethical. Were they that desperate for this man's help that they too would stoop to a lack of ethics? And if so, weren't they actually acting as he described? That thought made her unhappy.

Bob must have noticed this and finally said something: "That's great and all, but what if the world is fundamentally not reasonable?"

Peter replied, "Oh, but it is, my friend, it is. Now let us begin talking about the proposal. I shall explain why space interests me so much. You see, this world shall not last forever. Oh no, eventually this world has to end. Perhaps a floating asteroid will strike it, or a catastrophic drop in oxygen content and runaway climate change will snuff out its humanity. These crises have happened in the past, my friends. It is my destiny to not perish with the Earth. The self-made man understands that this world is but one card in a deck. There are an infinite set of cards in the deck of reality. This Earth is where we evolved, we were born, we were raised, and where we live our lives, but the Earth is but a temporary place—a place slowly built up by the self-made men who did their best to craft it and nurture it as we could. The self-made men of the past labeled this action a duty placed on them by God to protect his creation. But we need not invoke such superstitions these days. It is true we evolved here; it is true here is where for now we are trapped, but out there in the stars we will one day travel. We must escape this world and the inferior beings whose need for hierarchical bureaucratic society to support their laziness and sloth drags us down. We—the superior beings armed with our life-preserving self-interest, pure capitalism, and reason—will leave this place and create a true utopia among the heavens where no institutionalized form of economics, politics, religion, or sex will be needed, because self-made men will naturally treat each other ethically based on the reality of the ethical need and not the baseless illegitimacy of authority. One day this world, and all its inferior beings who need civil institutions to live their lives, will be cleaned out by a passing asteroid or comet like the way a dog rids itself of fleas by being hit by a passing car. That is why I seek the stars—only there can humanity be free to live as it truly needs to live. What do you say to this, my visitors of the day?"

Tammy had reached her breaking point and was the first to speak: "I have to admit all this social philosophy interested me in my youth going through school. I went to school to become a worker for the government—the kind of institution you apparently despise. As I say I've tried to read about society. I've sat down and poured my soul into the collective works of philosophers who pondered on what makes a society function. I'm all about the plan. If there is one thing I know how to do, it is how to plan. I want to know if society is well planned out. Will the train from Cleveland arrive in Akron on time or won't it? Will enough people be able to afford a ticket? Are there enough logistical reasons to need trans-portation from the two cities? Will we need more trains in the summer or less in the spring? The supply and demand—is it there, or do I need to create it, and can I create it? I worry if I've forced it upon people who don't actually need it. To me social commentary is all about the good plan. Will today's plan work tomorrow, and can the plan move to meet today's and tomorrow's plan? In the end, after countless hours of reading, I have come to one solid conclusion about the value of books of social commentary and the philosophical writers: no matter how profound and well thought out they think their social commentary is, the central message tends to get distracted from when it is recited out of the mouths of cute bunnies. In the end they all seem to be a lot of fluff here and there that works good on paper, but then everyone thinks they have a good plan until they get hit."

Peter replied, "Exactly. All those fools and their stupid books. Don't believe a word from them. Believe me. But enough wasting time on pointless other people's philosophy that has never done man a lick of good. It is time for you to explain your great idea to me. How will you help me leave this dead world?"

Tammy looked at Bob. Bob looked at Mitch. Mitch looked at his lobster he was eating, but his lobster, while yummy, wasn't up to explaining space trains after a good solid boiling. Mitch looked at Bob. Bob looked at Tammy. Tammy looked at Peter and decided she would apologize for Phil's rather boastful plan that wasn't their plan at all. Just then the music started. The three of them turned and stared down the long table. There at the end, completely unnoticed to each of them, had sat Phil Flip the whole time. He stood up from the table. Screens came down from the ceiling to cover the mirrors on the walls near him. A projector from the ceiling started playing a movie. A speaker in the distance spoke over the movie. There was dramatic music in the air. The whole thing had really nice production value. The narrator was talking about a space train. The movie showed a train huffing and puffing through space. It picked up people on a ball labeled Earth. It traveled through the solar system while passengers dined, slept, and disco danced onboard the space train. Then the space train halted, and the passengers were dropped off on a red ball labeled Mars. The people on Earth seemed unhappy and unpleasant sorts. As they arrived on Mars they became transformed into shiny, happy space people who looked a lot like Peter McKinnon. The movie was impressive; if you didn't know it was total bullshit, you might actually believe Phil or anyone in the room knew how to actually do this.

Tammy looked over at Peter McKinnon. He was eating it up like a little kid eats up stories about monsters under their bed. She looked over at Mitch, and he seemed so giddy with entertainment he might start dancing with his half-eaten lobster. Then she looked over to Bob who was sitting with his head in one hand trying to cover up what appeared to be complete embarrassment. Still, thought Tammy, it was working somehow—lying and dishonesty were working where all else had failed. It seemed like some kind of miracle. Perhaps a horrible miracle, but maybe since it was for the greater good it was OK that she was compromising all her ethics for it. Heck, even Lazarus had to die first before Jesus would help him. The proposal was coming true. True, it was not the actual proposal. True, it was a complete fantasy that Tammy didn't understand because to understand it was impossible. And yet somehow at that moment all those lonely days in her office seemed worth it. She had taken action. She had not let the plan die. She had decided to make sure if a good plan came to her, she would do what was needed to get it done. And she had done it, sort of. It was the greatest day in her life, and then something rather odd happened. Philip Flip started sinking very slowly into the floor. At first it was barely noticeable, and then more and more Tammy could tell Phil was sinking.

Tammy shouted out, "I think Philip is sinking!"

Peter shouted back, "I said this is no time for social moralizing; this idea is the greatest genius I have ever witnessed in full-length movie form!"

Then Bob looked up and said, "No, I think she means Phil really looks to be literally sinking into the ground."

Peter replied, "That's impossible, for there is no ground really. Below us just the deep of the ocean—not real ground."

Phil had been waving a laser pointer randomly at things on the screen during the presentation, part conductor and part drunk guy at bar playing air guitar. Now he stopped. He assessed the situation and said, "You know, I think Tammy is right. Screw the presentation; I'm heading over where you—"

It was too late. A huge gap running straight through Xanadu opened up in the island. Phil and his half of the room plunged into the depths of the ocean below. The three of them sprang up from their chairs to the edge of the carnage. Looking down into the gap that had opened up, they saw that where once Phil and that part of the mansion had stood was now loose debris and ocean waves. The music of the presentation still played on in the background. Really, its production value couldn't be beat.

Peter shouted, "That is impossible; my engineer assured me that did not just happen. I suggest we ignore it and get on with the presentation."

The other three people turned to look at the totally delusional Peter McKinnon in disbelief. Philip Flip was likely dead or dying, and all he could think about was space trains? However, before anyone could comment, the island shook even more violently than any time before. All four of them were thrown to the ground. In the distance, explosions could be heard. The engineer had been right—well, before he was paid to lie and go away.

When the shaking stopped, Tammy said the incredibly obvi-ous: "I think this is really happening, and I think we should plan on getting out of here."

Peter didn't wait to discuss it with anyone; he was already run-ning for the door and the helicopter.

Mitch said, "I wonder where he is headed?"

Tammy replied, "He's the only one of us who knows how to get off this island; follow him!"

The three of them ran out the door and down a maze of halls and rooms, catching glimpses of Peter from time to time. Peter was slick and fast, and there was a fear that he might get out of sight as they followed him through the maze that was the remains of his house. Finally they saw Peter bolt out the door. The door was the one they came in from the garden.

Tammy said, "I think he's planning on heading for the heli-copter!"

They finally caught up to Peter mid-garden. He was stand-ing looking at another huge fissure that had opened in the island. Between the four of them and the helicopter tower was a gaping hole. Only a steel girder straddled the ocean void to the other side.

Peter said, "Thank God you three are here. We need a man of action and integrity to test that steel girder to see if it is safe for me to cross. Mitch, get out there and show us what you're made of."

Mitch acting without thinking said, "Don't worry, I am a self-made man, and I'll show you." Before Bob or Tammy could stop him, Mitch climbed onto the girder and started across.

Bob closed his eyes and waited for the eventual splash of Mitch. About halfway across Mitch slipped and landed on his round midsection. He was now straddled the girder, off balance but still alive. The waves lapped below him. He noticed that he was both rather high up and on a rather narrow steel beam. He didn't know what to do.

Peter shouted at Mitch: "You lazy idiot. Pick yourself up by your bootstraps and cross that beam for me!"

Tammy had a plan. She screamed, "Don't try to get up; bear hug that beam for all it's worth. Just get as strong a hold as you can, Mitch. Then while still on your stomach, try to scoot yourself across. Remember to squeeze. I've been to your house—I know you know how to squeeze, Mitch!"

Mitch squeezed the beam hard in a bear hug. He thought of charging it ten dollars for the privilege of being squeezed, but he didn't know where to send the bill. Then he realized he got his balance back. So Mitch slowly scooted himself across the beam and reached the other side. He had not died. Now Peter pushed Tammy and Bob aside and yelled, "I'm next!" Peter straddled the beam like Mitch had and scooted himself across. Tammy and Bob followed suit. Bob arrived in time to see Peter running off again without them.

The three of them caught up to Peter trying to use the elevator on the helicopter pad. But it was no good as the electricity was dead, so the lift could not carry them to the top. On the pillar that held the pad in place was a small rope ladder to the top.

Peter said, "It looks like this is the only way up. I think I should test it first. After all, I don't want you all thinking Mitch is the only brave man here. Peter started to climb up the rope ladder. Halfway up another violent wave of vibration shook the island. Peter was knocked almost off the ladder. One hand clung to the rope. He was dangling high above the three below. Tammy gasped. The shaking stopped, and Peter managed to regain his full hold on the rope. He reached the top and pulled himself onto the platform above. The other three got set to climb up too.

Just then the rope ladder fell to the ground at their feet. Peter look over the edge of the helicopter landing at the three of them below. Peter then let out a mighty oratory statement that would have done Senator A. J. Brown proud: "My friends, I know I am a morally superior self-made man and have to live in the moment for myself. You see, in one of those great ironic twists, I now agree the needs of the many outweigh the needs of the few or the one. I am a man of vast importance and knowledge. The poor fools who occupy this world simply could not survive without me. You are all very pleasant people, and in time I feel I could have shown you how to be morally superior, self-made people like me, but there is only so much sand in the hourglass. The sand here represents time, if you're not familiar with how an hourglass works. Since, you know, it is the future postmodern world, I am making sure you are all up to snuff on your arcane references to ancient time-pieces that utilized common material from the lithosphere. Time is at this moment a very precious commodity. For the sake of this world and the people in it who I love as an acquaintance who I don't know well or like, I must leave in all haste or risk denying this world my presence. The world can surely spare you three, but the world could never spare me. I am not willing to sacrifice my-self to this world I created just because I built it of inferior-quality material. I shall not let my vision of the world I created be distorted by the reality of its actual creaky, leaky, under-strengthened, and falling-down nature. I will not be questioned by those who have never achieved. The value of self-interest above all I have learned is the value that allows me to truly be alive. While I may lose my freedom-loving island I built single-handedly to the sea, I shall never lose the knowledge that man's proper place in this universe is, as the recipient of a low-taxed dividend, a pigheaded determination for other people to do whatever comes to my mind to tell them to do, and that my mind's vision will always travel the unlimited railways of space and time. I shall not let the sun go down on me, baby. I will not let my sun set into the swamp of your hopelessness, the marsh of your approximate, bog of your maybe-later, the moor of your not-quite, the mire of your not-yet, and the morass of your not-at-all. I will never let the action-packed superhero that is my personal soul to perish, even if I don't believe truly in religion and thus don't really believe I have a soul to perish. You see, I used *soul* in the previous sentence more symbolically rather than literally. The truly gifted like me shall never perish in your lonely frustration to achieve the life I actually deserved, but have never been truly been able to reach. For all I have—and trust me I have a lot—I know so long as you have a little something too there must still be more I need to have. So long as I survive this incidence, and I shall, I swear I will have it all! There are two paths that I have now come upon in the yellow woods. Lucky for me I am rich enough that I can afford to purchase three poorer people and let them walk down the less-traveled path for me and find out what will be its fate. I need not stay with you and travel your path to your fate. I will check your progress on that road and the nature of your battles from a relatively safe distance and height. The world I desire can be won, it exists, it is real, and it's also very dry and not sinking. If you all are also made out of that special steel inside, it might be yours too." With that, Peter climbed aboard his helicopter and took off without them.

Helplessly Tammy replied, shouting upward as loud as she could to the helicopter fading into the distance, "Not to nitpick, but you know you could have planned that better. In the time it took you to deliver that stirring point of social philosophy, we could have all climbed up the ladder to the helicopter too."

"You know, that guy is kind of a dick," added Mitch.

Chapter 9:

All Bad Things Come to an End Too

I'm not afraid to die; I just don't want to be there when it happens.
— Woody Allen, Hollywood type

anny Vazquez had grown up in a small village. His house was constructed of sheet metal with a floor of dirt. The village had no running water, and a nearby stream was used for drinking water, cleaning, and irrigation of the fields. There was no school in the town, nor did most villagers even know what it was to dream of one. One worked the land, ate when there was food to eat, and died when hardship came. But Vazquez's father was different. He had three sons already and more than enough to work the fields and get through hard times. So he sent Manny Vazquez to walk six miles every day to the larger neighboring town to go to the local church. The priest at the church was no genius, but he could read, write, and even do some basic math. For a few hours between priestly duties, he would offer what knowledge he could to the kids who were willing to listen. Manny discovered he liked learning. Knowledge was, as his dad had told him over and over, the only gateway out of his little town in the middle of nowhere and the poverty that inflicted the town. Manny dreamed of true upward mobility.

There was only so much Manny could learn in his current poor, remote existence. His dad wanted more for his son, as any dad would, so one day he told Manny to run away from his family and his current life to try his luck in the big city. At first Manny did OK just to find enough work to pay for someone so young to eat. Life was as hard as in his remote village. Manny was willing to do any odd job and do it right. He gathered a reputation as a hard worker. Soon people in the city who hired children for odd jobs sought Manny out because of his reputation. He saved here and there to have enough money to attend the local school for night classes. At the age of sixteen, he figured he had done as much as he could in the city. He needed to migrate further away to a larger city in another more prosperous country with better chances to learn if he wanted to continue his father's dreams.

So he moved. In the new city, life at first was the same as before, but hard work was soon rewarded. He found a night vocational school that would allow him to work a job during the day and train him for a true vocation at night. Now sometimes he was earning enough to keep a roof over his head when it rained. But Manny was not satisfied. One day Manny heard a rumor that even further north there was an airline company servicing its fleet offshore to save money. They were looking for hard workers like Manny willing to learn new skills, not drink too much, and not expect too much pay. Manny moved there in hopes of better learning opportunities and more chances for upward mobility.

Manny worked hard for the airline and was eager to try any new job the shop foreman would allow him to do. The job was the best he'd had yet. It allowed him to be fed constantly and to always have a roof over his head, regardless of the weather. He soon found himself graduating from airplane repairs to helicopter repairs. He was not satisfied with just repairing them and soon found a night school willing to train the local workers to fly the planes and helicopters they worked on during the day. Manny had studied hard his whole life, passed the entrance exam to the school, and soon learned to fly.

Manny was still not satisfied. One day he saw an advertisement to move and work on a private island. This island needed many new skilled workers. One of the openings was for a person trained in helicopter mechanics and piloting helicopters. Manny left his job at the airline and traveled with the hope of landing this new promotion. Manny was a hard worker and a skilled pilot who was willing to work for less than many others with the same skill set. He didn't mind living far from home with no prospect of seeing his family. They hired Manny.

Now one day Manny received a message from a certain Alexis who was the maid in a certain Nigel Lancaster's mansion. Alexis wanted him to come over and see her. Manny knew Mr. Lancaster would not be home, ever. Manny was supposed to replace the fuel line on the helicopter that day. It had been running a little rough that morning. However, the fuel line was still within two sigma of its maximum recommended lifetime, and on average it probably still had a few good flights left. Manny was by now a self-made man. Manny did what any other self-made man would do when faced with the decision to spend an afternoon in a trillionaire's empty mansion with a beautiful young woman who wanted him or fix a plastic part in a fuel line that might have a another few days of life. After all Manny was a self-made man and knew any other self-made man would check the helicopter maintenance out himself before using it. There was such a thing as personal responsibility, and what fool flies around in helicopters trusting other people to follow recommendations and regulations—particularly on an island that was free of such bureaucratic bullshit anyways. Who was likely to fly it besides Manny anyways? And Manny wouldn't do so until fixing the plastic part. So what was the problem? After all fixing the helicopter was not for Manny's benefit today, but visiting Alexis likely was. The choice was not a hard one for a self-made man. After all the odds were that the plastic part would survive if something unusual happened and someone flew that helicopter without Manny fixing it.

In the fuel line was a small plastic part. The plastic part had a recommended and maximum lifetime. The recommended lifetime was created because not every plastic part made it to one hundred percent of that maximum lifetime. There was always the underachieving plastic part. A plastic part doesn't know if it is the plastic part that would break early or not. Many places have regulations on such things as maintenance of plastic parts, but the plastic part didn't get to choose to belong to a place with such regulations. On average this plastic part had a fighting chance of making it to the mainland in one piece. Unfortunately for this plastic part, somewhere over the vast empty ocean it failed. The plastic part didn't know how rich the passenger was, it didn't know he was a self-made man, it didn't know the passenger was better than it, it didn't know it should likely have lasted longer so as not to deny the world of the passenger's presence, it didn't know it was supposed to work more without more, it didn't know right, it didn't know wrong, and it didn't know anything because it was just a plastic part. And thirty minutes after takeoff, the plastic part, the helicopter, and the passenger fell from the sky into the ocean never to be seen again. All in all it was a bad day for the plastic part.

Their fate now looked pretty grim with no way off the island. Bob tried to stay optimistic. He looked at the other two and said, "OK, you two, we're not dead yet—don't look so hopeless. Screw that guy—the three of us working together can still get out of here. The question is, what do we need to do to get out of here? Anyone have a good plan?"

Mitch wasn't paying attention. He moped on the shaking ground. Finally he said, "That guy stole the whole train proposal; without it we will all be finished. By the time we get back to mainland, he will have declared the whole thing his idea, and we'll have done all this for nothing. What is the use of escaping if all this was for nothing? That stupid dick will just say it was all his idea after we're dead. I know he will because I know I would. Oh, why couldn't he have saved me too? I am rich and important too."

Tammy said, "Shut up, Mitch, we don't need to feel sorry for ourselves; Bob is right—what we need is a plan to get out of here. Don't worry, Mitch, if there's one thing I'm good at, it is planning. Look over there." Tammy noticed something moving behind the tall trees on the neighbor's land.

Bob and Mitch glanced over to the trees at the end of the property. The ground shook again violently. Through the shaking slowly Bob could make out what Tammy was pointing at. Someone or something was moving.

Tammy said, "I think it is some of the island workers. There must be boats somewhere. Those rich might fly themselves around, but they probably boat in the cheap help for this place. Who else would know where these boats are but all the servants who really run this island? If that is a person in the distance, I bet they know the plan to getting to those boats—they know how to escape. The engineers probably built evacuation ideas into the island even if the rich never knew it. While the rich ate and gave themselves a self-congratulatory reach around (or automatic software upgrades in the case of Nigel), the servants probably did countless evacuation drills, hurricane drills, and fire drills. When in doubt follow the people that had to follow rules and regulations designed for your safety in the real world and probably didn't give up the habit here too."

The three followed the distant figure. He or she was clearly heading in one direction. The breeze was picking up. They were heading toward the open ocean. Finally they arrived at a wooden dock on the shoreline of the fake, sinking island. They could see it was an old man they had been following. The dock was filled with workers and servants from the island who were piling into boats. Many carried life jackets. The dock was designed for large ocean vessels, but at the moment, to everyone's misfortune, only smaller boats were at the dock. Most of them looked full already; many had already set sail from the dock. The three of them ran toward the dock and hopefully safety.

They came upon a small wooden boat that had yet to shove off from the dock. On the boat was an old man with a large bag of loot that he had acquired from the island before fleeing. The old man looked at the bag of loot. The old man looked at the three of them. The old man made a cross in the sky as the priests had taught him to do. Then slowly and reluctantly he picked up the bag of loot and placed it on the dock. There was now room for the three of them on the boat. Mitch climbed aboard the boat.

Tammy paused a second on the dock and said, "Wait, the bag might have something useful in it. She pulled out several promising things from the bag and placed them in the boat. She chose things that she planned on being handy later on. Then she climbed aboard. Bob untied the craft from the dock and climbed aboard. The four of them watched the island slowly sink into the vast ocean. They were adrift in the ocean in a helpless and small boat like many other boats from the island.

Mitch said, "I can't believe we made it. Then again, what do we do? Surely we won't last long out here in this."

Tammy said, "Clearly not if we don't work together to survive, so let's take a look at what we have for our survival."

The old man said, "I always keep a water jug in the boat for when I go fishing. I also have my fishing pole, but sadly I do not have any hooks in here. I wasn't planning on fishing today."

Tammy asked Bob, "I know you are sometimes manhood-challenged not being able to drive and all, but do you think you could turn this earring into a hook?"

Bob said, "Yeah, that looks rather doable. But if we are to catch any fish out here, we are going to need bait. Anyone have anything that can be used as bait?"

Mitch then said, "This a stupid plan; can't we just go to the store and buy a fish? Why are we using this pole thingy?"

The old man said, "The pole is to catch the fish. The fish out here aren't in store-purchasing form but swimming about free to be or not to be caught."

Tammy said, "Mitch, you must have known that; I mean you paid someone to fish for you."

Mitch said, "Honestly I thought they just sailed out to a big fish store in the middle of the ocean where the fish bought and sold themselves on the open market. I thought the fish's job was to fatten itself up so as to put food on the table for the little fish. Come to think of it, funny enough, when we were in the dining hall I saw these Cheezy Pufferz and thought it would likely be a long flight back, and so why not take them and save them for the flight." Mitch pulled out the bag of oddly yummy artificial cheese filled with air.

The old man scratched his chin and looked at the bag. "I have never known a fish to eat these things. However, I have known men to eat whole bags of these in a single sitting. You can't eat just one. If this Darwin guy was right and we are descended from fish, then maybe we both share the common weakness for Cheezy Pufferz."

Tammy recommended that the four of them wet their pants and place them on their head to protect from heatstroke in the midday sun. The old man got to work at fishing while Bob and Tammy sorted out the other things they had. Bob thought with the water jug and the hollowed metal oar material, he might be able to make a still that evaporated sea water so they could drink. Bob tied them together with the rosary he had gotten from Father McNally. Bob also thought possibly they could warm it in the midday sun by using the silver platter they took from the bag as a mirror. They gave Mitch the task of using his round body to shape the platter into a parabola. Bob had seen Elizabeth "Beast" Horn-Jabber do it on her outdoor nature-survival show *Horn-Jabber Hates On Nature in 3-D*. That was the show where they filmed Horn-Jabber surviving impossible odds in remote areas of the planet armed only with her pocketknife, her camera woman, her makeup artist, their crew, their personal trailers, their mobile food-catering service, and the devious, adventurous nature of the mind that comes from a life spent living on the edge.

Things went as well as expected. To everyone's surprise they caught a small fish, and they all agreed it was better to perhaps save it for the next day and use it to try and catch an even bigger fish. The still actually made a few sips of water for each person. It went well enough, but it wasn't that great. But it was all they had. How long could it last? Night soon fell on the four ocean voyagers.

The sky was cloudless, and the stars shone brightly in the sky like nothing the three city dwellers had ever observed before. They were amazed at the absolute blackness of the night and the brilliance of the stars in the darkened sky. The old man, who lived much of his life without electric light, had learned to hate the dark and the unknowns it brought. The old man said, "I do not like the dark; please someone say something to take our minds off this terrible situation."

Tammy started the conversation. She said, "You know, I dreamed about writing. I always wanted to write a book about cats solving murder mysteries on trains."

Bob said, "My dream was always to get the proposal passed, but I guess there isn't a lot of hope at the moment for that. How about you, Mitch?"

Mitch, however, was still stuck on the book idea and asked, "Whose cats would they be?"

Tammy replied, "I never saw my cats as being owned by anyone. In the cat's world, the indignity and evils of human cat ownership, as a title recognized by the state, had finally turned people off. Not immediately, but slowly cat champions had risen to fight and even die so all cats could be free to purchase train tickets and then be murdered so that there would be mysteries to be solved by other cats."

Mitch then asked, "Couldn't they just rob something grand in a complex, physiological thriller of priceless paintings, beautiful women, and a puzzling cat-and-mouse game with the police? Why do they have to murder each other?"

Tammy said, "I don't know. I just think sales are generally better with a few murders."

Mitch was still not satisfied: "Would the animal enthusiasts also free the dog and the pig, or would only cats be freed from the bonds of human ownership? Would they wear clothes like humans or walk around violating public decency? Did anyone ask these cats if they even wanted to be free? I can't think of anyone that could speak cat to ask them. The book leaves so many mysteries about cats left unanswered. I'm not sure I can buy into your cat world. Cats to me just assumed they are already free, and being cats they naturally took whatever rights they desired."

Tammy explained, "Well, with every book there are of course logical loopholes. A book can't be perfect. I figured in this world, try as they might, while people learned to respect the freedom of the cats, the people couldn't get the cat to respect to rights of mice. A clever person could probably see that as a metaphor for something, but the cat probably just saw it as lunch."

Mitch said, "I find books a little creepy. People in them don't talk the way they talk in real life. Do you know what I mean? The story is all contrived bullshit, like someone wrote the end first and figured out how to get there. If I knew how things were going to end, I should never do anything since things always seem to end like a pair of cheap socks for me. Another reason I don't like books is that people fart much more in real life than in books. I can't remember the last book I read with a really good breaking of the wind."

Tammy was puzzled, "Would you like the author to write 'pthpthpthpthp' or something from time to time? Wouldn't it distract from the incredibly well-crafted story? Here let me give you an example: 'I think the meowderer is pthpthpthpthp you, Mr. Frisky.' See, random words of nonsense being mixed in distracts from the message."

Mitch said, "I don't know. Just seems like *Emma* would have been more entertaining if Jane Austen would have let them let out a little steam in the form of a good fart every now and then."

The old man spoke, "Please, would you change the topic. I do not like this topic." The four of them again sat silent looking into the night sky for a while. The boat drifted, bobbing up and down in the waves. They did not hear the other boats that had left the island. They were alone in the world.

Then Mitch spoke, "You know, looking at all those stars up there, you have to think this huge greater world is filled with other worlds. Lots of space aliens without good train service, and crap like that. Think of all the money I could make selling it to them."

Bob replied, "The problem with that, Mitch, is that most of those worlds probably don't have anyone on them to sell stuff to. It could be just a lot of empty planets. I'm not saying life might not be abundant in the universe. But all we have to judge this on is the only place we know life exists—here on Earth. But on Earth it took billions of years for complex multicellular life that would be capable of buying and selling your stuff to exist. If Earth is just an average planet with life, then on average we should expect most life to be only simple life forms since most life-bearing planets won't be favorable for life until four and a half billion years after their creation. Only a very improbable set of events would create a world favorable to complex life. One of those places was Earth with its amazing ability to stay within the solar system's habitable zone for a long time; its largeness so important molecules wouldn't reach escape velocity too often; its unusually large moon; its magnetosphere to protect the surface from radiation; plate tectonics to turnover material; and the favorable chemistry of its atmosphere, lithosphere, and its magic water in three states. There might be other unknowns that made life work long-term here on Earth too. I'm not saying there aren't planets out there with these things too; I'm just saying there won't be very many close enough to matter."

Mitch said, "Still all the same, there are probably some nasty space aliens out there hellbent on universal domination!"

Bob sighed, "People always worry about advanced space aliens traveling the vast universe to invade Earth. The aliens are always portrayed as violent, deceptive, greedy, selfish, and militaristic. The aliens, despite having the energy to travel the mind-bogglingly vast openness of interstellar space, are oddly horrible resource managers. They are always envisioned attacking the Earth for its resources. Although the composition of Earth is not so different from surrounding solar systems' resources, the aliens choose to skip the easy pickings of Mars or the moons of Saturn to attack the only planet that might think to fight back with its guns, knives, and—worse—viruses. Think how bad a few rats chewing wires can be to a ship at sea—well it would be far worse to have a few humans mucking about the works of your interstellar spacecraft. The worst feature of these aliens is their poor driving skills. They can take their ship to Alpha Centauri and back but can't fly around the New Mexican desert without crashing. Then being stuck here, apparently the only thing they could do with their incredible advanced space technological mind is pile rocks together in desert location so hacks can write books about ancient alien cities."

Tammy said, "Still an alien might attack Earth. Earth is the only planet with a species so greedy you could bribe it to stupidly give the aliens things the aliens would have to work for on Mars or Venus."

Bob replied, "I guess so. Why would one worry about such a scenario though? Any society that took to space without the ability to regulate and mitigate its violent, deceptive, greedy, selfish, and xenophobic militaristic tendencies to properly manage its resources was highly likely to die a slow, silent death at its own hands somewhere in the eons-long journey through extremely resource-poor interstellar space long before it ever reached Earth. Societies that don't learn to solve their problems where they are do not solve their problems by escaping to form new utopian societies somewhere new. Their problems always travel with them. For example take the pilgrims who headed to the New World in search of religious freedom. Sure their own homeland was intolerant of their religious beliefs, but remember that they were also intolerant of the beliefs of those around them. They thought they would set up a religious utopia in America. But they didn't—they brought their religious intolerances with them. Despite many early Americans trying their best to create religious utopias, they never did. Even today where due to codifications such as separation of church and state—and trust me it is better here than many places—intolerance still exists to this day based on religion in this country. Our ancestors didn't solve their problems; they just brought them with them, and now we have to solve them here. There isn't a moon base, Mars colony, island, or alien-invasion fleet that doesn't have the same basic problem. Any alien civilization that can make it through the eon-void journey is likely one that has solved society's age-old questions of how to regulate and manage resources, stem violence, and mitigate selfish excess. It is impossible to remove these things from society, but that is why we have rules and regulations. The question is: Can we trust ourselves enough and pay attention enough to make sure we self-regulate fairly and intelligently?"

Tammy replied, "I have always worried about that trust part. It feels like the government doesn't work; it can't be trusted. I work every day trying to make life better for people, and no one seems to notice me working for them. It's like the everyday ordinary tasks the government does, people just ignore because it is ordinary. So they only focus on the extreme. Everyone wants a moon base, but no one appreciates the weather or GPS satellite. And when they don't get either due to bickering over the big extreme idea, they say see government can't work together to solve our problems; we can only trust ourselves. So what do they do about it? These people gather together to form like-interest groups and foundations that then build TV networks, radio stations, Internet sites, and activist groups. They do this all under the idea that people can't work together and be trusted, so they need a government that understands these principles. So these people work together in an organized fashion to inform the voters to elect people that don't believe government can work because people can't be trusted to work. You think it would be simpler for these people to just realize their very existence proves people can at times work together for a common cause, even if that common cause is a really ironic and stupid thing. Still the idea of moon bases and Martian colonies are rather romantic. Is there any room for romance in the world?"

Mitch agreed, "You're right—the government can never be trusted to work. That is why I only elect people that guarantee me it won't work. I think this country would be much better off if more people who don't believe in the concept of government actively ran for office in the government to lobby against more government jobs like the ones they will have. I believe it is time to put to work in the government people who don't think the government can work so that we go about the hard work of fixing this government that doesn't work."

Bob asked, "But then aren't you just going to end up with what you voted for—a government that doesn't work? I agree with Tammy—the government, despite the bad press it gets, does do a lot of positive work. I just wish someone in the government, you know, spent some time telling people that more. Too many people confuse freedom with anarchy. To have freedom you have to have a basic framework in which that freedom exists. For example, a free market still has rules and regulations just as a free American society does. What makes America special is that in America we the people get to vote for those who create the framework of our society. To listen to some people on what makes our country great, they claim that it's because our forefathers envisioned a society without a framework and then ironically use the very document that calls out this framework, the constitution, as the example of this. Without any framework all you have is anarchy. Anarchy may feel like freedom, but any slight imbalances in an anarchic society tend to lead to the vast majority quickly getting the shaft, and that does not make the majority freer. Total anarchy of the press ends with a small handful of people owning all the press and denying free people access to have their views heard. Total anarchy of free speech allows vastly wealthy corporations to simply drown out common people's voices in the marketplace. Total anarchy in a free market simply leads to vastly uneven boom-and-bust cycles that average people can't afford to live through. Totally anarchy might feel like you are freer, but that freedom is short lived without some basic framework and rules. What makes America great is that in theory you have a direct say in the rule making. When you say, 'Get your federal government out of my Medicare,' there is something wrong with your understanding of how our government's framework operates in society, not the actual government."

Then Mitch stopped mid-non-thought because he had a horrible idea. "But Peter McKinnon said we were just idiots riding on a dog that likes to play in the road. Don't we have to leave this dog—the Earth—or else be eventually struck by a passing car?"

Bob replied, "Well sure, eventually all things come to an end. The Earth has around five billion more years. It might have two hundred fifty million to five hundred million more years where its surface environment is hospitable for life as we know it. It could be shorter or longer as projections of the future five hundred million years from now are likely to be off. The point is that there is a lot of time. There is so much time that it is impossible for you to imagine how long it is. These people are all in a rush to leave, but they never think what leaving might mean. As climate change shows, dumping stuff into the atmosphere has consequences. A vast rocket fleet flying through the atmosphere to space stations, moon bases, and Mars colonies every day puts a lot of pollution into the upper atmosphere where we generally don't pollute at all now. You never hear anyone explain how they are going to actually study that before they do it or what they might do to mitigate that. If the mass exodus of Earth hurts the Earth, then what good did it do you unless you're a heartless dick like Peter McKinnon and don't care about the people you left back on Earth? People always want to dump things into the atmosphere to mitigate the stuff they already dumped in the atmosphere, yet they never seem to talk about how the new stuff might affect the air-ocean interface, the changing composition of the ozone layer, the changing composition of the upper atmosphere, and stuff like that. I mean do we ever sit down and think things out proper before we hand out some stupid prize and tell billionaires to 'go get them, tiger'? They talk like space will be an endless dumping ground for self-pleasure, capitalism, and their junk. Space debris is bad enough now; think what it will be like with daily trips to the space zoo for rich space mom and space dad. Even the incredible vastness of near-orbit space needs carefully thought-out ideas, mitigation, and regulations. Orbital space and the upper atmosphere is not your personal toilet for your dreams of utopia. The question to people is: Who do you want designing your future—your government in which you get a voice and a vote for and whose science projects must pass peer review and be abided by regulations before implementation, or a group of trillionaires who may or may not have your best interests at heart? It's our future too. Shouldn't we get a say in it?"

Tammy added to the conversation, "So you think we are doomed to go down with the ship? I can tell you, I plan on not having that fate!"

233

Bob said, "Seriously, I'm not a pessimist. I just don't think adding the word *space* in front of stuff makes it the actual future. In the end I never think there are any traveling aliens out there in cramped ships. A real space-faring nation would explore and travel the universe like we do already with unmanned spacecraft. Think what might be possible a million years in the future with technology. We probably will send a person to Mars because humans have that kind of 'nothing-like-being-there' attitude. But I imagine a truly advanced civilization would travel world to world with their machines and tools doing the bulk of the work for them—just like we did since the beginning of space exploration and continue to do now. Our machines are getting better and better; we relatively are the same animals we were at the dawn of the space race with the same biological and logistical limitations to long-term space travel. Our tools will explore, find favorable places to inhabit, and start building life where they are programmed to land *in situ* if needed. It isn't as romantic as space invaders, but it is probably more probable."

Then Mitch replied, "Do you think these alien women will have really large space breasts?"

The old man spoke, "Please, would you change the topic? I do not like this topic." The four of them again sat silent looking into the night sky for a while. It was very late now, but none of them could sleep. The lack of food was unlikely to elevate the quality of the conversation.

Then Mitch said, "Did I ever tell you guys I developed ESP?"

Tammy did not believe in such nonsense. "Please, Mitch, I am almost certain you did not develop ESP. You already said you were bad at predicting the future."

Mitch said, "It isn't that kind of ESP. I can read thoughts. I can. Just try me."

Tammy said, "Fine. What am I thinking about right now?"

Mitch said, "OK, give me a minute." Mitch concentrated very hard. He put his hand to his head. He felt for cosmic vibrations, but nothing came to him. He held his hands out in front of him. No cosmic vibration. He felt for Tammy's aura, but the boat rocking made it hard. "I'm sorry, I guess it doesn't really work on you. But trust me, I can read thoughts. Well, I know for sure I can read my own thoughts. They just pop into my head."

The old man spoke, "Please, would you change the topic. I do not like this topic." The four of them again sat silent, looking into the night sky for a while. Tammy decided she needed to get ahead of Mitch on the subject list of things worth talking about adrift in the ocean with little hope of a long future. Then Tammy said, "You know, Luke was starting a new self-help thing. It was called 'the three people that hold you back.' There is Mr. Fear, Mr. Worry, and Mr. Doubt. He says he is working on eliminating these things from his inner being and thus finding true happiness."

Bob asked, "Did Luke ever tell you why he was so interested in self-help and finding inner happiness?"

Tammy replied, "Well, he did explain it to me once. He read on the Internet that wealth correlated with happiness. He wants to be wealthy, so he has worked hard to become happy first, thinking wealth will soon follow."

Mitch said, "I've been around rich people my whole life, and I've never seen them happy. They are always complaining about some poor person doing this, taking that, wanting this, or smoking that. If that's happiness, I must not know what the word means."

Tammy replied, "Mitch, you don't know what the word means. Look, you sit in a wonderful garden all day surfing the Internet. Trust me—be poor for a few days, and you'll see comparatively a little complaining doesn't mean as much as the total despair that comes from starvation and the loneliness of having nothing."

Mitch replied, "They should be happy to have nothing. I read happiness is not getting what you want and need, but wanting what you get even if all you get is nothing. There is nothing I like giving more to other people than nothing, and think of all the happiness it creates!"

Tammy said, "I doubt pretending to be thrilled you are lost at sea and likely to die is a good way to be happy. I think it is bound to lead to frustration."

Mitch said, "I guess. It's sort of like this whole train thing, huh. It is like seeing your dream in the distance and moving halfway to it only to see you are halfway there. So you move halfway closer to your goal and see you still are only halfway there. No matter how much halfway closer you move, you eventually find you still have half the distance to go. Every halfway step I got temporarily happy thinking it was almost over, and yet it still isn't over. It seems frustrating; still, either you get happy with where you are or accept perhaps happiness is overrated."

Tammy replied, "Mitch, if you have nothing, not even a dream, then there is no path to feeling temporarily happy and then frustrated. Happiness might be a cycle, but you need at least something to even get on the track."

Then Bob said, "You know, I read that also, and it's true wealth and good health do correlate with happiness. But I'm pretty sure happiness doesn't cause wealth, good health, transformational religious experience, or anything for sure. I think seeking happiness through these self-help, soup-de-jour methods just leads to people seeking positive, reinforcing information instead of creating paths to real self-evaluation. Affirmation generally just leads to ill-health ideas, Ponzi schemes, pseudoscience, and possibly bankruptcy. None of those things are likely to lead to happiness, but instead are likely to lead to despair."

Tammy reconsidered the topic for a moment. She then said, "Still thinking about it a little more, doesn't Mitch have a point? Didn't Siddhartha find happiness from asceticism?"

Bob replied, "Well, no, he found happiness from being a rich merchant, banging hot chicks, and occasional bouts of asceticism.

Happiness is the sum of the whole of life's journey, not the absence of the opportunity to ever have a life's journey."

Mitch said, "I listened to that book on my PPED; it would have been better with more lotus-position farting. Hey, you know what leads to happiness? A really big penis leads to happiness. A guy with a big penis is always happy. For years the only things a man had to compensate for a small penis were a Frisbee dog with a scarf on, a large gas-guzzling truck with maximum tire size, or an open-carried maximum-bullet-shooting gun. I'm glad in the postmodern world we have Doctor Willy's Penis Enlarging Cream. It is surely the greatest invention in human history because it creates the most happiness!"

Bob said, "I hate to tell you, Mitch, but countless medical studies have shown the penis cream does not work to enlarge your penis."

Mitch said, "Really? When I rub it on my penis, it always gets bigger!"

The old man shouted at them, "You three are the worst storytellers of all time! I wish I had listened to my worry, fear, and doubt, for I would not find myself here in the middle of the ocean, probably to die soon. I was happy in a small village. I sent my good son out thinking the world was better somewhere outside my poor existence. One day many years later, he wrote to me telling me he had found paradise, and I should come and he would take care of me. My other poor sons told me to stay, work the land, and continue to build the small village for our people. They were worried, for they feared that my young son had become delusional with wealth, and they doubted for my safety outside the village. Well, I failed to teach my good son about the problems of greed that come with opportunity, and as you have been saying, I didn't find a utopia in this new place. I found only in the end this boat and you three horrible people. Now my son is probably lost to the sea, and I shall never see my other sons again."

Tammy smiled to him, although in the dark it might not have been seen. Tammy said, "You should not be so negative. Be happy because had you not come, we would never have found this boat. It was you we followed to find the dock. And had Mitch not come, we would not have had the Cheezy Pufferzs to catch our fish and the promise of more fish in the future. Had I not come, we would not have the fishing hook and platter to use to get food and water. Had Bob not come, we wouldn't have had someone who could make our water still and craft a fish hook. Maybe everything doesn't happen for a reason, and sometimes the world is a crazy, unreasonable place. But if you're lucky, you find people willing to work together to make do with the crazy world as it is and try to build it up to be a better place. Sometimes the world is a small village, sometimes it is a whole country, sometimes it is a poorly constructed artificial island, and sometimes it is a small boat in the sea."

The old man was now happy. "You are right—you are not such bad people. I am sorry. We do work together, and though it might be in vain, we might still be rescued because we have not pan-icked and begun to get greedy. This boat is not unlike my small village. You have many skills that have helped me here on this boat, but you all lack one important skill: you all suck at telling stories. Since you are not good at telling stories, I will have to tell you a story instead.

"A man goes to a remote wilderness park in a far distant land located in a vast, wild jungle to see the da xiang. The park gives the man a number to see the da xiang. The man sits down and waits and waits in the hot sun. The man is patient, and he waits on a bench because he wants to see the da xiang. Finally, after hours on the bench, the authorities call his number and he is ready to see the da xiang. Well, not really. The number is just to allow the man to stand in line to see the da xiang. The line is long, and the man must stand in the hot sun. They sell him hats to block the sun and food and drink because the line is very long. So the man is patient, and he waits in the line because he wants to see the da xiang. Finally the man gets to the end of the line, and there at the end of the line he sees the da xiang, right?

"Well, no. There he sees a rope cart—a cart suspended about three thousand feet above the forest floor stretching over the hilltop. It's a two-seat cart, and it doesn't stop to let you on. So the man needs to time the jump as it passes him. If he mistimes the jump, down he falls into the forest below. The man does not care; he jumps because he wants to see the da xiang. Now the cart was built many generations before; it sways and creaks, and at random times it starts to vibrate. The vibrations are horrible, and they travel through him until he thinks his fillings might fall out. But he sits patiently and doesn't panic because it is all OK as long as he gets to see the da xiang. He reaches the crest of the hill he was traveling to, and there he sees the da xiang, right? Well, no. He sees that the rope cart has another two kilometers to travel. So he relaxes and sits, and he waits and waits as the cart creeps, sways, and vibrates while hovering three thousand feet above the forest. He does not worry because he wants to see the da xiang. Then finally he sees a building at the end of the line. Yes, finally he has arrived, and he is going to see the da xiang. So he jumps off the cart that never stops so people must jump out and pray they don't fall into the forest floor. There in the building, he sees the da xiang, right? No, he sees a sign above a long staircase that reads, 'This way to the da xiang.'

"So he starts to climb the stairway. He climbs one hundred steps, then two hundred steps, and finally three hundred steps. They are big wooden steps, and on each step there is a little traction grids cut into them to prevent a person from slipping. The man does not give up; he keeps at the steps because he wants to see the da xiang. He goes slower and slower as the steps increase in number. He gets to the bottom of the steps. Finally, he thinks, I am going to see the da xiang. But there is no da xiang there either. No, he sees another sign that says, 'Go across the field, and at the end of this field will be a terrace.'

"So the man travels across the field because he wants to see the da xiang. He has to climb out onto a terrace, for the terrace overlooks a wild forest river valley. So he heads out on that terrace. He looks out into the river valley, and he sees a beautiful and ancient wild forest river flowing through the valley floor. He scans the ancient valley riverbanks for a sign of the da xiang. And there on the edge of the wild river shore, in the river valley across the field, down the stairs, on the other side of the rope carts at the end of the line that he waited to get in, he sees absolutely nothing. The man is puzzled, and he says, 'Where is the da xiang! I want to see the da xiang. I came all this way to see it. I do not accept at the end of the long journey there is nothing!' Now a worker at the park comes up to him with a camera in hand and says to the man, 'I am sorry. There is no da xiang. But you need not worry, for we will take your picture next to the riverbank, and then we will digitally place a da xiang into it for you.'"

Mitch said, "I don't get it. What was the da xiang thing?"

The old man said, "It is a just story; not every story has deep meaning."

Bob said, "Life would be simple if the same thing was the right thing to do no matter what the situation."

Tammy said, "You know, I think I have come up with a plan. If there is one thing I'm good at, it is planning. If we survive this, I think I know how to get this proposal passed now. The process of life has taught me a lesson. I think I understand the system now. I don't like it, but it is the only system I got. The system may suck, but it sucks less than all the other fantastical, supposedly better systems people dream of, and I think I understand how to use it."

Bob said, "If so, you're the only one in the world who understands it."

Mitch said, "I learned something too. I'm going to place one of those da xiang things in my garden back home and double the prices of my garden-visiting experience for my guests."

The four of them fell asleep dreaming of the possibility of being rescued and not about the horrible prospects that might await them the next day.

The press announced that there had been some disaster at sea. The now late, but still great Peter McKinnon was lost and presumed dead. There was a brief mention of international government cooperation in an effort to recue survivors, but really none of them—except the great computer heir Nigel Lancaster—was sensational enough to be worth mentioning. Nigel Lancaster's computer was saved, it was said, by a helicopter pilot and his fiancée. Many thought a Congressional Medal for Being an Awesome Cool American should go to them for such a great act. However, one snag in the gossip was that the computer, the pilot, and the fiancée were not actual American citizens and thus not at the moment eligible for the medal. Apparently Mitch Boetner might have been saved, but the press he owned always liked his father more than him. So if it was true, it wasn't front-page material.

In other news Congress had officially left their lame duck session for a much-needed Christmas break before the war on Christmas would officially begin. There was a general cheeriness in the air that year. Congress had tooted their own horn, for they had been productive—or so they claimed. Peter McKinnon had been proven correct and had gained a kind of grand productivity in death. The Congress had just passed the Peter McKinnon Memorial Act in honor of America's greatest and noblest job creator who had recently and tragically passed away. The president had quickly signed it into law. The act officially declared October 13 Peter McKinnon Remembrance Day. The act also allowed preschools to sell pornography after dark if they chose to; increased the faith-based charity amounts to be donated for the fiscal year; raised the pay of the Senate 2 percent; placed a one-dollar tax on large, sugary drinks to help pay for door widening on federal land; granted American citizenship to Nigel Lancaster's computer, its savior, the savior's fiancée, and the savior's father; and finally, last and least of all, it had some possibly pork-barrel thing tacked on that the press ignored because of its complicated details. All they reported was that it had to do with trains—or grains—and scheduling, or something like that. They didn't know for sure, and after all who really pays attention to what the government actually does?